When Mansfield's fingers moved to caress her cheek and edge tantalizingly down her neck, Cassandra jumped to her feet. "It is time for you to leave, my lord," she said firmly, disregarding the trembling of her knees. "It is late, and I wish to go to bed."

He smiled, and she did not like the look of it, at all—the look of a large, sleek cat about to pounce. "Do you?" he said. "I will be more than happy to accompany you."

"Thank you," she said primly. "But that won't be necessary. I wouldn't want you to break the promise you made to me."

His reaction was immediate and explosive. In one swift motion, he grasped both her wrists and pulled her roughly against him. She closed her eyes. His effect on her senses was too much. His breath moved her hair as he laughed, and she could imagine his cynical mouth grinning down at her.

"The devil take that promise," he growled. " 'Tis easily broken, as are all promises, my love."

Easily broken—as well might be her heart. . . .

Miss Drayton's Downfall

Miss Drayton's Downfall

by

Patricia Oliver

A SIGNET BOOK

SIGNET
Published by the Penguin Group
Penguin Books USA Inc., 375 Hudson Street,
New York, New York 10014, U.S.A.
Penguin Books Ltd, 27 Wrights Lane,
London W8 5TZ, England
Penguin Books Australia Ltd, Ringwood,
Victoria, Australia
Penguin Books Canada Ltd, 10 Alcorn Avenue,
Toronto, Ontario, Canada M4V 3B2
Penguin Books (N.Z.) Ltd, 182–190 Wairau Road,
Auckland 10, New Zealand

Penguin Books Ltd, Registered Offices:
Harmondsworth, Middlesex, England

First published by Signet, an imprint of Dutton Signet,
a division of Penguin Books USA Inc.

First Printing, March, 1994
10 9 8 7 6 5 4 3 2 1

PROLOGUE

The Long Wait

"Oh, come on, Cassie. Let's go home. It will soon be too dark to see the road, anyway."

Miss Cassandra Drayton turned briefly from her intense perusal of the road below to gaze anxiously at her sister. What Drusilla said was quite true, of course. The winding road that connected the seaport of Deal to the tiny village of Walmer, two miles inland from the coast, was fast disappearing into the encroaching September twilight. Even as her eyes resumed their scrutiny, Cassandra realized that the ornate stone entrance to Seven Oaks was no longer clearly discernible in the dusk.

"It must be nearly dinnertime, and Mrs. Hill will be wondering where we are. Perhaps Stephen will be here by tomorrow. After all, he did promise to come, didn't he?"

Cassandra sighed, rising to her feet and brushing the dry grass from her serviceable blue gown. "You are right, Dru," she replied, trying to hide her anxiety. "But Stephen said he would be back within two weeks, and it is now almost three since he left for Nottingham. With his neck-or-nothing style of driving, I expected him much sooner. I fear that something must have gone wrong."

"Cheer up, Cassie," Drusilla told her sister. "In all likelihood, Stephen stopped in London on his way south to purchase a ring for you. I declare, you are making a great fuss over a trifle. It's not like you at all. What possibly could have gone wrong, pray?"

"Any number of things," Cassandra replied. "His brother may have refused to countenance our marriage, for one."

"The earl may be a dreadful, black-hearted rogue, if rumors are to be believed, but when he sees that Stephen is adamant in his desire to marry you, Cassie, what can he do? Surely he wouldn't cast his only brother into the Ravenville dungeons?"

"There are no dungeons at Mansfield Grange, silly. Stephen assured me of it."

"What a bouncer! They are mentioned in all the Guide Books, as you well know," her sister insisted.

Cassandra refused to be drawn into an argument, however. She gathered her light woollen shawl around her shoulders and turned toward the vicarage. "Lord Mansfield could always refuse to increase Stephen's allowance, and he cannot comfortably support a wife on his present income. Stephen does not come into his great-aunt's inheritance until he is twenty-five, you know."

"That's only two years away," Drusilla remarked nonchalantly. "If the worse comes to worst, you can wait until then. After that, not even the almighty Earl of Mansfield can do a thing to stop you."

"Oh no! I cannot wait that long. I mean"—she amended this rash statement as her sister stared at her in surprise—"it is unthinkable that we be forced to wait two more years on the whim of that obnoxious tyrant. What possible concern is it of his whether we marry tomorrow, or in two years' time? I hope Stephen has made it quite plain that, eventually, we will marry, regardless of Lord Mansfield's wishes."

Drusilla glanced at her curiously. "You couldn't marry tomorrow, in any case, Cassie. The banns have not been posted."

"Stephen promised to obtain a special license," Cassandra volunteered reluctantly.

"Whatever for?" her sister demanded. "I hear they cost something like five pounds, which I daresay Stephen does not have in his pocket at the moment. Why the sudden haste?"

Cassandra turned to glance one last time at the entrance to Seven Oaks, more to conceal her flushed cheeks from her sister's sharp eyes than with any expectation of sighting the carriage she had hoped might arrive that afternoon. How could she explain to her innocent sister the real reason for her anxiety? She could barely believe it herself. She was still at a loss to understand what pernicious fate had induced her—a vicar's daughter—to conduct herself with such complete disregard for modesty and propriety.

"Well?" Drusilla insisted. "Aren't you going to tell me why you must be married by special license?"

With a slight shrug, Cassandra turned to walk down the hill beside her sister toward Walmer, the small coastal village where their father had been vicar for as long as she could remember. "It was Stephen's idea," she said softly, pulling her shawl more closely around her to ward off the cool evening breeze that blew in from the sea, heavy with the tangy smell of salt and seaweed. "You know how impetuous he is, Dru. Always rushing his fences. I can't say I blame him, though. We've been betrothed for ages, after all."

No, she thought, much as she would like to, she could not blame Stephen's impetuosity for her present predicament. At least not entirely. Of course, had it not been for Stephen and his repeated assurances that they would be married before she could turn around, she would not be in the embarrassing condition she was in. If, indeed, she was in any condition at all, she kept telling herself, stubbornly refusing to believe that fate had dealt her such a cruel hand. He had been so endearingly tender that last evening, and so confident that he could talk his brother into not only allowing the match but also permitting the newlyweds to take up residence at Seven Oaks with a substantial increase in Stephen's allowance. He had been so full of enthusiasm that Cassandra had been quite carried away.

She should have known better, of course; she *did* know better. But there was no use crying over what was past mending. The idea of being separated for two whole weeks had been unbearable for both of them, and the happy assumption—fueled by Stephen's promise that there was nothing to fear from his brother—that they would soon be one, had worked its insidious magic. Stephen's kisses, usually so sweet, had become unexpectedly urgent, and her defenses had been flimsier than she had imagined.

"Father won't like it, you know that, don't you, Cassie?"

Cassandra knew it only too well. Their father might be unworldly, his nose forever buried in the obscure tomes of philosophy that lined the shelves of his study, but he was bound to question the necessity of such extravagance as a special license, when banns would have been so much more the thing. The special license had, indeed, been Stephen's idea, and Cassandra remembered the rush of tenderness she had felt at her betrothed's touching show of concern for her reputation. Besides being quite devastatingly handsome, Stephen Ravenville was lighthearted and generous to a fault, and Cassandra loved him dearly, but had occasionally wished he were more practical. On that last evening together on their favorite hill, however, he had surprised her. After the enormity of what they had done sank in, Cassandra had—quite uncharacteristically—succumbed to a fit of wracking sobs that she had been unable to control.

Her dear Stephen had seemed as shocked by the unexpected change in their relationship as she had been, but he had risen to the occasion with a firmness that had allayed her worst fears. Cradling her in his arms, he had bent his blond head and gently kissed her wet face and stroked her hair until she had regained her composure. Then he had told her firmly not to be a silly goose; in two weeks' time she would be his wife, and nobody need know of their little indiscretion. It was then that he had mentioned the special license, and Cassandra had felt her heart swell with emotion for this man who had promised to love and protect her for the rest of her life.

This happiness had endured undiminished for the first two weeks of Stephen's absence. As the third week dragged by, however, a flutter of anxiety began to assail her, and during the past three days she had spent every hour she could steal from her other duties up on Oak Hill, scanning the road from the north. But no Stephen had materialized.

"How will you explain this unseemly haste to Father?" Drusilla interrupted with her usual directness, forcing Cassandra to tear her mind away from her somber thoughts.

"I shall leave Stephen to do that, Dru," she said, feigning a calm she did not feel. "He will undoubtedly have Father believing that it is all the crack to get married with a special license."

"I do wish he would hurry up and come back," Drusilla remarked, stooping to pluck a daisy from beside the path. "I can't wait to see the two of you settled at Seven Oaks and holding dinner parties and balls and such. I think it most unreasonable of Stephen to dally so long."

Cassandra heartily agreed with her sister. Stephen's presence was the only thing that would relieve the growing uneasiness inside her and put a stop to the ridiculous fears that had begun to plague her. Only this morning she had had the sudden premonition that he might not come back at all. Might he not have found London more entertaining than the quiet country life in Kent? she wondered. How could plain, ordinary Miss Drayton, a country vicar's daughter, hold a candle to those fashionable, pampered Beauties who flocked to the Metropolis to find wealthy husbands? She knew she was being unfair to Stephen, but try as she would, the nagging doubts remained.

Drusilla's childlike chanting momentarily diverted her. "*He loves me. He loves me not. He loves me. He loves me not. He loves me. He*—Oh, pooh!" Drusilla stopped abruptly and regarded her sister defiantly. "What a silly superstition this is, to be sure." She hurled the mutilated daisy from her in obvious disgust, but Cassandra felt as though a chill hand had touched her heart. *He loves me not,* she mentally completed Drusilla's chant and pulled her shawl more closely around her. Now she was being utterly missish, she thought angrily.

So absorbed was she in her own misery, that Cassandra did not notice that her sister had suddenly stopped in her tracks, her head cocked eagerly in the direction whence they had come.

"Oh, Cassie," she squealed excitedly. "Did you hear it?"

Cassandra whirled about and gazed expectantly up the hill. Then she heard it—the faint rattle of a carriage, traveling at high speed. Her heart suddenly light, she took off after Drusilla, who was racing back to the top of Oak Hill. Out of breath and with a pounding heart, she was just in time to glimpse the twinkling lights and dark bulk of a chaise sweep recklessly through the stone pillars of Seven Oaks and disappear up the winding driveway.

She stood quite still until the sound of the horses' hooves could no longer be heard in the distance. Then Cassandra turned to her sister and hugged her tightly, tears of relief running down her cheeks.

"He came back," she murmured disjointedly. "Stephen is back again. He came back to me, Drusilla. I am the happiest female alive."

"You are a totty-head, Cassie," her sister giggled self-consciously. "Of course Stephen came back. What else did you expect, you goose? Come, I'll race you to the bottom of the hill," she added, bounding off down the path.

Without the slightest hesitation, Cassandra hoisted her skirts and followed suit, feeling her heart and her feet had suddenly sprouted wings.

CHAPTER ONE

The Unexpected Guest

After several anxious days and restless nights Cassandra slept deeply and dreamlessly the night of Stephen's return, waking only when Sally appeared at her usual early hour the following morning with a steaming cup of chocolate.

"Good morning to you, miss," the little maid exclaimed cheerfully, setting the cup on a rosewood table beside the bed. "And a wonderful morning it is, too."

As Sally bustled about opening the heavy curtains at the casement window, Cassandra lay snuggled under the covers idly wondering why it was she felt so full of happiness that morning.

"Seems as though a carriage arrived at Seven Oaks late yesterday evening, miss," the maid remarked, slanting a sly glance at her mistress. "No doubt Master Stephen has returned from his visit to London."

Stephen! Cassandra sat up abruptly and stared out at the patch of clear sky visible from her window. Of course! Stephen was back! How could she have forgotten? She threw back the covers and slid her feet down to the cold floor. Struggling into the warm robe Sally held for her, she took her chocolate over to the window embrasure and settled down in her favorite daydreaming spot. She would not have much time for her fantasies this morning, she thought. Stephen was bound to ride over before the family sat down to breakfast, as he had done so many times in the past. A soft smile curved her lips as she remembered her father's teasing remarks about young Ravenville's ubiquitous presence at the vicarage breakfast table. How fortunate that her father got on so well with Stephen, she mused. Unlike his brother, the present earl, whom Cassandra had not seen since she was fifteen or sixteen, and then only to be virtually ignored, Stephen Ravenville was loved by everybody in the neighborhood. She had always found it difficult to associate her golden-haired, amiable, easygoing fiancé with the dark, taciturn nobleman she had encountered so briefly years ago.

Her recollection of that brief encounter had dimmed over the years, but the one thing about the notorious Earl of Mansfield she could not forget—or forgive—was the contemptuous glance he had raked over her, as if stripping her of her dowdy brown riding habit in his mind and finding her wanting. Involuntarily, Cassandra shivered. The shock of his lordship's impertinent stare had lain dormant in her memory for some time now, but her present dilemma had revived the unwelcome specter of those cold, hard, cynical eyes that had flicked so offensively over her and then dismissed her, as if she had been a mere servant girl.

A tremor of apprehension ran through her. Had Stephen been able to convince this unfeeling monster that she was worthy of a Ravenville? she wondered. Or had the earl dismissed her, as he had done long ago, as beneath his notice? Perhaps she should have listened to Stephen, after all, and run away with him to Gretna Green. With their marriage a *fait accompli*, the black-hearted earl could hardly allow his only brother to live in penury, could he? Cassandra was suddenly not sure. If her memory served her correctly, there had been not the least shred of humor or softness in the earl's eyes. Nor on his thin lips. He had stared down an imposing aquiline nose at the awkward young girl on a placid pony, given her the smallest possible nod, and ridden on, a mortified Stephen trailing at his heels. As the memory of that awful scene came flooding back, Cassandra recalled that she had sat, as if turned to stone by the Gorgon's head, until the two riders had disappeared from sight.

She had raced her pony all the way home, she remembered, quite as if the devil were at her heels. And perhaps he had been, she thought, finishing her now tepid chocolate and ringing for Sally. The Earl of Mansfield had certainly resembled the Angel of Hell, with his black hair tumbling in disarray around his bare head, and his eyes boring into her soul as if he would rip it out and consign it to eternal perdition.

Cassandra grimaced. Now she was being absurdly fanciful, she chided herself. But it was only too true that those piercing eyes— whose color she distinctly remembered as a sinister grayish green, like the murky depths of the sea after a storm—had haunted her dreams for many a night thereafter.

The arrival of the maid with a jug of hot water dispelled these morbid thoughts, and Cassandra threw herself into the agreeable task of selecting one of her less outmoded gowns in readiness for Stephen's visit. Even the knowledge that the simple morning gown in green kerseymere, modestly embellished with a single flounce at the hem and a gathered ruff of cream ribbon at the high neckline, was at least three years old did not diminish her pleasure. And when she was able to contrive a semblance of order in her unruly auburn curls, Cassandra felt ready to face what was to be—she resolutely told herself—the happiest day of her life. On impulse, she added a green ribbon to her hair and clasped her gold locket around her slim neck.

As was his wont, the Reverend Drayton was already perusing the *Morning Post* when his eldest daughter made her buoyant entry into the small breakfast parlor. He lowered the paper and greeted her with his sweet smile.

"Good morning, my dear Cassandra," the vicar remarked, regarding her unusually neat attire with interest. "We *are* tricked out this morning, aren't we? Am I to understand that we can expect young Ravenville to join us for breakfast? Or is this finery for my benefit only, dear?"

"Why of course it is, Father," Cassandra responded brightly, giving her father his morning kiss before taking her place at the other end of the table and pouring herself a cup of tea. "I had to forgo my ride this morning because Elektra cast a shoe yesterday. Jeb promised to take her over to Mr. Hawkins to be reshod, but you know how that will be. I don't expect her to be ready until late this afternoon."

"Hmmm. I see," said the vicar, returning to his paper. "I wonder if you would have time to drop in on old Mrs. Mason today, Cassandra? When her daughter brought the eggs over yesterday, she told Mrs. Hill that her mother was feeling poorly. I would go myself, but I have to finish my sermon. I don't know how I come to be so behindhand this week."

"Of course I will, Father. And I'll take the Masons a dozen of those pork pies Mrs. Hill made yesterday. With all those children in the house, they will be welcome, I'm sure." Cassandra glanced affectionately at her father, knowing from experience that he had heard little of what she just said. She was surprised that he had remembered Mrs. Mason's ailment at all, since he had become increasingly absentminded of late. His parishioners had long been in the habit of applying to her for advice when the need arose, and

Cassandra worried that after she and Stephen were married, Drusilla would have to take her place in supporting their father.

"You're a good lass, Cassie," her father murmured, almost to himself. "I hope I live to see you safely married and settled down in a home of your own, my dear," he added, quite unexpectedly, a worried frown on his kindly face.

Cassandra looked up from her coddled eggs in surprise. It wasn't often that her scholarly parent expressed any concern at all for the ordinary matters of life. When Mrs. Drayton was alive, she had taken care that the vicar was permitted to pursue his studies unhampered by the trials and tribulations of daily existence. Cassandra had naturally assumed that responsibility after her mother had been taken from them unexpectedly five years ago.

"Don't worry your head about me, Father," she remarked cheerfully. "I shall probably do very well, and Drusilla will doubtless make a magnificent match. She is the beauty in the family, you know." She wished she could confess that she had every expectation of soon becoming Mrs. Stephen Ravenville, but her betrothed had insisted that he be allowed to approach her father first, as convention demanded.

"You underestimate yourself, my dear," was the vicar's laconic reply before returning to his paper, and Cassandra saw that the matter of his daughters' future had already receded from his consciousness. She smiled at this enviable gift her father had for relegating unpleasant thoughts to the back of his mind and wished that she had inherited his knack. Under the circumstances, however, such a luxury was impossible, and she glanced nervously at the clock. What was keeping Stephen? she wondered. He should have been here by now. She was torn between anxiety and annoyance at her lover's absence. Surely he would not be still abed at this hour, would he? He, of all people, must know that her nerves would be ragged with worry. Thoughtless and immature he sometimes was, she had to admit, but he had never been unkind, and it was nothing if not unkind to leave her in suspense like this. Cassandra found that her appetite had quite deserted her.

So had her bubbling good humor of less than an hour ago. As a result, she welcomed her father's removal to his study and greeted the entrance of her sister with a patent lack of enthusiasm, which caused Drusilla's merry expression to fade.

"Whatever has put you into such a pucker, Cassie? I do declare you look exactly like old Lady Braithwaite when that smelly pug of hers gets indigestion from eating too many comfits." She sat down next to her sister and smiled encouragingly. "Buck up, dear," Drusilla added, glancing at the clock. "Stephen will be here any moment now, and you surely do not wish him to find you looking so positively lumpish, do you?"

"He should have been here already." Cassandra refused to be consoled and pushed her half-finished plate of eggs away impatiently. "I cannot imagine what is keeping him, Dru. He must know I am sick with worry."

"Only because you have become a complete widgeon, dear," Drusilla said teasingly. "Why on earth would you be sick with worry? You are not making any sense at all, love. I do hope that I never fall in love if it is going to addle my brains and take away my appetite, Cassie. I want no part of such nonsense." She proceeded to fill her plate with a generous helping of coddled eggs, slices of York ham, and two kippered herrings.

Cassandra felt quite ill by this time, and Drusilla's cheerful words only made her feel worse. How she wished that she could confide in her little sister. For all that she was over five years younger, Drusilla was blessed with a sunny disposition and a practical turn of mind, and would undoubtedly forgive her sister once she had recovered from the shock of discovering that Cassandra was guilty of the unthinkable. But that was the one thing she must avoid at all costs. How could she bring herself to sully her sister's tender ears with such a confession? It was bad enough that her own innocence had been lost, she mused, watching Drusilla tuck into her breakfast with hearty unconcern. But her sister was right to call her a silly widgeon. What did an hour or two of delay matter, after all, when the happiness of a whole lifetime with Stephen stretched before her? Stephen would come when he was ready, and she must wait for him calmly instead of fretting herself to ribbons like a brainless ninnyhammer.

Her inner composure somewhat restored by these sage arguments, Cassandra poured herself a cup of fresh tea and gently reminded her sister that it was unladylike to shovel one's food, even if one were on the point of starvation, which Drusilla obviously was not.

By the time the grandfather clock in the vicarage hall had struck the hour of one, however, Cassandra's nerves were raw. She had kept herself feverishly busy all morning, going through the clothespress for frayed sheets and other household linens that required mending or replacing. Then she had attacked her own wardrobe, going over her gowns with a critical eye and selecting those that might not put her to the blush when she was installed at Seven Oaks as Stephen's wife. After a while this occupation began to pall, since it reminded her that Stephen had not yet put in an appearance, and until he did, there would be no wedding.

By midday she was reduced to such a state of nervous anxiety that she could do little more than nibble at the cold pies Mrs. Hill had set out for the girls' nuncheon and absolutely refused to taste the raspberry tart their kindly housekeeper had prepared to tempt her appetite.

"If he does not appear soon, I shall drive over to Seven Oaks and box his ears for him," she declared with uncharacteristic sharpness. "This is inexcusable. I cannot understand—"

"Please don't fly off the handle at the poor man," her sister interrupted gently. "Perhaps something unexpected has come up and Stephen has been delayed, dear. He will come eventually, never fear."

"Eventually is not good enough," Cassandra snapped, her nerves taut as fiddle strings. "I've a good mind to tell the wretch that I have changed my mind and cannot marry him after all. He deserves no less for leaving me to kick my heels all morning."

"You know you do not mean that, Cassie," Drusilla pointed out calmly. "You are overset, that is all. Why don't you lie down for an hour or two. I promise to call you the moment Stephen arrives."

"*If* he arrives, you mean, don't you?" she replied irritably and flung out of the room, disregarding her sister's startled glance and careless of the spectacle she was making of herself. From the dining room she went directly to the kitchen, where she set about reorganizing the pantry with much clattering of jars and pots, accompanied by occasional muttered imprecations on the disgraceful unreliability of gentlemen in general and of one particular specimen of that sex in particular.

It was here that Mrs. Hill cautiously interrupted her, shortly after two o'clock, with the announcement that there was a gentleman caller waiting to see Miss Drayton in the front parlor.

For several seconds Cassandra stood perfectly still, her very breath suspended in her throat. So he had finally come, had he? Well, he was about to receive a piece of her mind, she thought, her anxiety turning unexpectedly to anger. Who did he think he was to treat her so cavalierly? And after all his promises, too. Mr. Ravenville would soon find out the extent of Miss Drayton's wrath, she decided, suddenly caught between the conflicting urge to ring a peal over his handsome head and to clasp that same golden head and kiss the rogue soundly.

"I will tell the gentleman you will be down directly, miss, if you are wishful of tidying yourself," Mrs. Hill said helpfully.

"There is no need for that, thank you, Mrs. Hill," Cassandra replied tartly. "He can hardly expect that I have been sitting in a state of frozen animation awaiting his pleasure."

Mrs. Hill eyed her critically. "You'll at least take off the apron, miss. It is stained with strawberry jam. You'll not want his lordship to take you for the scullery maid now, would you?"

"His lordship, indeed!" Cassandra snorted. "He is no such thing, and believe me, Mrs. Hill, I have a thing or two to say to that rogue that he will not like in the least." She doffed the offending apron and tucked a stray curl into the loose chignon on top of her head.

"But, miss," Mrs. Hill protested anxiously. "Take care what you're about, lass. He is not likely to take kindly to a scolding—"

"And if you think I care a fig for that, you mistake the matter, Mrs. Hill," Cassandra replied haughtily. "Out of my way, if you please. I can't wait to tell this gentleman what I think of him."

She swept regally out of the kitchen and marched down the hall, but halfway there her poise deserted her, and she broke into a run. Heedless of her outmoded gown and the stray curls that had come loose again to frame her small face, Cassandra flung open the door to the front parlor and bounded in, a sweet smile of welcome curving her lips even as her mind rehearsed the blistering scold she meant to administer to her beloved.

She came to an abrupt halt before she had taken two steps inside the room, her smile fading, and her prepared scold forgotten. For an interminable moment she gazed about the room, willing Stephen to materialize in place of the man who stood stiffly before the fire, his face set in a disapproving frown.

But Stephen was not there at all.

Reluctantly, Cassandra forced her eyes to dwell on the sole occupant of the room and felt her heart gradually freeze within her. The hard, cynical gaze of those gray-green eyes had not changed at all in the six years since last she had felt it slide insolently over her person. The aquiline nose seemed to have acquired an even more arrogant tilt to it, she noticed, but the expression on the lean, angular face, slashed by the thin line of taut lips, still reminded her vividly of the Fallen Angel. Instinctively, her hands flew to her breast, as if to protect her soul from the contaminating stare of the Earl of Mansfield.

Suddenly aware that she had been rudely staring herself, she shut the parlor door and advanced a few steps into the room.

"W . . . where is Stephen?" she whispered, mortified to hear the faint tremor in her voice.

The earl continued to regard her without moving a muscle. Then, with what appeared to be calculated rudeness, he brought up his quizzing-glass and examined her from the untidy mop of curls slowly down, pausing briefly on the curve of her breast, to the tip of her scuffed slippers. During this process Cassandra felt herself shrinking under the baleful influence of that enlarged eye, until she felt no larger than Mr. Shakespeare's Queen Mab, "*no bigger than an agate-stone on the fore-finger of an alderman.*" The illusion distracted her for a moment, until the earl cleared his throat ominously.

When he spoke, his voice was brittle with hostility. "Your manners are execrable," he said slowly and distinctly. "And that gown is an abomination."

Rigid with indignation, Cassandra threw caution to the winds. "So are yours," she snapped before recalling that this was Stephen's brother, and that their future depended to a large extent on his good will.

"Where is Stephen?" she repeated, valiantly suppressing her fury. "I've been expecting him since early this morning."

The earl's scowl deepened, and his eyes slid away from her to fix upon a point several feet above her head. Cassandra held her breath.

"Ah, yes," he murmured finally. "My poor brother, Stephen."

A frisson of panic shot through her. "What have you done to him?" she cried, her voice full of agitation.

The greenish eyes seemed to stare right through her. "I haven't done anything to him, Miss Drayton."

"Then why isn't he here?" she demanded. "He promised—"

"Yes, he told me all about his promises," the earl interrupted, and Cassandra heard a softening in his tone, which should have calmed her, but it only made her more apprehensive.

"Did he also tell you that we plan to wed with or without your approval?" she demanded.

"Yes, he did say something to that effect."

"And, of course, you disapprove of me, so you are trying to keep us apart. Is that it? You have thrown the poor lamb into the Ravenville dungeons. Admit it, you odious bully."

The earl raised startled eyebrows and regarded her blankly. Then he relaxed, and Cassandra could have sworn his thin lips twitched. "Ah, you have been misled by the infamous Guide Books, I take it? There are no longer any dungeons at Mansfield Grange, child. They have long ago been converted into excellent wine cellars. And I have not—as you put it—thrown my poor brother there at all."

"I am not a child," Cassandra retorted.

"No, so I gather," the earl responded coolly, reverting to his disapproving stance.

"And I apologize for calling you an odious bully. Even if you are one, it was not polite of me to throw it in your face." Belatedly, Cassandra realized that, as an apology, her words lacked a certain conviction.

The earl considered this in silence for several moments. "I am?" he asked, in a strangely flat voice. "Since I have had little opportunity to bully you, my dear, this must be Stephen speaking. Am I right?"

"Oh no. Not at all. Actually Stephen has quite a high opinion of you, my lord, although I cannot imagine why. But it stands to reason he must have feared you, for it took him forever to screw up his courage to approach you about. . . ." She paused, suddenly conscious that she had spoken rather too freely.

There was another awkward pause, during which the earl regarded her intently. Cassandra cast around frantically for something to say, and her eyes lit on the decanters clustered on the sideboard.

"May I offer you—"

"No, thank you, Miss Drayton," he interrupted brusquely.

Taking her own courage firmly in hand, Cassandra asked the question she needed him to answer. "Am I to understand that you refused Stephen's request? Is that why he is not here now?"

"No," he answered softly. "Under the circumstances, I could not deny my brother's request."

Cassandra stared at him in shocked silence as the implications of his words sank in. What circumstances did he mean? Could it be that Stephen had told his brother about—? No, he would never have betrayed her in such a way. And to a complete stranger, too. No, that was unthinkable.

"Then where is he?" she cried, her voice little more than a whisper.

"At Mansfield Grange," came the abrupt reply. "My brother will not be coming down to Seven Oaks again."

The silence that followed this pronouncement was absolute. Cassandra felt herself pale at the finality of the earl's cruel words. She swayed forward and clasped the back of a Queen Anne chair tightly to keep from falling. She could not believe that her worst nightmare was actually being played out in the comfortable setting of the vicarage front parlor. This coldhearted creature before her had—with a few cutting words—destroyed her whole life. She discovered that she had ceased to breathe and drew a shuddering breath, expelling it as a long, painful sigh.

"That cannot be true," she heard herself say with unnatural calm, as if she were addressing a child. "S-Stephen is incapable of such a b-betrayal." She could not stop her voice from faltering. "Our a-attachment is of long-standing, and he p-promised me . . . he would never . . . especially not *now*." The last words came out in what sounded perilously close to a wail of despair. She pulled herself together with an effort. She must not let this monster know the secret she shared with Stephen. He would suppose her only interested in blackmail, and if he offered her money to give Stephen up without a fuss, she would be sick, right here on her mother's best Oriental carpet.

"The deuce take it!" the earl exclaimed harshly, running his fingers through his hair until the black curls stood up around his grim face like some dark, devilish halo. "I am sorry, Miss Drayton. I seem to be making a confounded mull of this. Please sit down. There is something you should know." He gestured toward the small settee before the hearth.

Cassandra opened her eyes in dismay. Here it comes, she thought. The villain was about to give her a monumental setdown and cast her out of Stephen's life forever. "I prefer to stand," she said icily.

The Earl of Mansfield had turned to pace the length of the room, but at her words, he whirled on her, a flame of pure fury burning in the opaque green depths of his eyes. "This is not the time to trifle with me, girl. I said, sit down." He spoke softly, from deep in his throat, but to Cassandra—whose nerves were already at breaking point—it sounded too much like the warning growl of a cornered animal. She must have hesitated a second too long, for he suddenly grasped her round the waist and lifted her bodily, placing her roughly on the settee. "I do not like having to repeat myself, Miss Drayton. Please remember that for the future."

What future? she wondered, now thoroughly alarmed at such unconventional behavior. There could be no future for her without Stephen, could there? The man had clearly taken leave of his senses. She wondered uneasily if the earl could actually be deranged. Stephen had never mentioned such a possibility, but then, what family would wish it generally known that they harbored a madman in their midst? Cassandra racked her brains for scraps of information she might have gleaned from her readings on the treatment of those afflicted with mad starts and regarded Lord Mansfield closely. What would he do next? she wondered. Would she have time to rush to the door before he could maul her again? No, that was out of the question. He was standing far too close to her knees. She would be unable to stand up without bumping against him. Since the notion of touching the mad earl repelled her, she laced her fingers together and addressed him with all the calm she could muster.

"Pray tell me, if you please, my lord, what it is that I should know."

Lord Mansfield relaxed visibly and ran his fingers once more through his hair, creating an even more alarming resemblance to the Prince of Darkness. "I should have told you immediately, of course," he began, his eyes again fixed on the wall above her head. "But I am not adept at importing this kind of news. I could not find the right words."

He paused for such a long time that Cassandra wondered if he had forgotten her presence. "Right words for what news, my lord?" she murmured through suddenly dry lips.

He glanced at her and then strode over to the sideboard and poured himself a large brandy, which he threw down his throat without flinching. He poured a smaller portion in another glass and brought it across to Cassandra. "Here, take this," he said roughly. "You may need it."

"I never drink strong spirits."

"You will today, I can guarantee it." He placed the glass down forcefully on a round brass stand beside the settee. "Are you always so confoundedly obstinate, Miss Drayton?"

Cassandra looked up at him in surprise. She was growing somewhat accustomed to his black scowl and did not flinch from his gaze. "Only when provoked, my lord. Now, please tell me whatever it is you have to say. I am not precisely enjoying this interview."

This incautious sally was met with a harsh crack of mirthless laughter. "Neither am I, come to think of it," the earl growled. "What I have to say is every bit as painful for me as it will be to you, Miss Drayton, although I don't expect you to agree with me, of course." He paused to stare down at her, but his face had gone suddenly taut, and she clearly saw the muscles in his strong jaw clenching and unclenching.

"Just tell me what happened," she said softly, suddenly aware that the man before her—for all his studied indifference—was hiding some great sorrow.

Lord Mansfield let out a long sigh, which to Cassandra's ears sounded like either defeat or relief, she could not guess which. "My brother met with an accident just before he arrived at Mansfield Grange," he said tonelessly.

Cassandra gasped, but held her breath, knowing instinctively that there was worse to come.

"A fatal accident," the earl continued relentlessly. "We were able to get him up to the Grange, but he did not survive the night. I buried him a week ago in the family cemetery there."

Cassandra's dazed mind refused, during several agonizing moments, to accept the finality of the earl's words. When the enormity of what she had feared forced itself into her consciousness, she gave a soft little moan of despair and crumpled against the cushions of the settee.

CHAPTER TWO

The Promise

Since Cassandra had never swooned in her life and considered females who were forever indulging themselves in such maudlin histrionics to be beneath contempt, she was unprepared for the sense of disorientation that assailed her as soon as she began to regain consciousness. Cautiously, she opened her eyes and was startled to find herself being regarded intently by two green eyes in a harsh face that was alarmingly close to hers. She quickly closed them again, but was equally disconcerted to feel her head cradled in the crook of a gentleman's arm and a glassful of brandy being literally forced down her throat.

"Drink this," the earl's voice commanded, and Cassandra distinctly felt the warmth of his breath on her cheek.

"Don't defy me again, Miss Drayton," he continued roughly. "I am not a patient man, you know. And believe me, you will feel all the better for it."

The glass was summarily tipped against her parted lips, and Cassandra felt the fiery liquid invade her mouth. Obediently, she gulped and then choked violently as the brandy burned its way down her throat. The glass was removed, and she felt a handkerchief, smelling faintly of Holland water, pressed against her lips and then applied, none too gently, to her chin.

"I said, drink it, not spit it all over yourself," the voice remarked impatiently. "Now here, take another sip." The glass was pressed to her lips again, and Cassandra's weak protests went unheeded as her mouth filled once more with the strong drink, and she was obliged to swallow most of it. What little did escape and run down her chin was mopped up with brisk efficiency.

In an attempt to avoid being forced to drink a third time, Cassandra grasped at the hand that held the glass and turned her head away. Unfortunately, this evasive action only served to bury her nose in the earl's sleeve, a circumstance that caused her considerable shock and no little embarrassment. She jerked her face up again only to find the brandy glass pressed inexorably against her teeth.

"One more mouthful should do the trick," the earl remarked ruthlessly. "And then we need to talk, Miss Drayton."

So engrossed had she been with the novel sensations battering her senses that Cassandra had momentarily forgotten the announcement that had caused her distress. The earl's curt words brought it all back to her in a rush of desolation. She submitted numbly to the inevitable gulp of brandy and, belatedly realizing that she was still clutching the sleeve of the earl's finely tailored coat, allowed her hands to drop into her lap and opened her eyes.

Lord Mansfield put the glass down, removed his arm from behind Miss Drayton's head, and regarded his mangled sleeve with distaste. He rose lithely to his feet and stood gazing down at her from beneath hooded lids. He seemed detached from the tragedy that had just left her life in shreds, but Cassandra could not help but wonder if Stephen's brother was quite as untouched as his icy demeanor suggested.

"I trust you are not about to enact me a Cheltenham Tragedy," he remarked dryly. "I abhor watering-pots."

His sarcasm roused Cassandra from her lethargy of self-pity. "Have no fear, my lord," she snapped, "I rarely cry."

"Then I take it that you are sufficiently recovered to discuss your future."

Cassandra could not believe her ears. How could this arrogant stranger possibly be interested in her future? "My future?" she repeated. "I have no f-future without Stephen, and you have just i-informed me that"—she gulped back a sob—"that Stephen is . . . that Stephen is g-gone." She could not bring herself to pronounce the dreaded word and turned her face away to hide the bleakness she was sure must be mirrored there.

There was a short pause during which Cassandra refused to look at him. She had spoken the truth when she had told the earl she rarely cried, but this was one of those rare occasions when she felt an urgent need to cry her heart out, but it would never do, she thought resentfully. Not after he had made that quite odious remark about watering-pots. She steeled herself to look up into the earl's harsh face. "So you see, my lord, we have nothing at all to discuss."

"Are you quite sure of that, Miss Drayton?"

His voice had lost any trace of his previous hostility, and for a fleeting second, Cassandra imagined she caught a flicker of compassion in his eyes. But his words could not possibly mean what they appeared to mean, she told herself firmly. He could not suspect anything of her secret. Stephen himself had not known, and she had only this morning admitted to herself what her body had been telling her for several days now. Believing that Stephen had returned the evening before, she had looked forward to sharing this special secret with her lover, but now that he was gone from her life, Cassandra suddenly had a shattering vision of what her future would be. She quailed at the prospect.

"I don't believe I quite understand what you mean, my lord." She met his enigmatic gaze steadily, knowing her own to be filled with apprehension.

"Don't you, Miss Drayton?" he drawled softly. "Then perhaps I should tell you that my brother was conscious when he was found in the wreckage of his curricle." He paused, as if gathering strength to resurrect painful memories. "He remained lucid for perhaps an hour before the surgeon arrived. Toward morning, when he knew he would not survive, he talked to me about you."

Cassandra stared at him, emotion threatening to undo her. "Stephen talked about me?" she repeated in a strangled voice.

"I believe that is what I said," the earl remarked, relapsing into his previous curtness. "Incessantly, I should add."

With a sudden flash of temper at this callous remark, Cassandra rose to the defense of her lost love. "I can see nothing amusing about that," she said coldly.

"No, I don't imagine you would. The point I wish to make, however, is that in those few last hours of my brother's life, I learned far more about you than I ever wished to know, Miss Drayton."

The rudeness of this casual remark left Cassandra stunned with indignation. The man was boorish and uncouth beyond belief, she concluded. No gentleman with any claim to that title would dare to address a lady in such vulgar and offensive terms. Taut with anger, she rose unsteadily to her feet, but found that, inexplicably, her knees showed an alarming tendency to collapse. Determined to overcome this momentary weakness, she took a step forward and would have pitched into the earl's broad chest had he not caught her firmly by the shoulders. He was considerably taller than Stephen, his shoulders wider and more solidly built. Standing this close to him, she could clearly feel the latent vitality of the man in the touch of his fingers through the thin sleeves of her gown. The contact stirred a frisson of irrational panic in her blood as though some primitive part of her mind had sensed danger. She felt both fear and a strange exhilaration, which she quickly dismissed as shock at his unexpected rudeness.

"Let me go, sir," she snapped, trying vainly to jerk herself out of his iron grasp. "You are odiously rude. I refuse to be insulted in my own home, so I must ask you to leave at once."

Lord Mansfield might have been deaf for all the notice he paid to her angry request. "Do you not wish to hear the message Stephen entrusted to me, Miss Drayton?"

Cassandra ceased her struggling abruptly and stood passively in his grasp, staring up at him, the beginnings of real panic uncoiling in her stomach. "Stephen sent me a m—message?"

"You must stop this annoying habit of asking silly questions, my dear," he drawled. "Of course, he did. Why else would I mention it?" He pushed her back until she was once more seated on the sofa and walked over to pour himself another brandy.

"Stephen's last thoughts were of you, Miss Drayton," he remarked, coming back to stand before the hearth, his expression somber. "He seemed to feel the need for your presence, and since you were not there, he conjured you up with words. He described you to me in great detail." He paused, and Cassandra saw a cynical quirk on his lips as he examined her with what she considered quite extraordinary insolence. "With predictable exaggeration, I can assure you. I was quite touched by his devotion to you, however."

Overcome by the conflicting emotions of hearing Stephen's love for her recounted in what could only be seen as condescending terms, Cassandra instantly took umbrage. "You have no right to sneer at your brother's feelings," she exclaimed. "They do him c-credit." Her voice threatened to break, but she continued to glare at her tormentor. "W-why are you being so odious?"

"I have no wish to find myself saddled with a maudlin female," he replied bluntly, his brow lowering into a scowl.

"Are you always this unfeeling?" Cassandra burst out, her nerves ragged. "Don't you *care* that your brother is dead?" The dreaded word, once spoken, hung in the air between them like an invisible reminder of a past that could never be retrieved. No sooner had it left her lips, however, than Cassandra recoiled, horrified at her own callousness. "I do b-beg your pardon, my lord," she stuttered, mortified at the flash of anguish she glimpsed in Lord Mansfield's eyes. "I should never have said that. P-please forgive me. This news has shattered my life, and I am not myself."

Disregarding her apology, the earl glanced briefly over at the brandy decanter and then seemed to change his mind. He fixed his gaze on a point above Cassandra's head, and she wondered why he felt that he had to conceal his grief for Stephen under a veneer of cynicism. Stephen had been so open about his emotions, she remembered, especially after he had declared his love for her. She herself had a tendency to blurt out her feelings without regard for the consequences, as she had done just now.

"Of course, I care about Stephen," Lord Mansfield said with unusual softness. "He was my only brother, and life is going to be quite damnable without him." The softness passed quickly, and a hint of ironic amusement surfaced again as he added, "That is precisely the reason why I'm here now. He asked me to see that you were provided for, and I gave him my word."

Much as she resented the cynicism she detected in Lord Mansfield's words, Cassandra could not but react instantly to their implication that she was in need of any assistance from this impossible man. "Well, all I can say is that you have been put to a great deal of inconvenience to no purpose. I am quite capable of taking care of myself, thank you," she added with a calm finality she was far from feeling.

Lord Mansfield merely stared at her, and Cassandra had the uncomfortable impression that he could sense all her inner misgivings quite as clearly as though she had spoken them aloud. Then, quite unexpectedly, he smiled. It was the very faintest of smiles, as far as smiles went, but it lightened his expression and made him look less devilish. Unhappily, it lasted so briefly that Cassandra wondered if she had imagined it.

He sighed. "For your sake, Miss Drayton, and for mine, too, of course, I hope that you are right. But in order to discharge my obligation to my brother, I need to know for certain if . . ." He paused, and a glitter of sardonic amusement crinkled the corners of his green eyes. "If Stephen was correct in supposing that by now you might be in need of—shall we say—a more tangible token of support from the Ravenvilles."

Cassandra abruptly stood up and faced him, her face white with fury. "And for your sake, my lord," she spat, forcing herself to ignore the other—uncomfortably intimate—interpretation that might be placed on his words, "I hope you do not intend to subject me to a further display of your unspeakable vulgarity by offering money."

Although her violent reaction had evidently been unexpected, Lord Mansfield did not step back, and Cassandra found herself standing toe-to-toe with his lordship and glaring at him practically nose-to-nose. At least it would be nose-to-nose, she reflected irrationally, if she had been at least twelve inches taller, or he had been that much shorter. As it was, she felt at a distinct disadvantage. The man's towering bulk was disconcerting and made her feel dwarfed and somehow fragile as she never had with Stephen. When the earl let out a crack of laughter, she had the overwhelming urge to box his ears. Something in his eyes prevented her from giving full rein to her inclination, however. They appeared more gray than green upon closer examination, and there was a definite challenge in them as they surveyed her with cool amusement. Instinctively, she knew that his lordship had read her mind and was laughing at her.

"Nothing quite so crass as that, I can assure you, Miss Drayton," he said amiably. "But you have still not answered my question, have you?"

"I thought I just did," she replied ungraciously.

"Not the one about your future, Miss Drayton."

For reasons best known to herself, Cassandra was reluctant even to think of the future that awaited her, much less discuss it with a stranger. She brushed past the earl and went to stand by the window, wishing that he would just go away and leave her alone with her misery.

"Well?" His voice was implacable and made her nerves quiver. "I warn you, I am fast losing what little patience I possess, Miss Drayton. Will you kindly answer my question?"

"My future is no concern of yours, Lord Mansfield," she said quietly, her eyes fixed on the leaves of the ancient sycamore in the vicarage garden, which had begun to turn various shades of autumn yellow.

"If it was a concern of Stephen's, it is certainly a concern of mine."

Cassandra chose to ignore this odd remark and glanced at him over her shoulder. "You mentioned that Stephen gave you a message for me, my lord. What was it?"

Lord Mansfield strolled over to stand beside her at the window, causing Cassandra to feel positively dwarfish again. "He said a number of things I will relate at another time, but the one that most concerns you now is his express wish that you be guided by me in all decisions affecting your future."

Cassandra stared at him in frank astonishment. "I can't b-believe that Stephen w-would say anything so idiotish," she managed to say at last.

"You may believe what you wish, Miss Drayton," came the astringent reply. "However, he did say it, and as a consequence, I have undertaken this extremely inconvenient and tiresome journey into the wilderness of Kent to see that my brother's last wishes are carried out."

"His last wishes?" Cassandra murmured distractedly. "And what were those, my lord?"

The earl seemed to be fast approaching the limit of his endurance. "I am here to determine," he said between clenched teeth, "whether your reputation is in any danger of—shall we say—sustaining a major blemish in the near future." He showed an unmistakable reluctance to clarify this statement, and Cassandra could only pray that the blemish he mentioned was not the one she was beginning to think it might be.

"A major blemish?" she repeated, wondering if this crazy conversation was really taking place at all or whether she was in the middle of her worst nightmare.

"You are being singularly obtuse, Miss Drayton. Forgive me if I take this as deliberate prevarication on your part."

"Nothing of the kind," she replied in a voice that was barely a whisper. "It's just that I fail to see—"

"Try not to provoke me any more than is absolutely necessary, Miss Drayton," Lord Mansfield said with a silkiness that sent a cold shiver down Cassandra's spine. When she made no response, he regarded her intently for a moment before shrugging his wide shoulders as though he were suddenly bored with the whole issue.

"I was merely trying to spare your blushes, my dear, but if you insist on plain speaking, then plain speaking you shall get. It's all one to me. Now answer me this, Miss Drayton. Are you or are you not carrying my brother's child?"

Although she had feared for some minutes that this was what the earl had been leading up to, when confronted with a reality

she had tried to evade, Cassandra was devastated by the un
adorned bluntness of his question. It seemed to her overwrough
sensibilities that, by stating it so baldly, the earl had somehow
carved her shame in stone, which was a ridiculous notion if ever
there was one. She closed her eyes for a moment to gather what
little courage she had left, then turned to face the man at her side
whose harsh features were strangely expressionless.

"I fail to see—"

"If you wish to avoid being throttled, Miss Drayton," he
growled with barely controlled violence, "I advise you to answer
my question once and for all."

Cassandra realized she had been holding her breath. She let it
out in a long, gentle sigh. In a sense it was a relief to share her
predicament with someone else, although Lord Mansfield was the
last person she would have chosen for the role of confidant.

"The answer is yes," she said, wondering idly if this man, with
his black curls in disarray and his harsh, unforgiving countenance,
could be a messenger from Hell sent to extract her confession of
guilt and carry away her soul to eternal damnation. She cast these
fanciful notions from her mind and returned his gaze calmly.
"Yes," she repeated. "I am."

She had expected some sign from him, either of disapproval,
scorn, or even cynicism, but to her surprise he revealed none at
all. Instead, he strolled over to the sideboard and poured another
brandy.

"At least now we know what we have to do," he remarked in a
neutral voice.

In spite of herself, she was intrigued. "And what is that, may I
ask?"

"I must speak to your father immediately," came the unexpected reply.

Cassandra felt her cheeks go pale with dread. The man had run
mad again, she thought. At all costs, she must prevent him from
telling her father that his eldest daughter had brought disgrace
down on his head. "I see no reason for you to do that, my lord,"
she began, trying to keep the panic out of her voice.

Lord Mansfield drained his glass with a flourish and turned to
her, a mocking grin on his face. "Ah, but I do, my dear Miss
Drayton. We must not disregard a single tedious convention if we
are to do justice to Stephen's last wishes. And the inevitable interview with your father must surely be one of the most tedious."

Cassandra was beginning to get a sinking feeling about the direction the earl was taking. "Why would you need to interview my father?" she demanded, wondering if she would be forced to call on two of the stable lads to restrain him if he became violent.

"To make him a formal offer for your hand, of course," came the slurred, faintly sardonic reply.

Phineas Ravenville regarded Miss Drayton's startled face with wry amusement. His words seemed to have momentarily stilled her acid tongue, he thought, not without a flicker of relief. He could scarcely believe that he had actually uttered them. They were, if truth were known, the very words he had so studiously avoided for the past ten years, ever since he had come into the title at the tender age of twenty-one. He remembered all too well those first wild years he had spent on the Town, during which the young and dashing Earl of Mansfield had been courted assiduously by hopeful mothers, who considered him the catch of the Season. As the years went by, however, and his taste had run to flamboyant opera singers and scandalous demimondaines, prudent mothers had warned their young daughters to avoid the earl's rakish company.

And now, here he was, he thought with a touch of self-mockery, about to offer for a female he barely knew. The last thing in the world he had anticipated a week ago was to find himself here, in the wilds of Kent, about to be leg-shackled to one of the dowdiest, most ill-mannered shrews he had come across in a long time. He wondered briefly how different the future might have been for both of them had he been in London and not still at Mansfield Grange, his family seat, when news of Stephen's accident had reached him. He shuddered at the thought. His beloved brother would have died alone in a houseful of servants, and Mansfield would never have known the depths of Stephen's love for an inconsequential vicar's daughter. That might have been more convenient for himself, the earl had thought more than once during the mad journey down into Kent, but not for Stephen. The lad would have been denied the chance to unburden himself, and although Mansfield had never given much credence to the powers of love, he recognized that his young brother was well and truly besotted with his country wench. So, thanks to the most important promise the earl had ever made, Stephen had died at peace, confident that his precious Miss Drayton's reputation would be safe in his brother's hands. The consequences of that promise were only now beginning to loom before him in all their stark reality.

He noticed that Miss Drayton was recovering from her shock, horror and revulsion gradually replacing amazement on her pale face. To forestall the protest he knew was imminent, he broke the silence. "Where can I find your father, Miss Drayton? The sooner I can talk to him, the sooner we can put this business behind us."

His words seem to jolt her, and the earl saw a flash of anger animate her expressive hazel eyes. They were rather fine eyes, he realized and wondered cynically if Miss Drayton had perhaps used them, among other things, to seduce his brother into their secret betrothal. He had discounted Stephen's enthusiastic description of his ladylove as the deluded ramblings of a man in the throes of a grand passion, and had rather expected to find himself dealing with a brazen hussy who would not hesitate to lie about her condition if she saw that it might be worth her while.

He had been surprised in Miss Drayton. Although he knew her to be twenty-two, she looked much younger, and definitely virginal, although he knew she was no such thing. He would have known precisely how to handle a grasping hussy, having dealt with innumerable females of that persuasion during his lifetime of dissolution. A large sum of money would normally have changed hands, and Mansfield could have returned to London with a clear conscience at having fulfilled his brother's last request.

The Miss Drayton who had burst so inelegantly into his life, however, called for a different approach. Stephen had insisted rather pointedly that his Cassandra's mother was the daughter of a baron, an impoverished one of little account, Mansfield had recalled, but nevertheless, a member of the nobility. Thus, in Stephen's besotted eyes at least, Miss Drayton's breeding made her quite eligible for the younger son of a Ravenville. Mansfield had refrained from pointing out that her father, the vicar, was only the third son of an undistinguished country squire. If he could only have Stephen back, he thought with a twist of bitterness, he would give his blessing to his brother's marriage, regardless of the bride's connections or lack of them.

But that was patently impossible, and Stephen's betrothed was not the fortune hunter the earl had half hoped she would be. When she had shown commendable reluctance to admit that she was increasing with his brother's child, the earl found his options drastically reduced if he wished to save her from the consequences of

Stephen's impetuosity. As his interview with the lady progressed, it became clear to Mansfield that the only honorable way out of Miss Drayton's dilemma was to marry her himself.

"You have completely taken leave of your senses," Miss Drayton remarked scathingly. "There can be no question of . . ." she hesitated, her cheeks flushing angrily. "My father will never consent to such a ramshackle notion, you may count on it. And furthermore, I would rather die an ape-leader than accept such an insulting offer."

The earl found Miss Drayton's vehement rejection of his suit rather sobering and wondered what the more persistent of this year's crop of marriage-minded mothers would say if they could hear a little countrified chit throwing the Earl of Mansfield's offer of marriage back in his teeth with such aplomb.

"Nevertheless, you will take me to your father immediately, and let me handle the matter," he remarked, wishing—now that he had decided on a course of action that would satisfy both his promise to Stephen and his own conscience—to settle the issue at once.

"I will do no such thing!" she exclaimed, glaring at him furiously.

He felt his patience growing thin. "I suppose you propose to stay here, where everybody knows you, and cause your family the embarrassment of having a fatherless brat thrust into its midst?" he said with deliberate bluntness. "That is just the kind of bird-witted start I might have expected from a female who knows no better than to receive callers with her hair hanging down her back." He felt a sadistic pleasure at being able to pay her back in her own coin. Perhaps that would teach the chit to defy his authority in such a hoydenish manner.

"My hair is not . . ." she began, her hand flying to tuck in the numerous loose auburn strands floating around her face. "And even if it were," she continued heatedly, "It is not your place to tell me how to wear my hair, my lord. So I will thank you to keep your odious observations to yourself."

The Earl of Mansfield decided to take matters into his own hands. He strode over to the bellrope and gave it a vigorous pull.

"Whatever do you think you're doing?"

"I am summoning one of the servants to conduct me to your father, my girl. And if I were you, I would accept the solution I am offering you with good grace. Remember that Stephen's last request was that you defer to me in matters concerning your future."

"Surely he could not have meant you to go to such an extreme," she faltered, clearly beginning to waver in her opposition. "You cannot wish to marry me. We are s-strangers." This last was uttered in such desolate tones that the earl almost felt sorry for the wench. He attempted to reassure her. "Many couples are practically strangers when they wed," he said bracingly. "We shall brush through well enough. That is, if you try to control your annoying habit of contradicting everything I say."

"I do nothing of the sort," came the impetuous response, to which the earl merely grinned humorlessly.

"Stephen did warn me that you could be rather hot in hand when you were crossed, my dear. But I should remind you that I am not my easygoing brother and will brook no nonsense," he drawled, privately convinced that the redoubtable Miss Drayton would benefit greatly from a firm hand on the reins.

"What a whisker!" she exclaimed. "Stephen would say no such thing; we dealt exceedingly well together. He would certainly not have to *force* me into marriage. And I am *not* your dear," she added, casting him a scathing glance from beneath her lashes.

"You are right on that score, at least," he shot back. "But you mistake the matter if you think I can be fobbed off by your rag-mannered starts, Miss Drayton." He paused to survey her contemptuously. "My brother must have been castaway when he fell into your clutches, my dear," he remarked with deliberate sarcasm. "But he went to his grave confident that no child of his would be born on the wrong side of the blanket." He saw that his crude words had rocked her composure, for she went pale and gave a small gasp of distress. Most women he knew would have fallen into a fit of the vapors after half the cutting remarks he had thrown at her, and the earl experienced a reluctant glimmer of admiration at the chit's fortitude.

"You may well feel put upon, my dear," he continued in a kinder tone. "But you will only catch cold if you try to thwart me. I intend to keep my promise to my brother, come hell or high water. No child of his will be born a bastard if I have anything to say in the matter."

There came a discreet knock at the door, and Mrs. Hill appeared, an anxious expression on her face. "You rang, miss?"

Mansfield looked across the room at Miss Drayton, a quizzical half smile on his lips.

"Y-yes, Mrs. Hill," she stammered, refusing to meet his eyes. "Lord Mansfield wishes to speak with Father. Will you please show him into the study?"

"Good girl," he murmured under his breath as he walked past her and followed the housekeeper out of the room.

CHAPTER THREE

The Agreement

As soon as the Earl of Mansfield's broad back had disappeared, Cassandra stood for several interminable minutes, staring blindly at the closed parlor door. Her mind was a chaos of mixed emotions. The memory of her dearest Stephen, now lost to her forever, was like an invisible rapier deep inside her, inflicting a constant, twisting, piercing pain. She stifled a sob, wishing that she could flee to her room and let out her misery in a restorative bout of tears. But no such relief would be hers until this sorry muddle she found herself in had been settled one way or another. Even as she stood there, that veritable ogre of a man was closeted with her father, she thought disconsolately. Dared she hope that her father would refuse to consider the earl's suit? she wondered.

A ray of hope flickered for a moment in her heart and then went out. It would be unrealistic to expect her unworldly father to question the sincerity of the Earl of Mansfield, wouldn't it? The villain was bound to be adept in all the more nefarious forms of persuasion. She considered how he had so successfully manipulated her into allowing him—albeit reluctantly—to interview her father. Cassandra knew instinctively, from the brief yet devastating contact she had had with his lordship, that he would not hesitate to use any means at hand—his rank, his wealth, his overbearing personality, his specious arguments—to obtain his ends. Her father stood not the slightest chance of resisting an onslaught from such an experienced adversary. And if her father capitulated, she would be condemned to spend the rest of her life tied to a man she could only despise.

The only advantage she could see to such an unpleasant arrangement was the same one the earl had emphasized so strongly. It was within her power to provide a father for Stephen's child. The magnitude of his responsibility daunted her. How could she possibly justify refusing such an offer? She could not do so, of course, and the more she considered the circumstances, the more she realized that she was caught up in a situation over which she had no control. The infamous earl had her in his power, she thought resentfully. And worse yet, he had Stephen's blessing to arrange her life as he saw fit. Much as she hated to admit it, Cassandra knew she was outnumbered and outmaneuvered. There was nobody to take her part in this affair. The earl demanded her acquiescence, Stephen had countenanced it, her father would inevitably agree to it, and above all, the child would benefit from it. She must strive to keep that one thought in mind, she vowed. Stephen's child. She would do it for their child, and for Stephen, and for her dear father, who only that morning had expressed his concern for her future.

Her future, she thought with a sinking feeling in the pit of her stomach. What was it the earl had said in that odiously condescending way of his? "We shall brush through well enough?" Yes, that was it. Brush through, indeed. Well, perhaps they would if only he kept out of her way and did not try to rule her life for her. Would he expect her to remove to Mansfield Grange? she wondered. Probably so. She would much prefer to stay here in the vicarage with her father and Drusilla, but had little hope of the earl's consenting to that. He would undoubtedly expect his new countess to take up residence at his own estate. *His countess.* The practical realities of becoming his countess had not struck her before, but it had a disturbing ring to it. There must be innumerable things a countess was supposed to know, and Cassandra was suddenly quite sure she would do all the wrong things and bring the earl's censure down on her head.

And then, with sudden misgivings, it occurred to her that there was the other, intimate side of marriage. Surely he would not expect her to. . . . No, that would be too horrible to contemplate. She must insist upon the earl's promise that theirs would be a marriage in name only. Not that she expected him to wish it otherwise, of course, given his obvious dislike of her; but with gentlemen one could never be quite sure. It would be wise to make that one of the conditions to her acceptance.

She was lost in speculations on how this delicate matter might be broached to his lordship when the door opened again, and Mrs. Hill trotted in. "Bless you, Miss Cassie," she exclaimed in her motherly voice. "You look quite done in, dear. And here is your father wanting you to step into his study. Seems to be in high gig, the vicar does. Can't remember when I've seen him this lively before." She eyed Miss Drayton suspiciously. "You wouldn't happen to know what's afoot, would you now, missy?" she ventured with the confidence of the long-time dependent.

"I'm sure I have no idea, Mrs. Hill," Cassandra replied mendaciously. "We will have to wait and see, won't we?"

"You'll want to nip upstairs to tidy your hair, miss," the housekeeper suggested. "You're looking a mite peaked, deary, and you are wishful of making a good impression on his lordship now, aren't you?"

Cassandra made a halfhearted attempt to confine her wayward curls and then shrugged nonchalantly. "This will have to do, Mrs. Hill. And no, actually I don't care what his lordship thinks of me. If he doesn't like my hair, that is just too bad. I shall not waste time primping for the likes of him."

Leaving an astounded Mrs. Hill gaping after her, Cassandra flung out of the room and marched down the hall to the door of her father's study, which she opened unceremoniously. The sight that greeted her eyes as she stepped inside made her spirits sink, but she gritted her teeth and fixed a bland smile on her face.

"You sent for me, Father?" she inquired flatly, acutely conscious of the vicar's flushed face and happy smile. He was standing before the fire beside the Earl of Mansfield, who held a half-empty glass of Spanish sherry in his long, tanned fingers. Her father was also drinking sherry, a rare occurrence with him, and one he indulged in only when he deemed that a celebration of some sort was in order. Cassandra could well imagine the event that had sent him into his present celebratory mood.

The vicar looked at her over his spectacles and smiled broadly. "Yes, my love. I have some extraordinary news for you. Quite took me by surprise, it did, I must admit. Here I was sitting at my desk as I am every morning, struggling with a particularly obtuse passage from Hesiod's *The Works and Days*. You remember the one I mentioned to you yesterday at the dinner table—verses 760 to 764, the ones about gossip getting out of control once started. Well, I believe I have finally come to understand why Hesiod likens gossip to a kind of goddess. It is a fascinating notion, my dear. You will enjoy it when I tell you."

Midway through her father's digression on one of his favorite topics, Cassandra cast a slanting glance at the earl to see how he was bearing up under the onslaught of Greek erudition. She found his sardonic gaze fixed on her, and his mouth relaxed into something perilously close to a smirk.

"I'm sure I will, Father," she intervened smoothly to bring him back to the present issue. "But I doubt Lord Mansfield has any interest whatsoever in Hesiod's treatise on farming."

"His lordship tells me he is an Oxford man," her father stated with evident delight. "He has even read Greek with old Mathieson. Remember Mathieson, my dear? He visited us one summer when your mother was still with us."

Cassandra was sorely tempted to lead her father into a more lengthy discussion of his Greek scholarship which could very well last until dinnertime, but she contented herself with asking if Lord Mansfield had indeed read Hesiod.

"Yes," he replied smoothly. "But my acquaintance with him is limited to his *Shield of Herakles*."

"Ah, I see. You prefer blood and gore to the quiet life of a farmer, I take it?"

"Am I to understand that you are also a scholar, Miss Drayton?" the earl inquired silkily, his eyes full of silent mockery.

"My daughter has an excellent ear for the ancient languages, my lord," the vicar broke in proudly. "She has been a great help to me over the years. I shall indeed miss her if—" He stopped abruptly and glanced nervously from the earl to his daughter as if wondering what they were doing clustered in his study. Then his face cleared, and he chuckled. "I fear I digress, my lord." He cleared his throat. "Cassandra, my love, Lord Mansfield has come to me with a most flattering offer for you."

"Oh, really? How very opportune of him, to be sure," she murmured between clenched teeth.

"I don't recall you ever mentioning any understanding between you, my dear. Although it could have slipped my mind, of course. The earl tells me that your attachment is of long standing. I could have sworn that it was Stephen you favored, dear, but I must have been mistaken."

At the mention of Stephen's name, Cassandra turned for the first time to look directly into the earl's eyes, her own wide with shock. For reasons of his own, the monster had not told her father of Stephen's death, she realized. Abruptly she turned her face away and blinked back the sudden tears that burned at the back of her eyes. How she longed to tell her father that he had been right, that it was Stephen she had wanted to marry, not this cynical, callous man who thought nothing of deceiving her father with half-truths and honeyed promises. She swallowed hard, but could not trust herself to speak or look at either of them.

"Your father wanted to be sure of your wishes in the matter, Miss Drayton, before giving me his answer," the earl interjected smoothly, as if sensing her distress.

"Yes, my dearest Cassie," her father said, nodding his head sagely and taking his cue. "I have told his lordship that I can see nothing to object to at all in the match. In fact, I am quite delighted with the prospect of seeing you settled so comfortably. It appears that Lord Mansfield is prepared to offer an astonishingly generous settlement in spite of the fact that I confessed to him that you have no dowry to speak of. But I will abide by your decision, my dear, but I do urge you to consider your answer carefully."

An astonishingly generous settlement indeed! So it was going to be a question of money after all, she thought bitterly. And her father, consciously or not, had made it quite clear what he wanted her decision to be.

Quite suddenly, the whole situation became too much for her, and she turned away from the two men and walked slowly over to the window overlooking the vicarage garden. The rose garden her mother had so lovingly established and which Cassandra continued to tend in her memory now looked straggled and forlorn in the blustery September wind. She wondered if this could be an omen of some sort. The last vestiges of blooms were long gone, and she noticed that the bushes themselves would soon need to be pruned for the coming winter. Who would take care of her mother's roses when she was gone? she wondered. The thought of leaving her beloved home and family, and living in an unfamiliar place surrounded by strangers caused her throat to constrict. She gulped back a sob and felt her eyes grow misty with unshed tears. A great sadness filled her heart at the bleak future in store for her, but she knew, for her child's sake, she must overcome this missishness and do what had to be done. She took a deep breath to steady her nerves, but before she could turn around, she sensed a tall presence beside her. The earl took her hand in both of his, and it was then she realized she was trembling uncontrollably.

"My dear girl," he murmured, squeezing her fingers reassuringly and carrying them to his lips. "Do not, I beg of you, send me away with a broken heart." The kiss he placed lingeringly on her fingertips was surprisingly warm and caressing, but the words were deliberately mocking and designed expressly for her father's benefit. Her anger flared again, as he must have known it would, and she tried to wrench her hand away. He held her firmly, however, and, tucking her captive hand in the crook of his arm, led her back to where the vicar stood hesitantly before the fire.

"Well, my dear?" her father asked anxiously. "Have you allowed yourself to be persuaded?"

There was no better way of putting it, Cassandra decided. Between them they had made it easy for her to capitulate, and she found herself without the strength to protest any further against a future she had already persuaded herself to accept.

It was only when her father, taking her silence for acquiescence, folded her in his arms to congratulate her, that she let her tears fall unrestrained.

The sight of Miss Drayton's tears had the unwonted effect on the Earl of Mansfield of making him feel like a cad. This was a new and uncomfortable experience for him, one which he was able to shrug off easily enough as soon as the vicar had dried his daughter's eyes and told her not to be a silly goose. After all, he reasoned, females were noted for their emotional starts and, for all her claim that she rarely cried, Miss Drayton was no different from any of the other females of his acquaintance. For a moment there by the window, however, he had been afraid she would reject him out of hand. Her expressive hazel eyes had been glazed with tears, and she trembled quite noticeably when he raised her cold fingers to his lips. He had purposely made his kiss seductively caressing in the expectation—born of years of practice at such things—of melting her resistance. His deliberately flirtatious words, designed to bring her firmly under his control again, had produced quite the opposite effect. With a spurt of unexpected anger, she had almost wrenched free of his grasp, and her eyes, no longer misty with tears, glared up at him with undisguised hostility.

Well, well, he thought wryly as he led her back to her father. So that's how it's going to be, is it? The wench is unwilling, is she? Pity she was such an unprepossessing little creature, otherwise he might have looked forward to some sport in bringing her to heel. No sooner had this callous thought crossed his mind than Phineas regretted it. Had he become so depraved that he must needs prey upon an innocent chit to gratify his jaded senses? Not precisely innocent, he grimly reminded himself. If she had been, he would not now be in the unenviable position of getting himself leg-shackled to a female who obviously held him in distaste.

He glanced down at her small, unhappy face and wondered what the devil his London friends would say to this incongruous mismatch. Robert Heathercott, in particular, would rag him unmercifully when he found out that the notorious Raven—as the earl was known among his intimates—had succumbed to the wiles of a country vicar's daughter with nothing to recommend her aside from a pair of fine eyes.

He was startled out of his ruminations by that same pair of eyes—still filled with thinly veiled hostility—which regarded him fixedly.

"Before we go any further in this matter, Father," he heard his newly affianced bride state in a firm voice, "there are some points I need to discuss with his lordship."

The vicar appeared taken aback by this sudden contretemps. He looked anxiously from his daughter to the earl and seemed at a loss for words.

"Anything you wish, my dear," the earl interposed smoothly. "I am sure your father will grant us a few moments alone if that will set your mind at rest. Isn't that true, sir?" He addressed this last remark to the vicar, who declared himself more than happy to oblige his lordship."

"I shall certainly be glad to leave you alone for half an hour, my dear." He beamed dotingly at his daughter. "I must find your sister and tell her the glad news."

"Ten minutes will suffice, Father," Cassandra remarked dryly, but the vicar clearly had his mind set on other things and gave no sign of having heard her.

No sooner had the door closed behind the vicar, than Miss Drayton rounded on him, and Mansfield felt the full force of her anger. "I would like to know why you saw fit to deceive my father so cold-bloodedly," she demanded.

He had a fair notion that she meant his failure to inform the vicar of Stephen's fatal accident, but the temptation to provoke her was too strong to resist. "I assure you that I refrained from giving your father the impression that I am madly in love with you, my dear," he replied, watching for the flash of temper he knew would follow these mendacious words. "I thought under the circumstances, that would be doing it rather too brown."

Cassandra gave a moue of disgust and glared at him. "You know very well that is not what I meant," she fumed. "Why did you not mention anything about . . . about Stephen?"

He shrugged. "I saw no need to burden your father with a tale of tragedy when he was enjoying the prospect of finally settling his aging daughter so advantageously," he said carelessly, pouring himself another glass of sherry from the decanter on the vicar's desk. He smiled to himself at the splutter of rage that greeted these words.

"You are nothing but a conceited coxcomb, thoroughly beneath contempt. And I should point out to you, my lord, in case you had not noticed, that I have yet to accept your advantageous offer, as you choose to call it."

"By not rejecting it when you had the chance, my dear, you gave your tacit agreement. Your father apparently thinks so, anyway."

"I am not your *dear*," she snapped, swerving off on one of the tangents that made conversation with her lively if not exactly coherent. "So you can refrain from the sarcasm."

Phineas gave her a mocking bow and took a long pull on his sherry.

"You should also refrain from drinking too much," Miss Drayton remarked sententiously. "And good sherry should be sipped, not guzzled as one would a cheap ale."

The earl was so surprised and incensed by this unexpected piece of rudeness that he nearly choked on the offending drink. Before he could think of a suitable set-down, Miss Drayton added insult to injury.

"I trust you are not one of those odious men who spend all their time castaway," she remarked scathingly. "If you are, you will kindly say so now, and we can put an end to this farce. The last thing a child needs is a father who is forever bosky."

Although Mansfield often did indulge in the delights of Bacchus rather more than was strictly good for him, he rarely set out—as did some of his friends—to drink himself deliberately under the table. Miss Drayton's criticism struck a nerve, however, and he was quick to retaliate.

"You surprise me, Miss Drayton," he said coolly. "I had no idea you were conversant with the drinking habits of gentlemen."

"I am not, if you must know, my lord," she replied. "But I have heard that gentlemen can become very unpredictable when they are foxed."

He laughed unpleasantly. "If you mean that in our cups we often turn to lewd and amorous thoughts, my dear," he said silkily, "then you are perfectly correct." He was amused to see that his blunt speaking had brought a flush of color to Miss Drayton's pale cheeks. "But *you* need have no fear in that direction," he added with deliberate emphasis, hoping that she would understand the insult he intended. "No gentleman, even in his cups, would dare assault a vicar's daughter." He smiled wolfishly. "Not even I, who have done some barbaric things in my time, would commit such a faux pas."

Instead of the explosion of wrath he had expected, Miss Drayton looked relieved. "I am glad to hear you say so, my lord, because that touches on the issue I wish to discuss with you."

The earl frowned in puzzlement for a moment, but then his face cleared, and he regarded his betrothed expectantly. Unless he was very much mistaken, the chit was about to deprive him of his marital rights. To tell the truth, he had not given the notion any thought. Now if Miss Drayton had been a raving beauty, or at least had possessed a flirtatious and captivating nature, he would have looked forward to her seduction with a modicum of pleasure. But she was none of these things, and Phineas could not imagine himself, even in his cups, being so deprived of female company as to desire to bed the provoking, rag-mannered little chit he was about to marry.

"Well?" he prompted, beginning to enjoy her discomfiture.

She swallowed and took a deep breath. "I believe we are both aware that this marriage is purely a convenience, my lord, wouldn't you agree?"

"Oh, absolutely."

She seemed to take heart at his ready assent. "It will be convenient, indeed even desirable, for Stephen's child to be . . . to have . . ." She stumbled for a moment, but Phineas merely smiled in lazy amusement. "To be born a Ravenville, I mean. We both know this to be true. As for you and I, my lord—"

"You should really practice calling me Phineas, you know, my dear."

As was his intention, he had thrown her off stride, and she dismissed the interruption impatiently. "As for you and I," she continued, "this marriage is nothing but an inconvenience, I am sure.

But I am prepared, and I trust that you are too, my lord, to protect Stephen's child from—"

"You should also practice thinking of it as *my* child, Cassandra," he murmured gently, taking great pleasure in the confusion he produced in his intended with his improper suggestion and the use of her name.

"B-but it is *not* y-yours, my lord," she stammered, her face pink with mortification at the direction their conversation was taking.

"I beg to differ, my dear," Phineas said, thoroughly enjoying himself. "As soon as we are wed, it will be, and I intend to claim it as mine. The whole world will expect me to, as would Stephen." He regarded her keenly. "I trust you do not intend to gainsay me, Miss Drayton. That would raise the devil of a dust, believe me."

Miss Drayton's hazel eyes flew wide with alarm. "Of course not," she exclaimed crossly. "Why would I do such a bird-witted thing, my lord?"

"Pure contrariness, I would imagine," he replied. "It is a serious flaw in your nature, which I have already brought to your attention several times."

To his surprise and secret gratification, Miss Drayton lowered her thick lashes demurely. "I shall endeavor not to contradict you in future, my lord," she murmured. "And that is precisely part of what I wished to discuss with you."

He took another drink of sherry, gazing at her all the while over the rim of his glass, as if defying her to say what was on her mind.

She ignored the challenge, evidently absorbed by her own train of thought. "In an arrangement such as ours," Miss Drayton said hesitantly, "an inconvenient one for both of us, to say the least, perhaps we should try to keep out of one another's way. Don't you agree?"

He had been correct; she was working up to the intimacies of their inconvenient marriage. Rather than put her mind at rest immediately, the earl assumed a bland expression. "You are undoubtedly correct, Cassandra. Out of sight, out of mind sort of thing, eh?"

"Yes, that's it." He detected a note of relief in her voice.

"We could, of course, argue over the dinner table," he said mendaciously. "Or in the drawing room after dinner."

"I promise to make a special effort not to do so, if you will do the same," she offered.

"But we are bound to meet over breakfast."

"Not necessarily," she pointed out. "I could take mine in my bedchamber."

"Ah!" he exclaimed, unable to keep the amusement from his voice. "Your bedchamber, my love. Will we argue there, do you think?"

"You will have no cause to enter my rooms at all, my lord," Miss Drayton answered sharply, her color high. "Ours must be a marriage in name only, Lord Mansfield. I want your solemn promise on that point, or I shall tell my father I have decided not to marry at all."

"What? And disappoint poor Stephen?" he mocked her.

"I insist upon it."

The earl was beginning to be bored with the whole issue, which had never been of importance to him anyway. "Very well," he agreed. "But with one condition."

"And what is that?" she regarded him suspiciously.

It amused him to have the last word in their argument. "If Stephen's child—that is to say, *my* first child—is a girl, you will promise to give me a son and heir. Fair enough?"

She gazed at him for a long moment. "Fair enough."

CHAPTER FOUR

The Impromptu Wedding

Cassandra sighed for perhaps the fifth time since she had come upstairs after leaving the earl to discuss the final arrangements of their marriage with her father. She had intended escaping to her room to indulge in the ocean of tears she needed so desperately to shed for her lost love, but she found herself thwarted. A bewildered and belligerent Drusilla awaited her with a barrage of questions for which Cassandra had no convincing answers.

"Tell me that this whole thing is a nightmare," Drusilla pleaded, flinging herself tearfully into her sister's arms as soon as Cassandra entered the bedchamber. "Father must have taken leave of his senses. He says that you are going to be the Countess of Mansfield, which I do not for a moment believe. You always thought the earl a top-lofty, obnoxious creature, and besides, you are betrothed to Stephen. And where is Stephen, anyway? Why is he not come to claim you, as he promised?"

Cassandra tried to pull her wits together in order to comfort her sister, whose grief and confusion were understandable. But Drusilla's tears, added to the realization that she would have to tell her sister that Stephen was dead, made it impossible for her to restrain her own pent-up emotions. With a choking sob, she put her arms tightly round her sister's shaking shoulders and felt her own cheeks grow wet with tears. The past hour had seen her safe world and carefully planned future change from the comfortable anticipation of sharing her life with the man she loved to a tumultuous sensation of being carried along by dark forces over which she had little or no control.

"Lord Mansfield brought the most dreadful news, Dru," she murmured finally, groping for a handkerchief in the pocket of her simple green morning gown. "It's about Stephen," she added, when Drusilla stared at her, wide-eyed with apprehension. As succinctly as possible, she related the meager details Lord Mansfield had given her regarding his brother's accident.

Drusilla reacted with predictable consternation and distress. Stephen had been as dear to her as a brother, and at first she simply refused to believe that he was lost to her forever. Slowly, however, the indisputable fact that Lord Mansfield had come down to Kent personally to deliver the sad news forced her to accept the reality of the tragedy.

After her sister's paroxysm of grief had run its course, and Cassandra had dried her own tears, the sisters huddled together on the old-fashioned confident, their arms around each other for comfort.

Drusilla was the first to raise her tear-stained face, a puzzled expression clouding her pansy-blue eyes. "Doesn't Father know about Stephen, Cassie?"

"Not yet, dear. Lord Mansfield thought it best not to burden him with too many things at once. He preferred to leave the distressing part until after the other had been arranged."

"The other? *What* other?" Drusilla demanded, a note of alarm in her voice.

"He wished to make Father an offer, you see, and he—"

Drusilla stared at her in astonishment. "An offer? Do you mean to tell me that what Father told me was not a Banbury tale after all? Are you really to become a countess, Cassie?"

Cassandra saw the disbelief in her sister's eyes and smiled wryly. "It would seem so, Dru. I'm afraid it's true."

Her little sister seemed momentarily deprived of speech, then she rallied and demanded to know how such a thing had happened.

"I don't really know," Cassandra replied helplessly. "It seems that Stephen made his brother promise—or so the earl would have me believe—to protect my reputation." She paused, uncomfortably aware that this explanation covered but half of the truth.

Drusilla was quick to pounce on the inconsistency of this argument. "He does not have to wed you to do that, surely?" she pointed out, her expression puzzled. "And why does your reputation need protection? You were betrothed to Stephen, for heaven's sake. Everyone in the neighborhood has known about it for the longest time."

"It was a secret from Stephen's family, however," Cassandra replied. "And that's the rub, you see. We were not officially affianced, and a clandestine betrothal—even if it is widely known—can only be considered highly improper and perhaps compromising. The earl is doing only what he considers proper to rectify his brother's indiscretion." Again this was not the whole truth, but Cassandra had, for once, agreed with Lord Mansfield that no one else should ever be privy to the true circumstances behind their sudden and quite incongruous marriage. So, much as she longed to confide in her little sister, she held her peace, hoping that Drusilla would not tease her for further explanations.

Her sister regarded her solemnly, her deep blue eyes troubled. "Didn't you really love Stephen, after all?" she asked quietly.

Taken aback by the directness of the question, Cassandra felt her heart sink and tears start to her eyes. "How can you ask such a thing, Dru?" she whispered, her voice unsteady. "Of course I did. I still do," she added emphatically.

"Then how can you agree to wed Lord Mansfield, a man you actively dislike? I do not understand you, Cassie. How can you bear to accept another man in place of Stephen? One who will bring you—if half the rumors about him are true—only a lifetime of unhappiness," Drusilla exclaimed impatiently. "That is the most nonsensical thing you have yet come up with, Cassie. What do you take me for—Some ninny-headed schoolroom chit with more hair than wit?"

Since Cassandra could find no adequate answer to this, she took refuge in her damp handkerchief. Her sister's words had cut deeply, and she was quite unable to think coherently, much less try to explain the trap she felt closing around her. Her father's unquestioning acceptance of the earl's suit, and Lord Mansfield's arrogant dismissal of her objections had undermined her spirit. What use was it to continue fighting a destiny she herself had to admit would benefit Stephen's child? The thought gave her strength, and she turned to hug her sister impulsively.

"Of course I don't consider you bird-witted, Dru. You have more sense than most girls your age, but please don't tease me about why and how this has come about. I am depending on you to see me through this ordeal, dearest, and you cannot help matters by constantly pinching at me. Just believe me when I say that it is for the best." She brushed distractedly at an auburn curl that had come loose from her chignon, wishing she could believe in her own words. "We must both look a sight," she murmured. "Come, Dru. We cannot sit here like two watering-pots all afternoon. Let's decide what we should wear this evening, shall we? I think your new pink muslin would be just the thing, don't you?"

"New?" repeated Drusilla derisively. "That pink gown will be three years old this Christmas. Don't you remember? You had it made for me that year we were invited to old Lady Braithwaite's Christmas ball. We had to let it out last spring, do you recall? When I began to fill out the bodice rather more than you thought decorous." A sad little smile curved her delicate lips. "Stephen danced the country dance with me, remember? It was my first real dance at a proper ball."

Cassandra was remembering that long-ago ball too well herself. She had worn a green silk gown that had been her mother's in better days, cut down to fit her slight figure. She had been nineteen and in love, and Stephen's admiring glances had told her plainly that she was loved in return, as had the kiss he had stolen in the dark garden on the cold December evening. Their first kiss, she remembered with a painful flash of nostalgia, and she had shivered at the delicious sensation of his warm lips as much as from the cold. And Stephen had told her. . . . But what was the use of dwelling on those painful memories? she chided herself. Stephen was gone now, and she had his child to protect.

She sighed. "Yes, I remember, Dru. You quite dazzled all those country swains, particularly Gerald Whittaker."

"Pooh!" Drusilla dismissed this suitor airily. "Tell me, why do you wish me to wear the pink gown tonight, Cassie? Don't tell me that . . . that dreadful man is invited to dine with us?"

Cassandra wished she could have denied it, but her father—usually so casual about social formalities—had insisted that Lord Mansfield accept an invitation to dine at the vicarage that evening. She had not missed the ironic curl of the earl's thin lips that told her—better than any words—how little he looked forward to the event. She was not looking forward to it herself, but firmly put the thought out of her head and went to examine the contents of her wardrobe.

The dinner party was a disaster right from the start. The earl was already in the Draytons's small drawing room, seated at his ease before the hearth, a glass of sherry in his hand, when Cassandra entered with a reluctant Drusilla in tow. He rose as they approached, as did the vicar, prompted no doubt to this unusual gesture of respect toward his daughters by their guest's punctiliousness. After a quick glance at the earl's harsh, faintly bored countenance, Cassandra studiously avoided meeting his eyes. What did she care, she told herself resolutely, that this Town fop must think her a veritable country dowd in her old-fashioned bronze satin—the only evening gown she possessed? Did he think that she cared a fig for the supercilious disdain she saw reflected on his face as he bowed with studied courtesy over her hand? He had already called her morning gown an abomination, hadn't he? Well, she had no intention of giving him a chance to utter another rude remark about her present attire, although she might as well start getting used to his crude comments if she was to spend the rest of her life in his company. The thought filled her with such trepidation that she forgot her resolution to ignore the earl and cast him another furtive glance.

Lord Mansfield was not in formal evening attire, but had changed his brown riding jacket and buff corduroy breeches for an elegant coat of dark blue superfine and spotless white inexpressibles that hugged his powerful legs so snugly they seemed to be part of him. The odd notion flitted through her mind that she could not remember Stephen ever wearing anything quite so revealing. She had the uncomfortable impression that she had witnessed the gentleman in a state of undress. The notion was absurd, of course, but the indelicate nature of it made her blush and turn her eyes away hastily.

She heard her father presenting Drusilla to Lord Mansfield and her sister's short response. Drusilla had been predisposed to dislike the earl, and Cassandra knew her sister well enough to fear that she would make no attempt to hide her feelings. Cassandra glanced uneasily at her sister and was not surprised to see her beautiful, heart-shaped face set in disapproval. The earl had taken her small hand and raised it to his lips, unleashing upon her the full force of his rakish charm.

"Had I but known that Kent held such abundance of grace and beauty, I would most certainly have visited Seven Oaks more frequently," he purred softly, gazing from under hooded lids as Drusilla colored prettily.

"Fustian!" came the tart reply, as Drusilla snatched her hand away and turned to her sister with a moue of distaste. Cassandra was unaccountably cheered by the top-lofty lord's setback and found it impossible to keep her amusement from showing in her eyes as they took in the earl's discomfiture at this unexpected response to his flattery. Nevertheless, she felt impelled by good breeding to smooth over her sister's rudeness.

"Drusilla!" she cried in mock horror. "Do behave yourself, love. You should not treat Lord Mansfield as though he were that toad Gerald Whittaker, who is forever fawning over you," she said with a malicious glance in his direction. "I am sure his lordship merely intended to pay you a compliment, dear, and though undoubtedly he meant nothing at all by it, the gesture was prettily made. You are expected to show proper appreciation for his efforts to please."

Cassandra derived a surge of perverse pleasure at this heaven-sent opportunity to put the odious earl in his place and was able to meet Lord Mansfield's thunderous gaze with aplomb.

"If you expect me to simper and flap my eyelashes, Cassie, you are all about in the head," Drusilla answered belligerently.

"No, dear," Cassandra said laughingly. "Nobody is asking that you make a cake of yourself. But his lordship will have a very poor opinion of us if you insist on being so rag-mannered. I am already sunk beneath reproach myself and was counting on you to redeem me."

Reverend Drayton, who had been listening to this exchange with a bemused expression, interrupted his daughter at this point. "What is all this about Squire Whittaker's lad making a nuisance of himself?" he inquired, typically missing the main issue of the discussion. "Why wasn't I informed of this before now?"

"Oh, it was nothing, Father, I assure you," Drusilla supplied glibly. "Gerald is an insignificant toad, anyway. And after I pushed him into the duck pond last month, he is not likely to come skulking around here again soon. He was not amused by that ducking, I can tell you." She giggled, transformed instantly from a haughty young lady into the innocent country girl she was.

"I can well believe that," the earl murmured under his breath. "I trust that you are not afflicted with similar violent starts, Cassandra?"

Before she could think up a suitable reply to this query, Mrs. Hill appeared to announce that dinner was served, and the earl offered her his arm, which she took reluctantly.

Conversation over the dinner table was desultory to say the least. In a deliberate attempt to annoy Lord Mansfield, Cassandra encouraged her father to discuss, in exhaustive detail, an obscure manuscript he had been commissioned to translate from the

Greek. Since its author was anonymous and the treatise a tedious peroration on the vicissitudes of war, she was fairly certain that his lordship would be bored silly. He surprised her, however, by interjecting several knowledgeable remarks on similarities between the anonymous author's interpretation and that of Thucydides in his *History of the Peloponnesian War*. Impressed, in spite of herself, Cassandra relented so far as to pose tentative questions about Mansfield Grange, the earl's principal seat, which she knew only through Stephen's enthusiastic descriptions. For a brief period the conversation flowed smoothly, and although Drusilla still maintained her unrelenting reserve, Cassandra began to enjoy the chance to discuss intelligent topics with someone other than her father.

The fragile harmony shattered abruptly, however, as soon as the gentlemen joined the ladies in the drawing room. Cassandra sat at the small pianoforte, which had been one of her mother's prized possessions, softly experimenting with a difficult passage from one of Beethoven's sonatas. The earl strolled over to stand beside her, causing her fingers to fumble a chord.

"I had no idea you were so accomplished, my dear," he observed dryly.

Expecting nothing but snide remarks from him, Cassandra's response was immediate and cutting. "Musical instruction is not exactly a prerogative of London society, my lord. Out here in the wilds of Kent, culture has also made its inroads on the natives." She paused to execute a cluster of complicated chords with ease. "And I am not your dear, as I believe I have told you once before."

She did not bother to glance up at him, but could imagine the sardonic expression that must have softened his lean, aristocratic features. "I beg to disagree, my dear, but you are. And the sooner you stop fighting the bit, the easier it will be for us to pull off this charade."

"And the sooner you stop talking to me as though I were one of your horses," she hissed sharply under her breath, "the better we will go on, my lord."

He gave her a short crack of laughter at that, and Cassandra wondered why he should find her intended insults amusing. "That might not be such a bad fate, you know," he remarked easily. "I take very good care of my horses. Always provided they please me, naturally."

Cassandra felt the steel in the lazy inflection of his voice, and a tremor of apprehension ran through her. This man was not only cold and arrogant in his manner, but she suspected he could be entirely ruthless with all who dared oppose his will. The prospect did nothing to lighten her mood, but she made a brave attempt to appear unaffected by the earl's subtle threats.

"If you expect me to make any effort to please you, my lord," she said with a brittle laugh, "you have put your money on the wrong horse."

"What is all this about putting money on horses, Cassandra?" her father inquired, coming over to join them at the instrument. "Gambling is the curse of the devil," he continued mildly. "I trust you will remember that, my dear, when you leave us to take your place in London society."

Well accustomed to her father's vagaries, Cassandra regarded him affectionately. "I have never gambled in my life, Father, so it is highly unlikely that I will start now, don't you think?"

Her father abruptly seemed to lose interest in the devil's curse. He looked vaguely uneasy, an expression his daughter immediately recognized as the one he invariably adopted when he knew he should have done something but could not remember exactly what it was. With a murmured excuse, he wandered back to the fireside, where Mrs. Hill was busy arranging the tea tray.

Cassandra glanced up at Lord Mansfield in time to catch a quizzical lift of his eyebrow as his gaze followed the vicar across the room.

"My father has always been absentminded," she felt obliged to explain. "Since my mother died, he has immersed himself more than ever in his studies. It is not unusual for him to forget to eat and even sleep."

"I trust he had remembered to inform you that we are to be wed tomorrow," the earl remarked coldly.

Cassandra fingers froze on the keys in a jangle of discordant sounds. Her eyes flew to Lord Mansfield's face. "Tomorrow?" she repeated weakly, feeling suddenly very vulnerable. "Surely you are jesting, my lord? That is impossible."

"You are wrong again, my dear," he said dryly. "Your father has already agreed to perform the ceremony tomorrow morning."

"But the banns—"

"I have a special license, of course. That was Stephen's idea, I must admit, but I thought it best to be prepared for the worst."

"For the worst?" she repeated, feeling stupid, but too upset by the implication of his words to think straight. So Stephen had told his brother *everything* after all. There could be no doubt of it now. The promise of the special license had been Stephen's way of assuring her of his love and protection. But with his casual remark, this callous, overbearing man had turned it into a furtive and even slightly sordid thing, to be used only as a last resort. Cassandra felt suddenly sickened by the whole affair. Something of the bleakness in her soul must have shown on her face, for Lord Mansfield cleared his throat uneasily.

Cassandra realized that she had been staring fixedly into the earl's dark eyes without seeing him. Her vision cleared, and she shook her head in disbelief and rejection. "I won't do it," she said through clenched teeth. "The devil take you and your special license. I simply won't do it."

Her stubborn refusal seemed to reassure the earl, for he smiled grimly as though relishing the opportunity to bend her to his will.

"Oh, yes, you will, my dear," he said. And once again, Cassandra was acutely conscious of the steel behind the softly spoken words.

Phineas had not anticipated any real rebellion from Miss Drayton. Her position was precarious, to say the least, and once she got over her fit of pure stubbornness—a trait she would do well to control in the future—he was confident that good sense would prevail. Besides, he told himself the next morning as his traveling chaise, with his bags already strapped up behind, came to a stop before the vicarage, he held all the trump cards. Miss Drayton might protest all she chose, but she would soon discover that when the Earl of Mansfield set his mind to a certain course of action, no mere female would cause him to deviate from it.

On the whole, he was rather pleased with the way he had brushed through what was—any way one looked at it—a deplorable situation. It was fruitless to wish that Stephen might have done things differently. Knowing his only brother as he did, Phineas had predicted a long time ago that the romantic, impulsive, often impractical Stephen was bound to find himself in the briars, one way or another. If only it had not been so heartrending and final, the earl thought, remembering his brother's pale, anxious face, the exhaustion and fading strength of his young body, and the growing awareness of death in his eyes. It had not been easy to sit by uselessly and watch his beloved brother slip away like a shadow, a faint apologetic smile on his lips at the end, as though he regretted the trouble and pain he had caused.

Impatiently, Phineas jerked his thoughts into the present. There had been little enough he could do for Stephen in the past except to promise that his precious Cassandra would not suffer from his impetuosity. Now, in the present, there was something very definite he could do, and Phineas was quite determined to do it. He would wed the prickly Miss Drayton and give the Ravenville name to Stephen's child in spite of the unfortunate fact that the wench was obviously a shrew who thoroughly disliked him. Once the knot was tied, he consoled himself, he would take the chit up to London, get his sister Sophy to help outfit her in some decent clothes, and then pack her off to Mansfield Grange. His mother would be glad of the company; at least he hoped the two women would manage to rub along together without too much friction. In any case, he planned to spend most of his time in London for the Little Season and then off to Melton Mowbray with his crony Heathercott for the hunting. With any luck he would not have to see Miss Drayton—that is, his new wife—until the family gathered at Mansfield Grange for Christmas.

Having disposed of the immediate future to his entire satisfaction, Lord Mansfield entered the vicarage morning parlor with a condescending smile on his face. Even the glum expression on the plain visage of his beloved—he grimaced at the misnomer—and the frank disapproval on the enchanting face of her sister, did not lessen the satisfaction he felt at disposing of this tedious business with all possible haste.

"Good morning, ladies," he greeted them casually, observing that his intended was again dressed in a truly hideous gown of dark brown kerseymere of no discernible style he could recognize. Her fingers were cold in his as he raised them briefly, and her eyes, very large and feverishly bright, held the same bleakness he had noticed in them last night. What was the matter with the silly chit? he thought truculently. Wasn't it enough that he had come all the way down here to save her from the consequences of her folly? Must she act as though he were some undesirable rogue with libertine propensities, waiting only for the knot to be tied to ravish her? He was unsure whether to be amused or disturbed by the image he had evoked. It had been many years since Phineas had bothered to examine his way of life, and he had never been given to useless regrets. Possessed of both good looks and fortune in abundance, the Earl of Mansfield had, from an early age, followed where his appetites had led him, acquiring in the process, the inevitable reputation of gambler and womanizer.

"I trust I find you in high gig, my dear," he drawled, amused at the blatantly inappropriate pleasantry. His betrothed looked anything but animated at the prospect of marriage to a peer of the realm or overjoyed at his presence. He wondered idly which rumors, if any, of his notorious exploits in the Metropolis could have reached this isolated spot in the Kentish countryside and poisoned the minds of the Misses Drayton against him. Why should he care? he thought, glancing around the room in search of a drink to sustain him through what promised to be a harrowing ordeal.

Miss Drayton must have read his mind, for she glowered at him. "It is customary to wait until *after* the ceremony to indulge in spirits, my lord," she said icily.

The devil take the wench, he thought angrily. He had only been in her company for two minutes, and already she was pulling caps with him. And this was just the beginning, he realized ruefully. A whole lifetime of being buckled to this arch-wife lay ahead of him. It was enough to make a man want to cry off, but this option, he knew, was not open to him.

Now if the intended bride had been the little sister, he mused, shifting his glance to Drusilla's comely form and finding her pansy-blue eyes fixed on him relentlessly. That might have offered a more lively challenge. Stephen must have had maggots in his head to have fixed his interest with the prickly elder Miss Drayton when this fairylike little morsel with rosebud lips was fairly begging to be snatched up. Both girls had plenty of spirit, of course, a trait he appreciated in a woman, but Phineas found himself wishing his brother's taste in females had been closer to his own.

He sighed and dragged his gaze back to his intended bride. "May I have a word alone with you, Cassandra?"

"No, you may not," Drusilla stormed at him. "You will treat my sister with respect or—"

"Please, Dru," Miss Drayton intervened hastily. "I am persuaded that I have nothing to fear from Lord Mansfield. And remember, you promised me you would not make a fuss, dear."

The younger Miss Drayton was plainly not convinced. She

huffed rudely, but turned on her heel and stalked out of the room, closing the door loudly behind her.

"Please forgive my sister, my lord," Cassandra murmured. "She is not generally this disobliging."

The earl would have termed Drusilla's manners rather more strongly, but he thought better of it. "Stephen informed me that you already have his ring, Cassandra. I suggest you give it to me before your father comes."

Miss Drayton gave a startled jump, and her hand flew to her bosom, where a slender gold chain disappeared into her unfashionably high neckline. She regarded him wide-eyed for several moments, her small teeth clamped on her lower lip, as if to still its trembling.

"You will use *Stephen's* ring to wed me?" she asked at last in a low, accusing voice, as if he had demanded that she remove her petticoats.

"Yes," he replied dryly. "That is the general idea." He saw the sudden hurt in her eyes and regretted his cavalier words. "Unless, of course, you prefer not to, my dear," he continued in a gentler tone. "It occurred to me that you might derive some small comfort from Stephen's ring since my brother is not here to put it on your finger himself." No such thing had ever crossed his mind, of course, but in a fit of whimsy, the earl found himself wishing that it had. He was not much given to considering the comfort of others, and he was startled at the effect of his careless remark on Miss Drayton.

"Oh, thank you," she murmured, gazing at him with eyes no longer bleak but full of emotion. "That was really very kind of you, my lord." Then she smiled, a small, tremulous smile to be sure, but a genuine one nevertheless. Startled, the earl saw it reach her hazel eyes and subtly transform her features into a softer, more feminine version of the stern-faced Miss Drayton he had come to expect. Phineas immediately felt a stab of guilt—another unusual experience for him—but he brushed it aside impatiently as irrelevant and mawkish. So he had lied, he thought, reverting to his usual cynicism. And if that was what it took to melt the frosty Miss Drayton into something approaching a normal female, then he would just have to lie more often, that was all.

Miss Drayton had withdrawn the gold chain from its hiding place beneath her gown, and Phineas saw that it held not only a small gold band but also an engraved locket. No doubt this is where she keeps a lock of Stephen's hair, he thought, faintly disgusted at his own contempt for such romantic notions.

"Stephen gave me this last June for my birthday," she explained, indicating the modest locket. "And here is the ring." she fumbled ineffectually with the clasp until Phineas brushed her hands away and released the fastener himself, acutely aware of the warmth emanating from her pale skin and the faint pulse in her throat. He saw by her intake of breath that his touch flustered her, and this should have soothed his masculine ego, but instead, it made him uneasy. This was a side of Miss Drayton he wanted no part of; he much preferred her when she was at daggers-drawn with him. He folded her gold ring into his fist, savoring the heat of the metal, derived, he well knew, from lying in that warm, intimate valley between her breasts.

"Is something wrong, my lord?"

Phineas realized he had been staring down at her, his mind caught up in the erotic images his imagination had so vividly conjured up of Miss Drayton's person. He gave himself a mental shake and smiled. "No, nothing's wrong, my dear." He opened his large palm and looked down at the ring, now warm with the heat of his hand. "I was just thinking how small the ring is," he said without thinking. "I can hardly believe it big enough to fit on a lady's finger." Impulsively, he reached for her left hand and slipped the gold band onto her second finger. "I can see that appearances are deceiving, however," he murmured, wondering vaguely if he had run mad. "The fit is perfect." He removed the ring and held it gingerly in his palm.

It was thus that the Revered Drayton found them when he bustled into the parlor, followed by Drusilla. The strange spell that had come over him was effectively broken, and all too soon Phineas found himself vowing to love, honor, and protect his brother's intended bride. Miss Drayton's responses were spoken in a calm, clear voice, accompanied by a stifled sob from her sister.

Overcoming a sudden reluctance, Lord Mansfield sealed his fate by resting his lips briefly on the upturned face of his new wife.

CHAPTER FIVE

The Wedding Trip

"I should be wearing mourning, shouldn't I?" Cassandra said tentatively, after they had been traveling for some twenty minutes without exchanging a single word. "But I had nothing in black. This gown"—she indicated the severe gown of dark brown kerseymere she had chosen that morning for her wedding—"was the only one I felt was appropriate enough." She hesitated, wondering if her new husband was feeling as cast down about their recently entered state as she was herself. He sat slouched in the seat beside her, his long legs in their impeccably fitted black Hessians stretched out before him, his eyes fixed on the passing scenery. Cassandra had the distinct suspicion that the earl was deliberately avoiding any commerce with her at all.

At her words, however, he turned to rake her with the same studied insolence she remembered from their first meeting so long ago. But this time, she was no green girl intimidated by the dashing and dangerous Earl of Mansfield, she reminded herself, returning the earl's stare with tight-lipped indignation.

"Appropriate?" he drawled, his eyes flat with disapproval. "Your wits have gone begging, my girl, if you imagine that . . . that relic to be appropriate for anything." His dark gaze came to rest on her bonnet, and his lips curled quite noticeably. "And do take that aberration off your head, ma'am. It offends the sensibilities."

"I will do nothing of the sort," Cassandra retorted hotly, incensed at this deliberate rudeness. "I happen to like this particular bonnet. I made it myself."

He laughed at this admission, but there was no amusement in the sound. "That is obvious to even the untrained eye," he remarked. "Now do as I say and take the thing off."

"I will not," she repeated pugnaciously.

He regarded her for a moment before saying in a voice that

held a distinct note of steel, "Believe me, Cassandra, you would not want *me* to take it off for you."

His expression was one of indolent unconcern, but Cassandra clearly recognized the implied threat. It chilled her to the bone. What had she got herself into? she wondered. She knew practically nothing about this man she had married except the dashing exploits Stephen had regaled her with each time he came back from a visit with his notorious brother. Yet here they were, wed less than an hour, and he was already displaying the precise kind of senseless tyranny she most despised in the male species. And she was legally bound to obey these oafish starts of his. That was what made her blood really boil. She would see this odious earl in hell before she let him get away with such bullying tactics, she vowed.

"You are perfectly horrid," she said through clenched teeth, her temper simmering dangerously.

He smiled his mirthless smile again. "I am so glad that you find me perfect in something, my dear," he drawled. "I was beginning to think we might not find anything at all to admire in each other."

Overtaken by one of her sudden furies, Cassandra snatched the offending hat from her head, and in a gesture of defiance flung it out of the carriage window. She was gratified to see that this unpremeditated maneuver took the earl completely by surprise. His languid air of boredom was wiped from his face like magic, to be replaced, first by shock, then by a thunderous scowl that drew his brows down threateningly over his elegantly patrician nose and his lips into a familiar thin line of annoyance.

"And you are a perfect hoyden, madam." His voice was dangerously flat, but Cassandra was past caring about his lordship's opinion of her behavior.

"I am so glad you have found something perfect in *me,* my lord," she replied in all sweetness. "I shall strive to cultivate that quality for your pleasure in the future."

"My pleasure?" His lips relaxed slightly, as though a truly amusing thought had crossed his mind. He glanced at her speculatively. "The only pleasure I expect to get out of *you,* my girl, is the day I throttle you," he said slowly, obviously savoring each word.

Cassandra shivered and looked away. She did not believe for a moment that he meant what he said. She knew very little about the laws of the land, but she was almost certain that not even an earl could get away with throttling his wife with his bare hands. Or could he? She glanced at him from under her lashes, but her precaution was wasted. The earl had resumed his indolent posture, and his eyes were closed, probably to discourage any further brangling between them, she imagined.

For the first time, Cassandra was able to examine her new husband at her leisure. Although he definitely lacked the classical beauty of his younger brother, whose blond perfection had charmed her for as long as she could remember, Phineas Ravenville possessed an animal vitality Stephen had lacked. She found herself both attracted and repelled by him. His attraction lay in his asymmetrical profile, in which aristocratic nose and rugged, aggressive jaw seemed at war with each other. At rest, his lips were well-shaped and gently curved, achingly reminiscent of Stephen's, she realized with a start of alarm. She pulled her eyes quickly away and concentrated on his brow, wide and unmarred by his all-too-frequent scowl. There was intelligence there, she guessed, although probably intolerance, willfulness, and uncertain temper, too. She had already experienced the effects of his strong will and arrogance, both defects in her eyes. The temper she could understand, having a healthy one of her own, but she deplored the cynicism, which seemed to reflect his prevailing attitude toward the world. And that was what repelled her about him, she thought. He lacked Stephen's sweet-natured spontaneity and generosity. Some kindness he had shown, she remembered, in allowing her to use Stephen's ring for their wedding ceremony. But in general, the Earl of Mansfield was irritable, despotic, and unrelenting in his disregard for anything but his own convenience. Clearly his flaws outnumbered his attractions.

With a small sigh Cassandra glanced down at her left hand. Stephen's ring, slender and delicate as he had been himself, looked as though it truly belonged on her finger. Now if only it had been Stephen who had put it there, she thought, twisting the gold band idly round and round. Without warning, she was shaken by the urge to cry, not only for Stephen, but also for herself and their child, now placed irrevocably under the protection of a man who didn't want either of them.

She was saved from these morbid thoughts by a strong hand, which appeared unexpectedly to clamp down on her nervous fingers, stilling her restless movements. "It is quite useless to repine over what cannot be mended," the earl said, not unkindly. "Stephen's gone, and although I admit I'm a poor substitute, this is what he wished for you, Cassandra. So let us make the best of it, shall we, my dear?"

Cassandra stared in consternation at the lean fingers covering her own. What his previous sarcasm had been unable to do, his present, quite uncharacteristic gentleness achieved. Her eyes filled with tears, and she choked back a sob.

"I s-still cannot quite b-believe that any of this has really h-happened," she gulped, scrambling for a handkerchief in her reticule and then accepting the large one he pressed into her hands.

"Neither can I, if you want to know the truth," he said in a tired voice. "Stephen was so much younger than I that, at times, I felt more like his father than his brother—especially when he was very young. Our father died when Stephen was twelve, as you perhaps recall, and I made a pretty poor substitute, especially in those early years. Later we grew to understand each other better."

He paused, and Cassandra, anxious to hear about the time Stephen had spent away from her at Mansfield Grange, urged him to continue. "Please tell me about those early years, my lord. There is so much about Stephen I don't know."

The earl looked at her reflectively and then smiled, a little sadly, she thought. "Perhaps we both need to exorcise some of these memories about my brother," he said at last. "You must know much that I don't about him."

Cassandra felt herself blush at the implications of this remark, but the earl seemed not to notice. "Where shall I start, then?" he demanded, his eyes already clouding over with memories.

"At the beginning," she prompted impulsively.

The earl smiled and began to unravel the past for her, at first in fits and starts, then more fluidly, until he seemed to immerse himself in each episode as though reliving it in the company of his dead brother.

As their journey progressed, Cassandra lost some of her reticence and was able to share with the earl some of the adventures she and Drusilla had experienced with Stephen during his summers spent at Seven Oaks. By the time they stopped at Canterbury for a change of horses and refreshments, she was feeling quite in charity with her new husband.

This harmony was threatened during their brief stop at the

Black Boar Inn when Cassandra, preparing to descend from the carriage, suddenly remembered that she had pitched her only bonnet into the road many miles back. She glanced apprehensively at the earl, who waited to hand her down, only to find his eyes fixed upon her with a glint of his old cynicism.

"Yes, my dear," he observed, as though he had read her mind. "That article of clothing, which I hesitate to call a bonnet, might well have added a degree of decorum to your entrance into the inn, but I daresay nobody will notice."

Miffed at this subtle reminder of her lack of countenance, Cassandra said stiffly, "If you are going to be horrid about it, perhaps I should remain here."

The earl merely signaled to the groom, who had ridden behind their coach and was even now waiting beside his master, a rather dejected-looking bonnet in his hand.

"Thank you, Jimmy," Lord Mansfield said, taking the dusty object and eying it distastefully. "We shall have to buy her ladyship a more suitable headpiece once we reach London. One that she will not be tempted to pitch out into the cornfields." He slipped a silver coin into the grinning young groom's eager hand and dismissed him. "Here you are, my dear," he said, handing Cassandra her bonnet. "Put this detestable thing on, and let us repair to the private dining room old Higgins has prepared for us. I am in dire need of sustenance."

"Are we really going to London?" she demanded apprehensively, as soon as they had been served and their host had retired to the taproom. "I understood you to say we were going straight to Mansfield Grange."

The earl looked up impatiently from the roast venison he was carving. "We must pass through the Metropolis to reach Nottingham, so I thought it advisable to make a stop there." His eyes strayed to her dowdy gown, and he grimaced. "You will need to be made presentable before you meet my mother, in any case."

Still not inured to his lordship's cutting ways, Cassandra blushed furiously. She was both mortified and outraged at his constant reminder that she did not measure up to his standards of fashion. "I concede that you may be right about this hat, but there is absolutely nothing the matter with my dress," she stated coldly, determined to keep her temper under control this time. "I see no reason—"

"It was one thing for you to look like a quiz in Walmer," the earl interrupted, with equal coolness. "But I will not have my wife become the laughingstock of London. You will consign that garment to the ragbag and behave like a countess if I have to dress you myself."

Cassandra was so taken aback by this high-handed rudeness, that it was several moments before she could speak. When she did recover the use of her tongue, she allowed it to run away with her. "I presume you will personally see to the selection of my new wardrobe," she said sarcastically. "I hear you are quite adept at the art of dressing females."

The earl went very still, his fork poised in the air, as he stared at her from beneath hooded lids. Cassandra could have bitten her tongue as soon as the rash words were spoken, but unexpectedly, his astonishment turned to amusement.

"Actually, I am better versed in undressing than in dressing, my love," he remarked laconically, lifting the morsel of venison to his mouth. "More practice, you understand," he confided nonchalantly. "And if that was an invitation, my dear wife, I confess you have me confused. I distinctly remember hearing you insist that you did not wish for such services." He grinned devilishly at her. "Your wish is my command, however."

Cassandra pushed back her chair and jumped to her feet, her face pale with fury. "You are intolerably offensive," she exclaimed hotly. "I will not stay here to be insulted by such a disgusting libertine." She made a blind rush for the door, but found his hand firmly on the knob before she could escape.

"Sorry, my dear," he said blandly. "But I disagree. You will sit down at the table, pour yourself a cup of tea, and try to behave like a lady." When she demurred, he scowled at her menacingly, and Cassandra whirled and marched back to her seat. He took his place opposite as though nothing untoward had happened.

"You seem to have heard all sorts of unsavory things about me, my lady," he remarked after a while, attacking another slice of meat. "So let me put your mind at rest. I will admit that at least ninety percent of those rumors are accurate; the other ten percent are somewhat exaggerated. Now, does that make you any happier?" When she made no response, he glanced up and sighed. "If you wish to avoid being teased, you should not fly off the handle so easily, you know. I find the temptation to shock you entirely irresistible. And as for the other matter, I intended to ask my sister

Sophy to accompany you to the shops rather than inflict my notorious presence upon you."

"Sophy?" Cassandra repeated eagerly, momentarily forgetting that she was furious with Lord Mansfield. "Is Sophy in London?"

The earl looked at her in surprise. "You remember Sophy, do you?"

"Of course. She came down to Seven Oaks the summer before she was married to Viscount Hart. Dru and I found her to be great fun." She paused, suddenly recalling something. "Your sister knows about Stephen," she added.

"About Stephen?" He glanced up, brows raised inquiringly.

"About our secret betrothal," Cassandra explained. She saw the flash of impatience that crossed the earl's face. "How should we explain our sudden marriage? Sophy will be sure to think it odd."

He shrugged. "No doubt I will think of something to fob her off," he said carelessly, his energies now focused on a raised pigeon pie. "In the meantime, I suggest you eat some of this pie. It will be dark before we reach London."

The Earl of Mansfield's eyes rested speculatively on his sleeping companion as the traveling chaise entered London by the Kent Road, crossed the Thames over Westminster Bridge, and made its way through the thickening twilight along Whitehall before turning off in the direction of St. James's Square. After their stop at Rochester for a change of horse, his new countess had seemed unusually subdued and had finally curled up in her corner on the soft velvet squabs and gone to sleep.

His countess, he mused. He had never given much thought to the qualities he might have looked for in a wife had this one not been thrust down his throat so precipitously. In truth he had studiously avoided thinking of marriage at all and had endured, with ill-concealed impatience, his mother's occasional hints that it was high time he set up his nursery. All that was a moot question now, of course. He was well and truly leg-shackled and—through no effort of his own—with a good start made on his nursery. His eyes flicked over Cassandra's slim figure and, for the first time, it occurred to him to wonder if perhaps this unpredictable, rag-mannered country miss had achieved what scores of marriage-minded mamas of the *ton* had failed to over the past ten years: trapped the hardened cynic Lord Mansfield into matrimony. The notion was unpleasant. Phineas did not like to be bested at any of the games he played, and this hand, which had been dealt and left unfinished by his brother, was uncomfortably new to him. A momentary glint of anger flickered briefly in his dark eyes, then disappeared. If this chit had bamboozled him into marrying her, he thought with grim humor, he would thoroughly enjoy sending her back to the vicarage with a bug in her delicate ear.

It was almost dark when the chaise drew up outside Mansfield Court on St. James's Square, and Phineas was obliged to reach over and shake his wife to wake her. "We have arrived," he informed her dryly. "Put on that wretched hat again before Dorset mistakes you for a governess or something worse."

The Countess of Mansfield opened startled eyes and gazed up at him blankly. He saw awareness of her surroundings dawn slowly in their hazel depths and a wary look replace her wide-eyed stare. "We are in London already?" she murmured, sitting up and trying ineffectually to straighten her riotous auburn curls. "Oh, I wish you had woken me sooner, my lord. I did so want to get my first look at the Thames. That was most inconsiderate of you." She clamped her mistreated bonnet firmly on her head and tied the ribbon under her small chin.

"Cease your chattering, girl," he said shortly. He felt tired and his temper was none too stable. Miss Drayton would do well to learn to keep her recriminations to herself, he thought.

"I am not chattering," she replied, predictably. "I was merely making a civil comment, so you have no business snapping at me, my lord. I am tired and hungry, too, you know."

Lord Mansfield had descended from the chaise during this speech, and now he turned to offer his hand to his countess. Her hand felt small and decidedly cold when she placed it in his, and Phineas grimaced in annoyance. "Where the devil are your gloves?" he demanded.

Cassandra glared up at him, evidently not intimidated by this harsh outburst. "Watch your language, my lord," she said sternly. "I must have dropped them on the floor of the carriage."

The earl gave a muttered oath and climbed back into the coach, emerging after a few moments empty-handed and with a thunderous scowl on his face. "There are no gloves there," he said, as if daring the chit to contradict him.

"Then I must have left them behind at the Black Boar," she remarked blithely. "It is of no consequence, my lord; they were hardly presentable anyway. No doubt you would have had me consign them to the ragbag along with my poor gown and bonnet."

There was an unmistakable hint of defiance in her tone, and Lord Mansfield had the urge to administer one of his most cutting set-downs. Unfortunately, he could think of nothing sufficiently chilling, so he took his wife by the arm and hurried her up the shallow steps of Mansfield Court.

By this time the front door had been thrown open, sending a welcoming glow of light out into the darkness. The portly figure of his butler stood ready to receive the Earl of Mansfield.

"Welcome back to London, milord," this worthy said with a warm smile on his rotund face. This smile disappeared as soon as he caught sight of Cassandra, to be replaced by a stiff look of reproof. Without another word he stood aside to allow his master to enter, his features schooled into the disinterested stare of the well-trained servant.

"No need to pucker up so, Dorset," Phineas remarked, amused at the butler's assumption that Miss Drayton was another of the light-skirts he introduced from time to time into his London residence. "I was counting on you to give your new mistress a warm welcome after her tiring journey. Meet the Countess of Mansfield, Dorset. My dear," he added and turned to Cassandra, realizing with something of a shock that his butler's gesture of disapproval had not been lost on her. "This is Dorset, who has been with the Earls of Mansfield for . . . what is it, fifty years now, Dorset?"

"Fifty-one last spring, milord," Dorset replied, although even so many years of training did not prevent the flash of astonishment the earl detected on his old butler's countenance. "Since your grandfather's time, milord." Turning to the countess, Dorset executed a stiff bow. "Welcome to Mansfield Court, my lady," he said smoothly, his face betraying none of his thoughts. "May I say that the staff will be delighted to welcome a mistress to this house after so many years."

The butler's remark—laced as it had been with an imperceptible hint of criticism—surprised the earl. It had never occurred to him to think about such matters; indeed, he had always assumed that his bachelor establishment, with his occasional gentlemen-only card parties and other less innocent gatherings, had suited his staff very well. It had certainly suited him, and the sooner he could make the countess presentable and pack her off to Nottingham to his mother, the happier he would be.

"I am happy to hear you say so, Dorset," he heard Cassandra answer warmly and realized that his wife's manner in dealing with the butler had been unexceptionable. If anyone were capable of intimidation, it was the stiff-necked Dorset, yet the countess had instinctively struck the right note with him. Either unaware or unconcerned that her plain, dowdy gown was several years out of date and that her bonnet was dusty and crushed from being tossed into the road, the Countess of Mansfield had addressed the formidable butler with unself-conscious and quiet dignity. For some odd reason, the thought that his wife had appeared to such advantage before the servants pleased him.

"Put her ladyship in my mother's suite," Phineas commanded. "And ask Mrs. Dorset if she can persuade m'sieur Gaston to send up a light supper tray for her ladyship."

"Yes, milord," came the quick reply. "I shall send for Mrs. Dorset immediately to show her ladyship to her rooms."

"No need for that, Dorset," the earl interposed. "I shall take her ladyship up. Please have the trunks brought in."

"Will you be dining at home yourself, milord?"

"I think not," Phineas replied, avoiding Cassandra's surprised glance. "I will probably dine at White's." He offered his arm to the countess. "Come, my dear. No doubt you are anxious for a bath and a change of clothes before you dine."

Ignoring her sudden silence, the earl led his new wife upstairs.

The news that Lord Mansfield would not be dining with her on their first evening in London took Cassandra by surprise. Unaccustomed as she was to the ways of the nobility, she had innocently supposed that her new husband would, at the very least, try to preserve the outward appearance of a normal married life. In this she had obviously mistaken the case, she thought ruefully as she allowed the earl to guide her along a wide hallway and throw open a door into what appeared to be an elegant private sitting room.

"My mother was particularly fond of this room," she heard him say as she stood gazing in wonder at the pale greens and blues that gave the room a particularly restful atmosphere. "You may wish to refurbish it to your own taste if we spend any time here in the future."

"Oh, no," Cassandra exclaimed quickly. She could not imagine any changes she might wish to make in the furnishings or arrangement of this delightful room. "It is perfect exactly as it is. And besides," she hastened to add, "I wouldn't dream of disturbing your mother's room."

"It is no longer her room," he said shortly. "And you may do as you wish. I shall instruct Dorset to have my mother's things removed to another set of rooms tomorrow. She rarely visits London, in any case."

For once, Cassandra could find no words to protest, and she thought the earl looked vaguely relieved. "Good," he said. "Your bedchamber is through that door to the left. I shall ask Dorset to send up one of the maids to wait on you until we can get you a proper dresser."

"A dresser?" Cassandra said in a startled voice. "I don't need a dresser, my lord. Pray don't be ridiculous. I have dressed myself for years and am well qualified to continue to do so."

"Nevertheless, you will have a dresser, my lady," came the caustic reply. "And let us not come to points on this issue, if you please." He looked quickly around the room and then strode over to the door, as if eager to make his escape before she could protest. "If there is anything you need, you have only to ask Dorset. And now, I will wish you good night."

Cassandra did not answer. Indeed, she could not, so bemused was she by this unexpected turn of events. As she listened to the earl stride away down the hall, she asked herself once again what manner of marriage she had entered into. Nothing she had ever seen or heard about the wedded state had prepared her for the deep sense of desolation that now invaded her whole being as she stood in the luxurious boudoir, staring at the door through which her new husband had disappeared so abruptly, after wishing her a curt goodnight. Just what she had expected, she did not know and furthermore, she was afraid to speculate. It struck her forcibly that she had unconsciously avoided thinking about this first night of her marriage to Lord Mansfield at all. What had she expected? she now asked herself ruthlessly. Hadn't she extracted from him the promise that theirs would be a marriage in name only? Just how would she have reacted had his lordship changed his mind and decided to take what was his due? The thought caused a strange shiver to run through her body, unlike any she had ever felt before. Feeling suddenly unsteady, she sat down in one of the wing chairs beside the empty fireplace.

She shivered again, and this time Cassandra was able to convince herself that she was cold. She was being uncharacteristically mawkish, she thought, striving to banish all thoughts of the earl from her mind. He would not be ignored, however, and Cassandra was forcibly reminded of his tall, masculine frame, standing at the door and wishing her good night. There had been nothing even faintly approving in his cold stare, much less any sign of interest, amorous or otherwise, in his new wife. The inescapable truth was, she had to admit, that the earl had been eager to escape her company. Clearly, the possibility of forcing his attentions upon her person had not even entered his head. Why it had ever entered hers, Cassandra was at a loss to understand.

With a sign she rose to her feet and entered the bedchamber where she surprised a neatly efficient maid turning down the covers. The girl bobbed a curtsy as soon as she saw her mistress. "Good evening, milady," she said in an awed voice. "I am Bridget, and Mr. Dorset says as how I'm to act as your lady's maid until you find a permanent one, milady."

"Thank you, Bridget," she replied, looking round the elegant room with its enormous four-poster bed at one end and the cluster of easy chairs around a warmly blazing fire, and wondering how she would ever grow accustomed to such splendor. "I am glad you have lit a fire. It was chilly in the sitting room."

"Your bath will be ready in a moment, milady," Bridget said. "And I have put a warm brick in the bed to take the chill off. It's been a while since her ladyship, the earl's mother that is, last visited us."

An hour later, warm and drowsy from the luxury of a leisurely bath and replete with the appetizing supper tray provided by the earl's French cook, Cassandra lay in the soft bed and told herself that she should at least be thankful for the material comforts her precipitous marriage to Lord Mansfield had brought her.

In spite of this eminently sensible resolution, the memory of Stephen and what her wedding night might have been haunted the new countess's restless dreams.

CHAPTER SIX

Town Bronze

The next morning Cassandra awoke to the unfamiliar sounds of the city long before Bridget appeared with her hot chocolate. Unable to go back to sleep, she had risen, wrapped herself in her ancient woollen robe, and pulled open the heavy velvet curtains to take her first glimpse of London. She saw that her bedchamber was at the back of the house and gave onto a small enclosed garden, but beyond this small oasis of privacy, the outline of the city loomed, harsh and almost threatening—or so it seemed to Cassandra, fresh from the open country—in the gray light of predawn.

Involuntarily she shivered. The dark city reminded her of Lord Mansfield, unpredictable and definitely dangerous, yet strangely exciting, too. Cassandra could not quite put her finger on the attraction of the city before her, but something pulled at her. Perhaps the excitement was sparked by the unseen danger she sensed lurking beneath the civilized veneer of those elegant houses, tall church spires, and forests of chimneys whose billowing clouds of smoke bespoke the early morning labors of hundreds of servants, but also reminded a vicar's daughter vividly of the fires of Hell.

These fanciful thoughts of Hell and its dark inhabitants brought the earl back into her mind. Cassandra shivered again, but it was not the thought of Hell's dark angels that caused her to pull her robe closer about her as she sat in the window seat. Where had he gone last night after he had left her so abruptly? she wondered. He had mentioned his club, but what had he done there? Had he met some of his dissipated friends and gambled the night away? Had he come home in the early hours, his lean, handsome face stupid with drink? This seemed highly likely to her since she knew—even from their brief acquaintance—that the earl drank heavily. She had not heard him come in at all, now that she thought about it, so perhaps her new husband had spent his wed-

ding night out on the Town. Or had he—she forced herself to consider the possibility—spent it in some other woman's bed?

Cassandra swiftly pushed the unpleasant thought from her
mind, but once conjured up, the vision of Lord Mansfield with another woman would not go away. Horrified and repelled by her
own prurient interest in his lordship's relationships with other females, Cassandra discovered that, despite all her efforts, her mind
seemed to have taken on a life of its own. Images of her husband's lean, athletic body crowded her imagination. All the tantalizing parts of him she had never even seen suddenly appeared to
her in all their masculine glory. Frantically, she glanced down at
her wedding band, hoping the thought of Stephen would erase the
immodest pictures of his brother that had invaded her consciousness. But Stephen had receded into some distant part of her mind,
and all she could see was Phineas. His brooding dark eyes stared
back at her, filled with a hot, suggestive gleam, while his lips—
heaven save her from such lips, she thought—full and sensuous as
she had never seen them, drew her mesmerized gaze until she felt
that she must either taste their promised delights or expire with
longing.

"Good morning, milady."

Cassandra jumped at Bridget's greeting and glanced guiltily
over her shoulder. She had been so immersed in her erotic fantasies that she had not heard the maid enter the room behind her.
"G-good morning, Bridget," she murmured, her voice strangely
breathless.

"I did not mean to startle you, milady," the maid said apologetically. She brought the cup of steaming chocolate over to her mistress and observed her anxiously. "My, you are flushed this
morning, milady. I hope you are not running a fever. Do you wish
for Mr. Dorset to send for the doctor?"

Cassandra hastily pulled herself together. "No, thank you, Bridget. I will feel better after I have my chocolate." She took the cup
from the maid and tasted it eagerly. She needed to concentrate on
these simple, everyday things in order to wipe that intoxicating
image of Phineas Ravenville out of her mind completely. She
would guard against such frivolous flights of fancy in the future,
she told herself sensibly. Not only were they disgracefully immodest and unlike her usual romantic daydreams, but they would
certainly impair her future dealings with the earl. How could she
expect to stand up to him with any degree of serenity if she were

beset by such pictures of that lithe length of him stretched out in-
dolently on her bed? No, she corrected herself quickly, her cheeks
flaming at the thought. Not *her* bed. Some other, faceless
woman's bed in another house, in another part of London.

Never in hers. Resolutely dismissing such thoughts from her
mind, she took another sip of hot chocolate.

Cassandra's tour of the Mansfield town house, conducted by an
enthusiastic and garrulous Mrs. Dorset, was interrupted just after
eleven o'clock by the news that his lordship's sister, Viscountess
Hart, had called and was awaiting the countess in the Blue Saloon.

All the misgivings she had ever entertained about her marriage
to the wrong Ravenville brother rushed back to her as Cassandra
followed Dorset's rigid form through the wide, cool halls of
Mansfield Court. She experienced a wild desire to turn and run
back to her room as the sedate butler threw open the carved door
to the Blue Saloon where the first confrontation of her married
life awaited her. Instead, she gave herself a mental shake for
being so missish and stepped resolutely into the room.

"Good God! Cassandra?" The lady who had issued this irrever-
ent exclamation stood poised in front of the crackling fire, where
she had evidently been warming her hands. She had turned
quickly when the butler had announced the Countess of Mansfield, but the polite greeting froze on her beautiful lips, to be replaced by the astonished ejaculation.

Cassandra could not help smiling at Lady Hart's amazement.
After all, the notion of Lord Mansfield choosing someone as ordinary as herself for his countess appeared ludicrous even to her.
How much more implausible would it appear to his family and intimates who knew his aversion for the wedded state and his pen-
chant for dazzling ladies of easy virtue.

"Cassandra?" the vision in a somber gray merino gown and
outrageously modish matching bonnet repeated in consternation.
"I don't believe it! What are you doing here, Cassie? Surely this
is another of my brother's absurd starts?"

Cassandra felt a stab of pain at the unconscious cruelty of these
words spoken in all honesty by someone she considered her
friend. Keeping her thoughts to herself, she trod across the Oriental carpet and took her visitor's outstretched hand. Even the subdued mourning she wore could not dull the viscountess's

loveliness, Cassandra thought without envy. Lady Hart had the kind of fair beauty that made men want to throw their hearts at her feet. Drusilla would look like this in a year or two, she realized, as soon as her sister matured a little, and if she had the proper clothes to complete the picture.

"Not at all, my lady," she answered, with more formality than they had used with each other in the past. "I fear that your brother has quite sunk beneath reproach this time." She smiled faintly at her own jest and saw the incredulity in Lady Hart's eyes slowly turn to bewilderment and then to embarrassment as she recalled her impetuous greeting. Cassandra saw the lovely face become suffused with pink and felt Lady Hart's eyes examine her in disbelief.

"Oh, what have I said?" she cried in distressed tones. "What a thoughtless creature I am, to be sure." She paused, regarding her hostess closely. "You really are . . . ? I mean, I had never supposed that *you* . . . Oh, what a coil! When I received that note from Mansfield last night, I never dreamed that it would be *you,* Cassandra. He did not say, of course. So like him to be offhand about all this. I confess that Hart and I very nearly died of curiosity when we learned that my brother had returned to London with a bride."

"Please sit down, Lady Hart," Cassandra murmured, not quite sure how she would find the strength to say what she must. "I want to offer my sincerest condolences on the death of your brother," she began, her voice betraying her toward the end in a slight quaver. "I know how much Stephen meant to you—"

"Stephen?" Lady Hart repeated disjointedly. "Thank you, Cassie," she said, pulling herself together. "That was a terrible shock to all of us. Mama is quite prostrated, and I cannot yet believe that it is actually true."

"Neither can I," Cassandra admitted softly.

Lady Hart looked at her sharply, a curious light in her eyes. "Yes, what about Stephen?" she demanded. "I knew there was something odd about this whole tale. I thought you had an understanding with Stephen, Cassandra. In fact, I *know* you did. How is it that you are married to Phineas if you were betrothed to Stephen?"

Cassandra's heart sank. What could she possibly say to explain this impossible marriage without sounding as though she had come straight from Bedlam? Where was Lord Mansfield? And why wasn't he here to help her through this outrageous farce when most she needed him? If only Stephen were here, she thought wildly. None of this would be happening, and she would have his loving support to see her through these first awkward encounters with his family. Quite at her wit's end and beleaguered by all kinds of doubts about her future, Cassandra unexpectedly burst into tears.

Lady Hart stood for a moment, her beautiful face frozen with shock. Then she stepped forward and Cassandra felt the viscountess's arms around her, urging her down onto the blue-striped settee before the hearth. Cassandra allowed herself to be cosseted for a few precious moments. It felt so good to let out her pent-up emotions, that she indulged herself without restraint until she remembered that at any moment Dorset would be returning with refreshments.

"Oh, please forgive me, my lady—"

"Why are we suddenly so formal with each other?" the viscountess cut in with a shaky laugh, her own eyes damp. "It used to be Sophy and Cassie with us, remember?"

"Yes, of course I do," Cassandra murmured, blowing her nose vigorously and wiping her wet cheeks. "I must look a sight, and Dorset will be back any minute with the tea. Oh, Sophy," she wailed, choking back another sob, "I am so mortified that I have behaved so absurdly. I don't know what came over me."

"We were speaking of Phineas, love, and I see that my odious brother has already done something to put you dreadfully out of curl. It doesn't surprise me, I must confess. He is the most selfish, tyrannical man alive. His black moods always terrified me, you know, and I'm his sister. I cannot imagine what he was thinking of to take a wife without telling us. He is such a care-for-nobody rake that mother had quite despaired of seeing him settled. And to someone like you, of all people—" She stopped abruptly, her face crimson. "I do beg your pardon, Cassie. I didn't mean that at all."

"Oh, you don't have to wrap it up in clean linen, Sophy. I am well aware that I am not at all in his lordship's usual style," Cassandra observed philosophically. "He has told me so several times himself."

Lady Hart stared at her aghast, her lovely mouth at half-cock. "I find it hard to believe that even Phineas would be so rag-mannered," she said in a shocked voice. "That is beyond anything shabby of him, Cassie. Where is the odious man anyway?"

Cassandra wished that she could answer that question, but she limited herself to what she had heard. "I believe he is at his club."

Lady Hart looked at her curiously. "And left you here to kick your heels alone, my dear? How unkind of him, but quite typical I'm afraid. My dear brother is notoriously careless of anything but his own pleasure. How you put up with him is a mystery to me. When do you expect him?"

Being unable to answer that either, Cassandra improvised. "Not until this afternoon. But I trust you will stay to have nuncheon with me, Sophy. I would like it above anything."

"Of course I will, dear. In fact, I have every intention of spending the entire afternoon with you. Phineas has requested my help in selecting your new wardrobe, Cassie. And I cannot think of anything that would please me better." She cast an appraising glance at Cassandra's plain gown. "I do not mean to be unkind, dear, but that gown is sadly outmoded."

"Oh, I know that only too well," Cassandra replied with a rueful smile. "His lordship has pointed that out to me in no uncertain terms. He has also severely criticized my choice of bonnet, so I am depending on you to rig me out in something that will not bring his recriminations down on my head."

Cassandra realized that her plain speaking had given Lady Hart pause, for she was regarding her hostess with an odd look in her brilliant blue eyes. "I can see that my brother has been his usual unpleasant self," she said finally, catching one of Cassandra's hands in hers. "But you must disregard his churlishness, Cassie. He has such an unpredictable temper and is so willful at times and no one dares to gainsay him. Mama and I are quite terrified of him when he gets into one of his black moods. I cannot tell you how thankful I am that dear Ned is nothing like Phineas. It is such a pleasant change to have one's wishes considered in all things and one's comfort regarded as a gentleman's primary concern." She smiled dreamily, and Cassandra recalled that Sophy's marriage last spring to Edward Greenley had been a true love match, much as hers and Stephen's would have been, she thought sadly.

"That must be most gratifying," she said, a wistful note in her voice that evidently did not escape the viscountess, for Lady Hart clapped her hands and declared that perhaps they should forgo nuncheon altogether and make do with the tea and cakes that Dorset was at that very moment setting out on the low table before his mistress.

"In that case, we can drive over to Madame Suzette's on Bond Street within the hour and enlist her aid in making up a selection of gowns that will dazzle even my starched-up brother. What do you say, Cassie?"

Cassandra looked dubiously at her friend, wondering how she could tell Sophy that nothing she wore was likely to impress the earl in the slightest degree, much less dazzle him. Cassandra was not even sure she wanted to dazzle his lordship. What would she do, she thought in sudden panic, if Lord Mansfield ever turned upon her that hungry, suggestive gaze she had imagined in his stormy eyes only this morning? She hastily pushed this disturbing thought from her mind.

"Well, Cassie?" Lady Hart insisted. "Do say you'll agree. My brother has misguidedly given me carte blanche in the matter, so we can shop to our hearts' content without feeling the least pang of guilt. And my own dear Ned suggested that I get another bonnet for myself if I see one that takes my fancy. I am perfectly certain that I will, of course. One can never have too many bonnets, wouldn't you agree, Cassie?"

Unwilling to tell the ebullient viscountess that she had never owned more than two bonnets at the same time in her life, Cassandra had to smile at her friend's innocent enthusiasm. She enjoyed shopping as well as any other young female, but until now had been guided more by practicality than exuberance. The thought of being able to select a few new gowns in the very latest fashions without worrying overmuch about the cost appealed to her sense of adventure. Before she could change her mind, Lady Hart had called for her carriage and whisked Cassandra out of the house.

In no time at all, or so it seemed to Cassandra, the two ladies were set down in front of Madame Suzette's exclusive establishment in Bond Street and welcomed by that lady with every sign of condescension. Cassandra soon found out that not only was Lady Hart one of Madame's most favored customers, but that the Earl of Mansfield was also a valued patron. No sooner did the quick-witted Frenchwoman discover that the new Countess of Mansfield required a complete wardrobe at extremely short notice, from formal ball gowns right down to nightwear and chemises, than she threw herself and her entire staff of seamstresses enthusiastically into the challenge. Even the restrictions imposed by the countess's mourning did not faze her. As a result, when the ladies left the modiste's salon several hours later, Cassandra found herself in immediate possession of three muslin morning gowns, two walking dresses, a deep lilac-striped carriage dress, and an evening gown in smoky gray silk trimmed with silver lace which Madame declared was all the crack this year in Paris. And these were merely those items that Madame was able to alter to fit Cassandra's slim figure without too much trouble.

Slightly aghast at the quantity of other gowns, pelisses, spencers, and intimate garmets Lady Hart insisted be made up later and sent round to Mansfield Court, Cassandra pulled her friend aside and whispered that surely the gowns they were to take away with them would be more than sufficient for her needs. This suggestion was met with a peal of amused laughter from her friend.

"My dear Cassandra," she cried, her magnificent eyes sparkling with humor. "You have yet to experience the press of invitations that will undoubtedly be showered upon you once the *ton* discovers that the Earl of Mansfield has finally acquired a wife. You will need all these and more if you are not to appear a dowd. Phineas would dislike that beyond anything, you can be sure. I consider this the very minimum, and we have yet to visit the milliners and bootmakers. Then there are shawls, gloves, stockings, fans, reticules, and dozens of other things I cannot recall at the moment, but which you will undoubtedly need if you are to make the kind of splash my brother has in mind."

Cassandra stared at Lady Hart in horror. "Did he tell you all of this in his note?" she asked in failing accents.

"No, of course not, silly. But why else would he ask me to see you rigged out in the first style of elegance?"

"Well," Cassandra said hesitantly, "I had understood him to say that he wanted to remove to Nottingham as soon as possible."

"What? And miss the Little Season?" Lady Hart looked incredulous. "That does not sound at all like Phineas, my dear. Surely you mistook the matter."

Cassandra was too tired and excited to argue, and it was only much later, as Lady Hart's carriage deposited them back in time for tea at Mansfield Court, that she recalled her friend's remark. Would the earl insist upon removing immediately to his country estate? she wondered. Or would he wish her to stay in Town for the Little Season? The idea of playing the charade of Countess of Mansfield before the whole of London society did not appeal to her, but she could not imagine that her preferences would influence Lord Mansfield's decision in the slightest.

At least he would no longer be able to rail at her poor taste in clothes, she mused as she and Lady Hart ascended the wide staircase, followed by two footmen carrying their numerous purchases. The knowledge that she now possessed several gowns in the first stare of fashion gave her spirits a boost. She would take Sophy's advice, she decided suddenly, and discard the old-fashioned brown kerseymere in favor of one of her new afternoon frocks in pale lilac silk before coming down for tea.

The Earl of Mansfield experienced an unusual feeling of guilt as he entered his residence a little after five o'clock the afternoon after his arrival in London. It was a new experience for him, one that he could not remember feeling since the days of his first years in London, when a particularly wild escapade of his came to the notice of the earl, his father, and brought a curt summons to present himself at Mansfield Grange immediately. Those interviews with his father lingered in his memory as reminders of too many years squandered in senseless and often highly reprehensible pursuits in the Metropolis. When he remembered the innumerable wastrels and spendthrifts from the very best families—and many who were merely hangers-on—who had professed themselves his bosom-bows and thought nothing of encouraging the young Phineas Ravenville to indulge his already dangerous predilection for gaming, drinking, and wenching, the earl grimaced. He had missed too many opportunities to get to know his father, whom he had idolized, in order to spend his energies raking about the countryside, intent on the ephemeral glory of besting the late earl's reputation as the most notorious rake and daredevil in all of England.

Had he achieved that dubious status? he wondered, handing his cane, gloves, and tall beaver to Dorset and requesting a bottle of brandy in the library. It was difficult to say, and in any case, did it matter anymore? The fifth earl had been dead for ten years now and Phineas never ceased to regret those years they had spent apart. His father had never insisted that he remain in Nottingham to learn the running of an estate as large as Mansfield Grange, nor had he reproached his son his frequent absences from family gatherings. But neither had he given his approval to his heir's obsession to follow in his footsteps. It had been left to his mother to ell him, after his father's premature death, that the late earl had wished for nothing more than to have his eldest son beside him in the bosom of his family.

By that time, when it had been too late to mend matters, Phineas had at first refused to believe that his notorious exploits had not found favor in his father's eyes. Again, it had been the countess who had gently informed him that his father's raking days had ended quite suddenly the evening he had laid eyes on his future wife, Lady Sybilla, youngest daughter of the Duke of Wexley, at her come-out ball so many years ago. Lady Sybilla had been strenuously cautioned against such a match, her son had learned for the first time, but she had persevered in her choice, he assured him, because it had been a love match for both of them, which had lasted until the day his father had died. The late earl's most treasured aspiration was that his heir would undergo the same miraculous experience and cast off his wild ways forever.

Well, Lord Mansfield thought rather acidly as he stood before the library fire warming the seat of his exquisitely cut breeches and watching Dorset pour a glass of brandy from the crystal decanter, there was no chance in hell of that ever happening to him. In the first place, he had never laid eyes on any lady who had tempted him, even fleetingly, to abandon his careless pursuit of pleasure. In the second—and here he grimaced at his scowling reflection above the mantel—his hand had been forced by unforeseen and, from his point of view, quite disastrous circumstances, to take a bride who was unfit in every conceivable way to be his countess.

"Her ladyship is taking tea in the drawingroom," Dorset offered in his quietly refined voice. "Lady Hart is with her ladyship, milord." Having dropped this piece of information into the silence in the library, Dorset regarded his master expressionlessly. "Shall I inform their ladyships of your return, milord?"

Phineas felt rather than heard the faint echo of reproof in his butler's toneless question. He raised his eyes from the fire to meet Dorset's bland gaze. Undoubtedly the butler—and quite possibly the whole household—was well aware that the earl had not come home last night. This in itself was not an unusual or noteworthy occurrence. Phineas had been in the habit of spending two or three nights a week away from his own bed, usually gambling at one of the exclusive gaming halls he patronized, but more often than not in the company of his current ladybird, Giullietta Rossani, the Italian opera singer who was the season's toast. Thoughts of the voluptuous Giullietta brought a sardonic smile to his lips.

"I shall join them presently, Dorset," he said gently, accepting the glass his butler offered him on the silver tray. "But allow me to fortify myself before maudling my insides with tea, if you please."

"Certainly, milord."

As soon as the butler had closed the door silently behind him, Phineas turned to gaze moodily into the flames. Dorset's implied criticism of his neglect of Lady Mansfield alerted him as to the source of his recent vague feelings of guilt. The deuce take the chit, he thought impatiently. He had vowed that his newly acquired bride would alter not one whit the life of unfettered freedom he had led for the past ten years or more. Yet here he was, already feeling defensive about spending a perfectly delightful and eminently pleasurable night with that seductive baggage Giullietta.

He drained his glass and set it on the mantel. He supposed he had better put in an appearance in the drawing room, especially since his sister Sophy was present. He wondered idly if Cassandra had allowed herself to be guided by his sister in her purchases. He had every confidence in Sophy's good taste; it was her one talent with which he had no fault to find, although it would be beyond even Sophy's enviable skills, he thought cynically, to turn a sow's ear into a silk purse.

The comparison was undoubtedly unkind and unwarranted, but it amused him, and on this note, the earl made his way up the stairs to join the ladies in the drawing room.

CHAPTER SEVEN

The Pearl Ring

Three evenings later, Cassandra stood before the cheval looking-glass in her luxurious bedchamber and examined her appearance critically. She was not at all convinced by what she saw, although Bridget had exclaimed rapturously over her mistress's latest acquisition. When she had tried the gown on at Madame Suzette's only yesterday, it had seemed to fit both her need to observe her state of mourning and her desire for a modish gown to wear at the dinner party she was to attend that evening at Hart House. Both Sophy and Madame had gone into transports over the elegant creation, which Madame had insisted made the young countess appear every inch *comme il faut,* as she put it.

Cassandra sighed imperceptibly and gave her bodice a discreet tug. She could not remember the neckline being quite so revealing when she had the gown on yesterday. Perhaps her sense of decorum had been lulled by the sophisticated atmosphere of the French modiste's salon, she thought wryly. Here, in the intimacy of her own bedroom, the low décolletage had given her a definite jolt of alarm. Could this be the same Miss Drayton who had arrived in London in that demure, outmoded kerseymere gown? she wondered. No wonder Lord Mansfield had been revolted by her sober attire if this was the kind of gown he was accustomed to seeing on his ladies.

At the thought of her husband, Cassandra sighed again. She had not seen the wretch since that afternoon, three days ago, when she had taken tea in the drawing room with Sophy after their first shopping expedition. She was feeling rather pleased with herself for taking Sophy's advice and changing into one of her new gowns, a flattering lilac silk with a darker shade of lace at the hem and neckline. They had been deep in plans for the following day's activities, and Cassandra had expressed some anxiety over the expense she was incurring. Lady Hart had dismissed this notion with an airy wave of her delicate hand, declaring that her brother had pockets deeper than most and wouldn't care a fig for the expense, when the door had opened and the earl had strolled into the room.

Sophy had jumped up immediately and rushed to embrace her brother enthusiastically. He had not seemed the least affected by this show of sisterly welcome and had disengaged her fingers from the lapels of his smart blue coat with a distinct air of distaste on his swarthy countenance. "Try not to behave like a hoyden, Sophy," he remarked, raising his eyes to meet Cassandra's gaze over his sister's golden head. Her heart had given an uncomfortable lurch, but she had managed to return his stare coolly. The thought that she was irrevocably tied to this dangerously unpredictable man frightened her, and she suddenly understood—as she stared into the depths of those hooded eyes—why Sophy had confessed to being terrified of her brother when he was in one of his black moods.

The moment of fear had been replaced by embarrassment when Sophy turned and caught her hand, pulling her to her feet. "What do you think, Phineas?" she demanded saucily. "We have been at Madame Suzette's all afternoon, and I trust that you are pleased with the results."

Cassandra had felt herself blush with mortification at being displayed so blatantly for his lordship's approval. She wished that she had not abandoned the shabbiness of her old gown, which had unaccountably provided a degree of safety from the kind of examination the earl had subjected her to that afternoon. To her immense chagrin, he had lifted his quizzing-glass and casually raked her person from head to toe in a most objectionable manner. It reminded her uncomfortably of their first meeting, and the humiliation she had felt then as a young girl swept over her now in the elegant drawing room. A black fury enveloped her and made her reckless.

"Do put that stupid thing away and stop being ridiculous," she had snapped before she could stop herself.

Sophy stared at her openmouthed, but Lord Mansfield had finally smiled and taken her hand in his. "Ah, my sweet Cassandra," he murmured, raising her fingers to his lips and placing a warm, lingering kiss on them. "I am glad to see that London has not daunted your spirit, my dear." Still holding her hand, he turned to his astonished sister and remarked blandly, "Isn't she a treasure, Sophy? Such an appealing way of bolstering a gentleman's fragile ego. I can't think how I came to be so fortunate."

Cassandra had instantly regretted her outburst and tried to withdraw her hand, but the earl held her fast. "I do beg your pardon, my lord," she said stiffly, wishing he would not regard her with such cynical amusement. "But you must agree that it is a coxcomb's trick to ogle anyone through that pretentious object. Don't you agree, Sophy?" She threw an appealing glance at her friend, who was regarding her in alarm.

"My sister has more sense than to lend her support to such an addle-pated notion, my dear," he drawled, depositing another warm kiss on her fingers before releasing her. "And now, ladies, are you going to invite me to join you, or must I return to my brandy in the library?"

Lady Hart, recovering from her astonishment at her brother's odd behavior, had begged him to accept a cup of tea, which Cassandra had poured for him, marveling at the steadiness of her hand on the silver teapot. He had only stayed long enough to drink one cup and give his approval to a projected dinner party at Hart House later in the week, before taking his leave of them. It was only after he had sauntered out of the room that Cassandra realized he had failed to comment on her new gown.

Well, she thought with a flicker of satisfaction at her own daring, he would be hard put to ignore this gown. The neckline, which dipped so low across her bosom that Cassandra felt in imminent danger of it dropping off altogether, was deep enough to titillate even the most hardened libertine, she thought smugly. Not that she had any experience with libertines, of course. Now, if only she could pretend unconcern at appearing in public with so little covering, she thought, gazing down in mild alarm at the wide expanse of ivory skin rising from the clinging satin of a purple so deep as to appear almost black, she would muddle through the evening without disgracing herself.

"What jewels will you wear, milady?" Bridget inquired, giving the fashionably narrow skirt a twitch to make it fall more snugly along the line of her hips. Or so it appeared to Cassandra, who was wondering how she was supposed to sit with any degree of comfort in such a gown. Jewels? she wondered. She had no jewelry at all, except for her wedding ring and the gold locket Stephen had given her. It would have to be that or nothing, of course, and Cassandra rather thought she would welcome anything around her neck that might distract from the disturbing view of her exposed person.

As if in answer to her quandary, there was a discreet scratch at the door, and when Bridget returned from attending to it, she carried a flat jeweler's box in her hands.

"That was Turner, his lordship's valet," she explained, a pleased expression on her kindly face. "His lordship sends you this,"—she indicated the box—"and says to remind you that the carriage is ordered for eight o'clock, milady. He will await you downstairs."

Cassandra took the jeweler's box hesitantly. She had just been thinking that as yet, her husband had given her no gift at all, not even an engagement ring. The idea that he had obviously planned to give her a piece of jewelry was rather endearing. She opened the box and smiled in delight. How he had known what color she would wear, she had no idea, but the delicate necklace of amethysts set in gold, with a larger stone pendant in the center, could not have suited her better. There was also a pair of small earbobs to match, which Bridget had barely enough time to fasten on her mistress's small ears before Cassandra heard the clock in the hall downstairs strike eight.

On impulse, she threw her new black velvet cloak over her shoulders to cover her décolletage before snatching up her gloves and reticule and descending the two flights of stairs to the entrance hall. Could it be that she feared Lord Mansfield's cynical gaze? she wondered, angry at herself for being such a ninny. What did she care if he approved of her clothes or not? It should be enough that he paid for them and that she enjoyed wearing them, shouldn't it? That was Lady Hart's philosophy, and Cassandra began to see that she must learn to please herself in this uncomfortable marriage she had contracted, because it was unlikely that she would ever please the obnoxious Earl of Mansfield.

The drive to Hart House was accomplished in silence. The earl barely acknowledged his wife's attempts to thank him for the jewelry.

"The Ravenville collection is pretty extensive," he said coolly in response to Cassandra's shy thanks. "Most of it is either in the safe at Mansfield Grange or with Hamilton, my man in business. My mother happened to leave the amethysts in London during her last stay here."

"Oh," his wife had exclaimed softly. "Are they hers, my lord?"

"No, of course not. They belong to the Ravenville estate and are now yours, my dear. I'm glad you like them."

He had stared at her in the dim light inside the carriage and thought that the new way she had fixed her hair became her. The auburn curls were piled in a sophisticated cluster on the top of her small head, with a number of soft strands escaping to fall against her neck. Her hazel eyes, large and faintly apprehensive, fell beneath his gaze, and the notion that perhaps his wife was adopting a more becoming modesty in her behavior gave him pause for thought. As he had several times had occasion to discover, Cassandra had the disconcerting habit of staring him down with a brazenness of a hardened doxy. He attributed this to lack of social graces rather than actual immodesty, but he was gratified to see that she could behave like a lady when she chose.

When the barouche came to a halt before Hart House, Phineas jumped out to hand his wife down himself and noted with approval that her small hand, correctly sheathed in a plum-colored glove, was warm in his. His thoughts flew back to the night of their arrival in London and his annoyance at her for losing her gloves. It seemed to him that annoyance was his predominant reaction to his wife's presence, although—by deliberate design—he had been in her presence as little as possible, particularly since that afternoon when she had accused him of being ridiculous for teasing her with his quizzing-glass.

Tonight, however, she had as yet made no sign of wishing to lock horns with him, and Phineas felt in a mellow mood as he escorted his wife into the warm hall and allowed a footman to relieve him of his hat, gloves, and silver-headed cane. He turned to find that the Harts's butler had already divested Lady Mansfield of her cloak, and the sight that met the earl's eyes startled him. The elegant female in the extremely fashionable iridescent plum-colored satin gown bore little if any resemblance to the taciturn girl in dull brown kerseymere he had brought up from Kent. Only her eyes were unchanged, Phineas thought, dragging his own reluctantly from his wife's unexpectedly beautiful neck and shoulders. But he had been premature in assuming that Cassandra's attitude had become any the less challenging. She was, even now, regarding him with faint, mocking amusement, very much as though he had been some callow youth in his first Season, caught staring, openmouthed, at a current Beauty.

Lord Mansfield allowed himself a derisive smile that did not get anywhere near his eyes, suddenly hooded and glittering dangerously. He offered his arm, cursing himself for his unguarded moment and perversely determined that no word of approval for his wife's quite stunning transformation would pass his lips.

"Come, my dear," he drawled, aware that Cassandra's subtle amusement seemed to have died. "Sophy will doubtless be impatient to see us." On impulse, he drew his wife's hand through the crook of his arm and kept a hand possessively over hers as they followed the butler upstairs to the drawing room.

"You are not nervous, are you, Cassandra?"

She glanced up at him, her eyes once more amused. "Of course not. Why should I be? Sophy tells me that her Ned is the kindest man alive. I am anxious to meet such a paragon."

The innocence of this reply made Phineas smile. Little did his lady wife know that Ned Greenley had, before his recent marriage to the earl's sister, belonged to Lord Mansfield's intimate circle of cronies whose philosophy of life included seducing every willing female of their acquaintance, going to their beds half castaway four nights out of five, gambling away every last penny in their pockets, never refusing a wager, however preposterous, and evading parson's mousetrap at all costs. So much of a rakehell had Ned been, in fact, that Phineas had at first vigorously denied him permission to pay court to Sophy. His sister had been adamant, however, and no amount of threatening or cajoling had made her deviate from her determination to have Ned Greenley. Unconvinced by her romantic illusion, shared by his mother, that rakes could be tamed, the earl hoped she would not live to regret her rash choice.

Absorbed with these thoughts, Lord Mansfield had advanced with his wife on his arm several feet into the drawing room before he realized that the party did not consist solely of Lord Hart and his lady. The sight of the two gentlemen who sprang to their feet and now stood staring at Lady Mansfield with undisguised admiration made the earl curse under his breath. Both his cousin, Robert Heathercott, Marquess of Gresham, and Mr. Willoughby Hampton knew about his precipitous marriage, of course. He had been almost constantly in their company since his arrival back in London. But Phineas had not been prepared—at least not yet—to introduce his new bride to two of the most notorious libertines of his acquaintance. Outside of himself, he thought with a flash of amusement.

But it was too late to retreat. Lady Hart had rushed to greet them and thrown her arms affectionately around Cassandra's shoulders, quite ignoring her brother.

"My dearest Cassie," she cried gleefully and with total sincerity, "you have quite put me in the shade with that marvelous gown. Madame Suzette was right; it is stunning on you. And you have cast the gentlemen into a state of speechless admiration. Isn't that right, Ned?" She addressed this last comment to Lord Hart, who had come forward to greet his guests.

"Just so, sweetheart," he answered, and Phineas was inexplicably put out by the glint of appreciation he detected in his host's gray eyes.

"What fustian!" he heard his wife reply laughingly. "Do spare my blushes, Sophy. You are being quite ridiculous."

"Nothing of the sort, I assure you, my lady," came a suave voice from beside him. He turned to see Robert Heathercott gazing down at Cassandra, his handsome face quite devoid of its usual bored and faintly sneering expression. "What are you waiting for, Raven? Introduce me to your beautiful lady."

Lord Mansfield frowned. Trust his cousin to get in a smooth compliment so effortlessly. "Much as I would rather not, Cassandra," he said, "allow me to present this rogue to you. My cousin, Robert Heathercott, Marquess of Gresham."

The marquess took Lady Mansfield's hand and carried it ceremoniously to his lips, which lingered on them for considerably longer than Phineas considered proper. "I am quite enchanted," he said in his most caressing voice. "Now I understand why Raven has been so reluctant to introduce us to you. He doesn't deserve this kind of luck."

"Raven?" Cassandra repeated, quite ignoring the marquess's compliment, Phineas noticed with a malicious glance at his bemused cousin.

"Yes," cut in Mr. Hampton, who had joined the crowd around the new countess. "Quite an appropriate sobriquet, wouldn't you agree, Lady Mansfield?" Willy Hampton was not as tall as his three friends, and his features were not as startlingly attractive as Lord Gresham's or as darkly fascinating as the earl's. His twinkling blue eyes and gregarious good nature had often been known to succeed with the ladies where the other two had failed, however. Although only the son of the third son of the Earl of Belton, he was quite indecently wealthy—thanks to a doting great aunt— and was known to spend quite as much on his clothes as on his horses, which were second to none, and was therefore always impeccably dressed and mounted.

Cassandra cast an inquiring glance at her husband, and Phineas obliged with ill-concealed impatience. "Mr. Willoughby Hampton, more commonly known as Sweet Willy," he said shortly. "Now if you don't mind, I am sure her ladyship would like to sit down," he added pointedly.

Phineas never knew how his cousin managed it, but by the time they were all seated, the marquess had positioned himself next to Cassandra on the settee, while Willy took a chair to her left. To his surprise, his wife appeared more amused than flattered at finding herself beset by two such eligible and polished gentlemen.

"So you are a marquess," he heard Cassandra say with total lack of self-consciousness. "I never would have credited it, my lord."

Lord Gresham looked slightly startled, but instead of the blistering set-down Phineas expected, the marquess's perfectly classical lips curved into a rueful smile. "I must apologize for disappointing you, my lady. May I inquire what you imagined a marquess to be?"

"Oh, much, much older, my lord. And definitely afflicted with gout."

Mr. Hampton burst into laughter and was joined by Lady Hart who had caught Cassandra's remark. "My dear Lady Mansfield," Willy remarked, casting a wicked glance at his bemused friend, "you may be sure that Gresham here will fit that description perfectly in another ten or fifteen years. He spends half his life with a bottle in his hand and is almost in his dotage already."

Cassandra turned her penetrating gaze on the marquess's face, and Phineas felt a frisson of apprehension. What outrageous remark would the chit make next? he wondered. Lord Gresham was not known for his forbearance, although Phineas doubted he would actually do violence to a guest in Lady Hart's drawing room.

"I think you must be jesting, Mr. Hampton," Cassandra said seriously. "And it is most unkind of you to call his lordship old when clearly he is nothing of the sort."

"Touché, old chap," Lord Gresham remarked dryly. "And you

well know that I have yet to drink you under the table, Willy." He turned to Cassandra, a sardonic expression on his face. "Thank you for coming to my defense, Lady Mansfield. I am touched."

Phineas held his breath, for he could guess what was coming next. He tried to catch his sister's eye, but Sophy was entranced at the countess's casual reaction to the handsome marquess. Typically, his wife came straight to the point.

"You shall disappoint me again, my lord," she declared in her clear, unruffled voice, "if you admit to being one of those repellent individuals who spend all their time under tables, besotted with drink." She regarded Lord Gresham steadily. The marquess was staring at Cassandra with a blank expression on his handsome face, and Phineas wouldn't mind wagering that Robert had never been addressed with such directness before.

Lord Mansfield felt obliged to break the awkward pause that had followed his wife's remark. "My cousin drinks no more than most gentlemen of the *ton*, my dear," he said easily, "so don't be hard on him."

"I have a pony that says you've never been called repellent by a lady before, Robert. What do you say?"

Cassandra turned to Mr. Hampton with a frown. "I did not call his lordship repellent, Mr. Hampton. Indeed, I would do no such thing, even if I thought he was. You mistook my meaning, sir, and—"

What his wife had been about to add was lost in the whoops of laughter that greeted her comment, and before anyone could say more, the Harts's butler appeared to announce that dinner was served.

Phineas sighed with relief and offered to lead his sister in to dinner, noting with some surprise that Lord Gresham had done the unexpected again. Far from being affronted, as the earl had expected, the marquess had offered his arm to Lady Mansfield, an enigmatic little smile on his lips.

Two days later, Cassandra was surprised to meet Lord Mansfield in the front hall as she was returning from taking luncheon with Lady Hart. She was even further astonished when he actually accosted her and invited her to drive with him at two o'clock.

"I have an appointment with Madame Suzette at that hour, my lord," she informed him, deriving unexpected satisfaction from being able to deny him. "I am sorry to disoblige you," she added mendaciously, conscious of the black frown that had immediately descended on the earl's brow.

"Do you mean to take the carriage?" he inquired.

"Oh, no," she replied, conscious of treading on dangerous ground. "Mr. Hampton kindly offered to drive me in his new curricle. He has just acquired a new team, which he says—"

"Yes, I know all about his new team," Lord Mansfield said between gritted teeth. He looked at her sharply. "Did he call here, perchance?"

"Not today," she answered truthfully, unwilling to inform the earl that both his friends had called on her yesterday for tea. "He called at Lady Hart's this morning while I was there." She refrained from adding that Lord Gresham had also been present, apparently undeterred by her unfortunate remark about his drinking the other evening.

"I shall take you to the modiste myself," he declared shortly. "And in future, if you need to go anywhere, and Sophy cannot accompany you, you may call on me."

Cassandra smiled. "You are never at hand, my lord," she pointed out blandly, wondering how much Mr. Hampton's invitation had to do with her husband's sudden gallantry.

Lord Mansfield glared down at her, and it was all Cassandra could do to meet his smoldering gaze without flinching. "Leave a message with Dorset," he replied abruptly. "I shall have my team outside at a quarter to two. Don't keep me waiting." With this abrupt command, he turned on his heel and disappeared into the library.

She would be damned in Hell before she communicated with her husband through the butler, Cassandra thought, her temper rising. What did this autocratic man think she was? One of his servants? Lord Mansfield's odd behavior occupied her thoughts as she went upstairs to her chamber and rang for Bridget to help her out of her lilac muslin morning gown. The notion of driving out in the company of her own husband should not cause this strange fluttering of her pulses, she told herself sternly. Perhaps it was the suddenness of the earl's invitation, which had flustered her, Cassandra thought, as she allowed her abigail to button up the smart forest-green merino walking gown she had not as yet had a chance to wear.

It was pure luck that she had allowed Sophy to talk her into purchasing the dashing green poke bonnet to complement the gown, and if Madame Suzette was as correct in this as she had been in her other prediction, Lord Mansfield would have nothing whatever to criticize in her choice of headwear. Secure in this knowledge, Cassandra slipped into her matching pelisse, gathered gloves and reticule, and ventured downstairs, her emotions mixed at the thought of having to cope with his lordship's ill humor.

She need not have worried, however, for Lord Mansfield was at his most urbane as he escorted her out and assisted her into the yellow-wheeled curricle standing at the door. Cassandra had often ridden in Stephen's curricle in Walmer, but she saw at a glance that her former betrothed's much lauded team of prime goers—as he used to call them—was no match for the earl's team of matched chestnuts, which stood fretfully waiting for his signal to go. The young groom sprang from their heads at a sign from Lord Mansfield, and Cassandra felt a moment of panic as the mettle-some team surged forward along the quiet thoroughfare of St. James's Square.

"Not scared, are you, Cassandra?"

She saw the earl was glancing down at her with an almost boy-ish grin on his face, one eyebrow cocked inquiringly. With some-thing of a shock, Cassandra realized that she had never before noticed just how devilishly attractive her husband was when he allowed his rare humor to reach his dark eyes and fill them with warmth instead of cynicism. For a heartbeat she stared into their laughing depths, quite enchanted by their radiance. Then she al-lowed herself to laugh with him, her spirits suddenly buoyant with delight at this first really happy moment shared with a man she would never have chosen to wed if things had been different.

"Bah!" she cried. "What kind of a missish goose do you take me for, sir? Of course I'm not scared. I know you to be a famous whip and member of the Four-in-Hand-Club to boot. What have I to fear?"

"And how do you know all this, may I ask?" he inquired, still smiling down at her in such a way that made her wish that he would smile at her just so more often.

"Stephen told me," she responded without thinking.

There was a moment of silence before he said, "Ah, Stephen." And Cassandra saw some of the light die out of his eyes, and their moment of harmony was gone before it had time to flourish.

When they arrived at Madame Suzette's salon, the earl handed the reins to the groom who had ridden up behind them and lifted her down with a quick, efficient motion. To her surprise, he entered the salon with her and was effusively greeted by Madame.

"Lord Mansfield, what a pleasant surprise," the modiste gushed as soon as she spied his tall frame beside the countess. "And my lady." She turned to include Cassandra in her effusive welcome.

"I understand my wife has a fitting with you, madame," he drawled. "I trust it will not take too long, as we have other plans for this afternoon."

Cassandra was amazed at the effect these few simple words had on Madame Suzette and her staff. In less than half an hour, the fitting for three new gowns—which would normally have occupied the better part of two hours—was accomplished, and Lord and Lady Mansfield found themselves being bowed out of the establishment with the obsequious condescension madame reserved for her preferred patrons.

"I see I must bring you with me every time I visit madame, my lord," Cassandra observed jokingly, as soon as they were once more in motion. "You possess a consequence I obviously lack in order to persuade her not to dawdle and waste time in idle gossip."

She saw his teeth flash in another smile as he threaded his horses through the congested traffic until they reached Piccadilly, where he put them to the smart trot.

"Where are you taking me, my lord? To drive in Hyde Park?"

"It is not yet the fashionable hour to be seen there," he answered, cocking an eyebrow at her. "That is if you wish to be admired by the *ton*. Is that your ambition, my dear?"

Cassandra laughed and gave a small snort of disgust. "You know, or you *should* know by now, my lord, that I care not a fig for such farradiddle. I would enjoy the chance to get away from all this noise and bustle. I am a simple country girl at heart, remember?"

Lord Mansfield shot her an amused glance. "Nobody would guess that to see you now," he remarked. "Madame Suzette has outdone herself."

Cassandra felt inordinately pleased. Faint praise though it was, this was the first compliment her husband had ever paid her. So, she thought with perverse satisfaction, the cynical Phineas Ravenville is not as unobservant as he would appear. She had not seen the earl since their evening together at the Harts's dinner party, but Cassandra was now more inclined to believe she had

not mistaken the glimpse of admiration she thought she had detected in Lord Mansfield's eyes when he had first seen her in the
plum-colored gown. It had been masked so quickly by his usual
cynical stare, that she had decided she must have imagined it, but
now she was not so sure.

She was recalled from her reverie when the curricle came to a
halt before an elegant building whose discreet, highly polished
brass plaque announced it to be the place of business of Duval &
Carrier, Jewelers. Cassandra looked up at the earl in surprise as he
again lifted her from the carriage and, offering his arm, escorted
her into the somberly furnished precincts of London's premier
jewelers.

"What are we doing here?" Cassandra whispered as they
waited in the tomblike silence of the reception saloon to which
they had been led by a black-clad clerk.

"You will see soon enough, my dear. I have been remiss with
you, Cassandra, as Sophy was kind enough to point out to me the
other evening. I intend to remedy the situation, that is all."

Since Cassandra could not for a moment imagine what he was
talking about, she would have demanded further enlightenment,
but they were interrupted by the entrance of a stout, soberly
dressed gentleman who greeted Lord Mansfield with enthusiasm.

"My dear, allow me to present Mr. Jacques Duval to you. Mr.
Duval, and his father before him, have been jewelers to the
Ravenvilles for generations, isn't that so, Duval?"

"*Indubitablement,* my lord," replied the rotund gentlemen in a
decidedly French intonation. "It is my very great pleasure to make
your acquaintance, Lady Mansfield," he added, favoring her with
a stiff, formal bow. "And may I be permitted to congratulate you
on your recent nuptials, my lord? How may I be of service to
you?"

"I wish to see what lady's rings you have, Duval. Something
special, you understand."

"*Mais oui, certainement.*" The Frenchman smiled, casting an
appraising glance at the countess. "Please make yourself comfortable, my lady. I shall personally see to it."

"What are you about, Mansfield?" Cassandra demanded
abruptly, no sooner had the Frenchman left the room. "You do not
have to buy *me* any jewels, you know." She met the earl's sardonic gaze coolly, although her throat had become inexplicably
tight. "I distinctly remember you saying that the Ravenville col-

lection was extensive. Why do you wish to purchase yet another ring? You must have dozens of them in the bank vault."

"I never gave you a betrothal ring, Cassandra," came the amused reply.

"We never were betrothed if I remember correctly, my lord," she said coldly, wondering why the notion of receiving such an intimate gift from the earl had shaken her composure. Any kind of intimacy with this man frightened her, she realized. When he was his usual cynical self, he could be cruel and hurtful, but when he was charming, as he had been with her this afternoon, he was doubly dangerous to her peace of mind. She must ignore his disdain and resist his charm, she told herself firmly. Otherwise her life would be unbearably painful. And since his reasons for wishing to give her a ring were decidedly unclear, if not suspect, she would simply refuse the gift.

Lord Mansfield's brows lowered menacingly. "You are not going to break squares with me on this, are you, Cassandra?" He spoke softly, but she was not misled into thinking she would prevail in her resistance without a serious brangle.

"I do not require a betrothal ring," she said, her chin lifting stubbornly. "Least of all from you."

"Perhaps not," he said, his glance now hooded, eyes reflecting an equally determined light. "But I *do* require you to have one. So let us not cross swords, my dear. Duval will think you the veriest shrew if you rant at me for wishing to surprise you with a gift.

"I am *not* ranting," Cassandra contradicted him crossly. "And I am *not* a shrew. It is you, my lord, who are being most provoking."

This exchange, which threatened to become a full-scale quarrel, was interrupted by the reentry of Mr. Duval with a velvet tray upon which sparkled the most beautiful collection of rings Cassandra had ever beheld. When the little jeweler placed the tray on the low table before her, Cassandra felt her breath catch in her throat.

She glanced apprehensively up at the earl and was not surprised to find him regarding her with a quizzical smile on his lips and genuine amusement in his dark eyes. He had seen her involuntary reaction to the glittering, bewitching jewels. Perhaps he had known all along, she thought with sudden insight, that she would not be able to resist the temptation he was dangling in front of her. She let out her breath in a soft sigh. He was probably right, of course. The idea of refusing anything as breathtaking as the rings spread out for her inspection caused an almost physical pain in her chest.

She felt rather than saw the earl take a seat on the settee beside her. "Don't be shy, my love," he said softly. "Try some of them on. You can have any one that takes your fancy." His lean fingers stretched over the tray and casually selected an enormous, glittering diamond. "What about this one?"

He had obviously meant what he said, Cassandra realized. The ring the earl was holding out to her was quite the most extravagant of the selection. She shuddered inwardly at the thought of what it must cost.

"No, I don't think so," she said slowly. Although she had not rejected this particular ring because it was her husband's first choice, but because the size of it disconcerted her, she felt his withdrawal and turned to meet his cool gaze. "It is exceptionally lovely, of course," she said, smiling directly into his eyes. "But it is not my style at all, my lord." He returned her smile, but Cassandra noticed that he regarded her dubiously.

"Your ladyship is quite right," Mr. Duval put in smoothly. "Something this ostentatious is certainly not your style." He picked up a stunning emerald set in tiny diamonds. "Perhaps something closer to the color of your eyes, my lady?" he said with Gallic charm.

Cassandra laughed into his twinkling blue eyes and suddenly felt less tense. "If I had eyes that color, Monsieur Duval, I would certainly agree with your choice. It is a beautiful ring." She took the emerald in her fingers and pretended to consider it, although she knew it was not the one she wanted.

She picked up several of the less impressive stones and examined them carefully, but was only tempted to try on a cluster of pearls sprinkled with tiny diamonds. The ring was too big for her small hand, however, at least in her estimation, and she withdrew it from her finger with a sigh of regret.

"Your ladyship has a preference for pearls?" Mr. Duval inquired solicitously. "Allow me to show you some particularly fine specimens we received recently from the Orient. Not all of them have been set as yet, but I believe I have one that will please your ladyship." He bustled out of the room and returned quickly with a small square box, which he opened to reveal the most glorious pearl ring Cassandra had ever seen. She knew instantly that this was the one she wanted. The pearl was exceptionally large, and its color reminded her of liquid ivory touched by summer moonlight. It glowed with warmth and a subtle mystery that enchanted her. She picked the ring up with reverent fingers and slipped it on, experiencing a frisson of excitement and pure pleasure at the radiant beauty of the gem. A myriad of small diamonds clustered about the pearl and studded the gold band with dozens of tiny points of glittering light. The ring fit her small finger as if it had been made for her.

Cassandra tore her eyes away from the mesmerizing glow of the milky pearl and stared wide-eyed at her husband. The bauble looked horrifyingly expensive, and she was suddenly fraught with feelings of guilt at choosing what must surely be the most costly ring in the establishment. Lord Mansfield was regarding her fixedly, and Cassandra wondered at the strange flicker of emotion she saw in his gaze. "Do you like it, my lord?" she asked breathlessly and stretched out her hand for his inspection. If he showed the least reluctance, she would feel obliged to reject it, she thought.

The earl took her hand in his, and Cassandra shivered at the odd tension that seemed to pass between them. He examined the ring for a moment and then raised her fingers and gently kissed them. "Very pretty indeed, my love. Is this your choice, then?"

"Oh, yes, please. If you like it, too," she added, sure that her eyes had betrayed her eagerness, for the earl's lips curled at the corners, and he smiled at her again.

"Very well. We will take it, Duval," he said laconically. "Am I right in assuming that you wish to wear it, my dear?" he asked.

Cassandra felt herself fairly melt with pleasure. She must have been transparent indeed for him to have guessed her thoughts. "May I?" she murmured, gazing up at him with her heart in her eyes, careless of the interested presence of Mr. Duval.

For the longest moment, Lord Mansfield stared down at her, an arrested expression on his lean face. Then he smiled and took her arm. "Of course you may, Cassandra," he said softly, nodding to the beaming jeweler and gently propelling her out into the mild September sunlight.

Cassandra found her voice as they pulled away at a spanking trot down Piccadilly in the direction of Hyde Park. "I d-don't know . . . I c-cannot find the w-words to thank you, my lord," she said disjointedly. "I have never received such a b-beautiful gift before. Ever." She glanced up admiringly at his handsome profile. "You are very, very kind," she murmured softly. "Even though you didn't have to," she added, almost to herself.

Lord Mansfield must have heard her, however, for he shot her an odd look from beneath hooded lids. "I wished to do so, Cassandra," he remarked in a neutral voice. "Now, shall we take a turn in the Park, my dear?"

At that blissful moment, Cassandra would have agreed to practically anything his lordship might have suggested.

CHAPTER EIGHT

The Kiss

If Cassandra had imagined, as indeed she had been tempted to, that the pleasant afternoon spent with her husband in Hyde Park and the exquisite pearl ring he had bestowed upon her as a belated betrothal gift might affect their relationship in any positive way, she knew she had mistaken the matter before the week was out. Not only did Lord Mansfield fail to appear at dinner that night, as she had half expected him to, but on the following evening he excused himself—through Dorset—from escorting her to a musical soirée at Hart House. It was only on the third afternoon that she caught a glimpse of him as she was driving in the Park with Lady Hart, Mr. Hampton, and Lord Gresham, but the sight brought her no joy at all.

Mr. Hampton had been entertaining the ladies with a suitably edited account of a recent pugilistic encounter both gentlemen had witnessed the previous afternoon at the Five's Court in Westminster, between the black giant Tom Molyneux and an unfortunate challenger from the colonies. Liberally sprinkled with boxing cant, Sweet Willy's enthusiastic explanation of the finer points of the manly sport had kept Cassandra so amused that she had paid scant attention to the many carriages, riders, and pedestrians who thronged the Park at that fashionable hour.

"A great hulking fellow he was, too," cut in the marquess, in response to a comment from Hampton regarding the performance of the challenger. "A barrel of a man, with forearms the size of Yule logs. But he lacked Molyneux's science and was finally milled down with his cork drawn and his daylights darkened. Too green by half, if you ask me."

"I think that is quite enough gore for one afternoon, gentlemen," Lady Hart exclaimed. "Oh, do pull up, Robert. There is Arabella Chatham, or Tottlefield as she is now. I had no idea she and her husband were back from their wedding trip." She turned to Cassandra. "Her mother, Lady Maria Chatham, is my mother's cousin, and I am curious to know if marriage has settled Arabella down at all. She was always such a delightfully saucy little minx."

By this time Lord Gresham's open landau had come to a stop, and as Cassandra watched, a small, exquisitely dressed lady, whose delicate face was framed with blond curls, cantered up and came to a prancing stop beside their carriage. She could not be above eighteen or at most nineteen Cassandra calculated, and her laughing, pixie face and clear blue eyes gave her the air of a happy child. She greeted Sophy with effusive cordiality before turning to the rather portly young man who rode up behind her.

"You remember Toby, don't you, Sophy?" she exclaimed gaily. "Toby darling, this is my cousin Sophy Greenley. We attended her wedding to Lord Hart last spring, remember?"

After Cassandra had been introduced to the vivacious Beauty, who impulsively invited her to join them one afternoon for a ride in the Park, she sat watching the scene with some amusement and not a little nostalgia. The Honorable Tobias Tottlefield hardly took his eyes from his bride except when addressed directly by Lord Gresham about the health of his uncle, the Earl of Ridgeway. The dreamy look on Mr. Tottlefield's ruddy face reminded her forcibly of Stephen, and her heart ached afresh for her lost lover. She barely listened as Arabella explained that their early return from the Continent was due to Lord Ridgeway's failing health. Her eyes wandered over the two newlyweds and were drawn into the distance where the rest of the Tottlefield's party of riders was approaching, evidently in high good spirits. The party consisted of two gentlemen who seemed to be vying for the attention of a dazzlingly fair Amazon on a dappled gray mare.

The lady had the kind of scintillating beauty that drew all eyes, and Cassandra studied her from afar, wondering who she could be. She had the air of a woman accustomed to being the center of attraction wherever she went and was dressed for the part in a military-cut scarlet riding habit trimmed in black astrakhan. Her tawny gold hair, arranged in curls that brushed her perfect ivory cheeks, was confined beneath a black fur shako, worn at a rakish angle. So magnetic was the dashing rider that Cassandra paid no heed at all to the two gentlemen who rode on either side of her, both seemingly entranced by her lively conversation.

Her attention was claimed by Arabella, who flirted prettily with

Mr. Hampton and repeated her invitation to Cassandra before wheeling her horse and cantering back toward the advancing trio, followed by her doting husband. Cassandra's eyes followed the couple enviously, and in doing so, her gaze focused on one of the gentlemen who was—she now saw all too clearly—smiling warmly at the dashing Amazon. The lady laughed flirtatiously at something the dark gentleman said and laid a gloved hand on his arm in a gesture that, even to Cassandra's inexperienced eyes, suggested an alarming degree of intimacy.

It was a smile she recognized—one she had herself basked in only the other afternoon. At that moment, however, it chilled her soul. After a horrifying instant, which seemed like an eternity, Cassandra turned her eyes away, all too conscious that her face must have registered her dismay. She found herself under the scrutiny of Lord Gresham's startling sapphire-blue gaze and knew at once, when he motioned his driver to move forward, that he had witnessed her humiliation.

Apparently the others had also noticed the Earl of Mansfield's presence beside the lady in scarlet, for Sophy swore under her breath and, turning to her sister-in-law, brightly insisted that Cassandra join her for tea when they returned to Hart House. Cassandra opened her mouth to refuse, feeling that to maintain any semblance of polite conversation would be beyond her, but the marquess interrupted to press Sophy's invitation with such charm that she capitulated.

The tinkle of the scarlet lady's silvery laugh echoed in her ears for the remainder of the afternoon.

The following afternoon, Lord Mansfield stood in the middle of his sister's morning room, a thunderous scowl on his lean face.

"I cannot recall giving you leave to dictate to me, Gresham." His tone was icy and held a distinct hint of steel.

"Robert merely expressed what we have all been thinking, old man," Mr. Hampton interjected hastily. "Deuced bad form to parade your latest *amourette* in the Park, of all places. And at the fashionable hour, too. Looked to me as though you actually wished to flaunt the wench in front of all those tattling Tabbies."

"And in front of Lady Mansfield," Lord Hart added gravely, his gray eyes fixed accusingly on his friend.

"You're a fine one to talk, Ned," Phineas snapped. "I can remember a time when you would have jumped at the chance to bed Chloe Huntington."

"Aye," Lord Hart returned shortly. "But I was not a married man in those days, Phineas. Sophy is most put out with you, I can tell you."

"My sister would do well to keep her meddlesome nose out of my business. Whom I ride with in the Park is none of her concern," the earl added coldly.

"If you insist on making a dashed cake of yourself, it's everyone's concern," Mr. Hampton protested, his usually placid features distorted into a frown. "What the devil got into you, Raven? It ain't like you to be deliberately cruel."

"Quite the contrary," the Marquess of Gresham drawled. "I would say it is exactly the kind of rotten, selfish behavior we might expect of my cousin, Willy." The cold disdain in the marquess's voice could not be ignored, and Phineas whirled on him angrily.

"You're another one to talk, aren't you?" he snarled. "And as for rotten, selfish behavior, I'd like to see anyone best you at that game, Gresham. So watch your blasted tongue before I ram it down your throat for you."

"Here, here, old man," Willy interrupted quickly. "At least Robert ain't married, you know."

Lord Mansfield glared at the marquess, his taut lips curled contemptuously. "No," he said silkily. "Although of late he appears to fancy himself in that role."

Barely had the words been spoken before Lord Gresham rose lithely to his feet, his fists clenched menacingly. "And what exactly do you mean by that snide remark, Cousin?"

"You know damned well what I mean," the earl snapped. "Were it not for your officious meddling, Cassandra would not have been in the Park yesterday. Stay away from her, Gresham, or I'll bloody that smug phiz of yours."

"Stubble it, the two of you," Lord Hart said forcefully, taking up a stand between the two irate gentlemen. "I'll not have my house turned into Jackson's Saloon. And if you make one more insulting insinuation about Lady Mansfield, I shall be obliged to take you on myself, Raven."

"And if it's a turn-up you've a hankering for, Raven," Willy cut in vigorously, "I'd be only too happy to oblige. Why pick on old Robert, after all? I've escorted the lady several times myself, in case you hadn't noticed."

"Enough!" Lord Hart exclaimed impatiently. "What kind of shabsters are we anyway, to drag a lady's name into our quarrels like this? Back off, Raven," he commanded brusquely. "You were out of line and owe Robert here an apology. And I aim to see he gets it," he added in dangerously quiet tones.

The earl knew that his friends were right, but the knowledge did nothing to improve his temper. He would have to apologize to Robert, of course. His accusation—both spiteful and unfair—had been thrown out in the heat of the moment, a result of his own feelings of guilt. He had not seen Cassandra since that moment in the Park yesterday afternoon, when he had glimpsed the stark disbelief and embarrassment in her hazel eyes before she had turned stiffly away. She had seemed so vulnerable in that instant, so innocent and ill-equipped to be the wife of a man like himself. It did not help to remind himself that Cassandra had been the one to insist on keeping their union platonic. He had not been sufficiently interested in her to raise any objections; in fact, he had felt somewhat relieved that he could continue his pursuit of the delectable Lady Huntington with a clear conscience.

A clear conscience! Good God! What kind of a fool was he to allow the prudishness of a vicar's daughter to distract him from his enjoyment of the fair Chloe? he wondered. And distract him she certainly had. Last night, for the first time, Lady Huntington had shown clear signs of her willingness to be drawn into an intimate dalliance with the rakish Lord Mansfield. And what had he done? Phineas cursed himself for a deuced slow-top when he remembered how he had fobbed the Beauty off and spent the night with his official mistress, Giullietta Rossani, on Curzon Street instead.

He sighed and ran his fingers distractedly through his hair. "You are right, Ned," he said ruefully. "I deserve to be drawn and quartered." He glanced at Lord Gresham and saw that the marquess had recovered his aplomb and was leaning nonchalantly against the marble mantelpiece, his handsome face inscrutable. His hooded sapphire eyes held the earl's gaze for a long moment. Phineas grinned and was about to step forward to offer his hand, when the door flew open and Lady Hart came into the room, her lovely face alight with amusement.

"Ned, dearest—" she began and then stopped dead at the sight of the group of gentlemen. "Oh, I didn't realize you were busy." Her eyes suddenly fell on her brother, and she grimaced in distaste. "You!" she exclaimed in arctic tones. "I am amazed that you dare show your face around here, you . . . you odious cad, you." She turned her back and swept out of the room, leaving Lord Mansfield with the distinct impression that he was persona non grata in his sister's book.

A week after what Cassandra referred to in her mind as the Incident in the Park, she returned from an enjoyable visit to the Artillery Grounds, where she had witnessed her first balloon ascent, with the anticipation of a quiet coz with her sister-in-law. The two ladies had been accompanied by Lord Hart and Mr. Hampton, and the latter had, in his unobtrusively charming way, managed to drive away—at least temporarily—the unpleasant memories that had haunted Cassandra all week. With his amusing explanations of just how the enormous basket, called a gondola, with its gaily colored silk balloon could be made to rise and descend at the will of the intrepid Mr. John Marrow who was in charge of the exhibition, Mr. Hampton quite diverted Cassandra from the unpleasant realities of her situation.

Although in public she had tried her utmost to maintain a studied indifference to the implications of that encounter with Lord Mansfield in Hyde Park, in her heart Cassandra could not deceive herself so easily. The unexpected sight of her husband in the company of a beautiful woman—and so obviously enjoying every moment of it—had jarred her sensibilities more than she liked to admit, even to herself. Neither Lord Gresham nor Mr. Hampton, both of whom had witnessed the shocking encounter, had, by so much as a flicker of an eyebrow, betrayed their thoughts on the matter. Could it be that they had seen nothing odd, she wondered, in a newlywed gentleman paying such marked attention to a beautiful widow? The notion that such callous disregard for propriety might be considered all the crack in London disturbed her. But what had hurt the most, she admitted to herself later, was that her husband had made no attempt to approach her carriage, but had ridden on beside Lady Huntington for all the world as though his wife had been a total stranger.

And, of course, they were strangers, Cassandra had reminded herself firmly in the privacy of her bedchamber that night. By her own express request, her marriage to the Earl of Mansfield was to remain unconsummated until after the birth of Stephen's child. And if that child was a son, perhaps it might remain so forever.

For some unaccountable reason, the thought depressed her, and for the first time, the full ramifications of the condition she had imposed upon her new husband dawned on her. Had she perhaps been overhasty in denying the earl her bed? she wondered. No, that was quite out of the question. Without his promise to respect her privacy, she would not have married the earl at all, despite his heavy-handed threats, would she? Then how could she justify her resentment of Lord Mansfield's attentions to other women?

These and other awkward questions had risen specterlike in her mind after the initial shock of observing her husband bestow on Lady Huntington that caressing smile she had—obviously quite erroneously—imagined was for her alone. She wished she could confide her misgivings to Sophy, but this was unthinkable without revealing the precise nature of the odd alliance she had contracted with Lord Mansfield. Cassandra shrank from such a step. Lady Hart, however, was not so reticent and made no bones about reviling her brother for subjecting his new bride to the spectacle of him ogling a widow whose reputation was not as spotless as it might be.

"He is an odious cad," Sophy declared sotto voce as the two ladies divested themselves of their warm pelisses and fur bonnets in the hall of her brother's town house. "And so I told him last week when he had the effrontery to present himself in my drawing room."

Cassandra stared at her friend in consternation. "Oh, Sophy, surely you did no such thing," she protested. "How very brave of you, to be sure. But you should not brangle with your brother on my behalf, since I am convinced there was no real impropriety involved. It's just that being a vicar's daughter, I am unfamiliar with the ways of the *ton* and—"

"Nonsense, Cassie," Lady Hart exclaimed as they made their way up the sweeping staircase to the Green Saloon, where Dorset had been instructed to serve their tea. "You are an innocent, of course, I'll not deny that. But when you know my brother as well as I do, you will not hesitate to believe him capable of the grossest improprieties. Why, only six months ago he set up a liaison with that Italian singer we saw at the Opera House last week. Giullietta Rossani I believe she calls herself. She used to be old Lord Westbury's *chère amie* and nearly ruined the poor man with her demands for baubles. She would have done the same to

Simon Weatherby, Ned tells me, had not the earl come into his cousin's ducal title and married the duke's widow last winter."

Cassandra stared at the viscountess in stunned amazement as Dorset threw open the doors of the cozy saloon for them. A most unpleasant sinking feeling began to invade her stomach, and she suddenly found that the tea and cakes she had ordered no longer appealed to her. How much of her sister-in-law's highly indiscreet revelation had the butler heard? she wondered, paling at the thought.

"What nonsense you do talk, Sophy," she murmured disjointedly, coming to a halt just inside the saloon to stare at Sophy in disbelief. "You are quizzing me, I am convinced of it. And it is very unkind of you to come to me with such horrid tales about your brother. I won't believe a word of it," she added stiffly.

"What are these horrid tales you refuse to believe, my dear?" came a drawling voice from behind them.

Both ladies spun around guiltily to discover the Earl of Mansfield lounging unobtrusively before the crackling fire, one elbow poised negligently on the green marble mantelpiece. So unexpected and unusual was his presence at the tea table, that Cassandra could only stare at him in consternation.

And he was certainly worth staring at, a perverse little voice within her pointed out with disarming honesty. After one quick glance at the scowl on his lean face, Cassandra's eyes dropped nervously to his lordship's boots, but found no comfort there. Polished to a miraculously high gleam and crossed casually one over the other, they seemed to her fevered imagination to represent all that was callously autocratic and dangerously masculine about this man who had so suddenly become the focus of her life. How could she doubt—if indeed she ever had—that he would think nothing of trampling her every sensibility into the ground if it suited his purpose? Hadn't he already done so in bullying her into this travesty of a marriage? Of course, his arguments had been sound, and perhaps his intentions toward his brother's betrothed had been honest, but did he realize that, in marrying her, he had forced her to give up everything she held dear? In exchange for what? she wondered, her eyes sliding up his thighs, encased in skin tight breeches that left nothing—absolutely nothing she thought guiltily—of his muscled strength and masculinity to the imagination. Hastily, she lifted her eyes to his face and saw that his scowl had been replaced by a sardonic expression, which suggested that he had read her mind all too clearly.

"Well?" A hint of steel lay beneath the softly spoken word.

With an effort Cassandra pulled herself together, but before she could utter a word, Lady Hart gave a very ill-bred snort and flounced over to the green satin settee beside the fire. "You may as well take yourself off to one of your odious clubs, Mansfield," she remarked coldly. "Cassie and I have no intentions of inviting you to take tea with us."

Cassandra saw a thunderous frown twist her husband's aristocratic features and rushed into the breach. "You cannot mean that, Sophy," she said quickly, seating herself in a green brocade chair and hoping that Dorset would hurry with the tea tray before the earl decided to strangle his sister.

"It matters little whether she does or not, my dear," the earl drawled. "And you have as yet to answer my question, Cassandra."

"Question?" Cassandra repeated mendaciously. "What question do you refer to, my lord?"

She was rewarded with a thin smile from the earl, which came nowhere near his dark eyes, focused on her relentlessly.

"What horrid tales about me has our Sophy regaled you with?" he repeated bluntly.

Cassandra glanced at her friend and was dismayed to see that Lady Hart had gone pale and was nibbling nervously at her lower lip. She presented, Cassandra thought helplessly, the very picture of guilt.

"We were but jesting, my lord," she said calmly, her strength bolstered by her friend's obvious panic. "Sophy was sharing some rather naughty gossip with me, that is all. About Miss Rossani, if you must know," she added with sudden daring and was rewarded by a tightening of the earl's jaw. "Ned and Sophy invited me to hear her sing last week," she continued blandly. "She is truly magnificent. Have you heard her sing, my lord?"

Without any warning, Cassandra had suddenly begun to enjoy herself and returned the earl's rigid stare with studied nonchalance. She was even able to relax her lips into a faint smile as she looked at her lord expectantly. Let him get himself out of this coil if he can, she thought smugly, watching the flicker of annoyance that flashed briefly in the earl's surprised gaze.

"Exactly what naughty gossip did my sister relay to you?" he demanded quietly, ignoring her question completely.

Cassandra shot an amused glance at Sophy, who was staring at her with eyes as big as saucers, her lovely mouth open in dismay.

"Oh, something about the prima donna's insatiable yearning for diamonds, was it not, Sophy?" She cast her husband a mocking glance from under lowered lids. "I'm sure you know the details better than either of us, my lord," she added. "According to the rumors that have reached our ears, Miss Rossani ruined poor Lord Westbury last year with her extravagant demands. The new Duke of Ashford seems to have escaped the same fate by the skin of his teeth they say." The glowering expression on Lord Mansfield's face warned her that she had already passed all bounds of propriety, but Cassandra felt herself in the grip of her rebellious temper and could not stop her unruly tongue.

"One wonders who will be the next dupe to fall into the fair diva's clutches," she added sweetly, conscious of Sophy's startled intake of breath at her temerity in broaching such a forbidden topic. "I daresay it will be public knowledge before long. Don't you think so, my lord?"

There was a moment of charged silence during which Lady Hart appeared to be solely concerned with pleating the folds of her lilac walking gown. Cassandra gazed limpidly into her husband's blazing eyes for what seemed like an eternity.

"You would do well to concern yourself less with gossip," he snapped. "And as for you, Sophy," he added, glaring fiercely at his sister, "*you* would do well to remember that you are a lady, not a kitchen wench. Where did you hear these rumors, may I ask?"

"Oh, Ned told me, of course," Lady Hart replied waspishly. "I understand Simon Weatherby was one of his particular friends before he fell in love with the Duchess of Ashford and reformed his ways. Why? You don't think that I make a habit of listening to gabblemongers, do you?"

"Hart tells you such things?" Lord Mansfield sounded more than a little put out by this revelation. "Well, that's what you get for choosing to wed a rake," he remarked coldly. "Don't say I didn't warn you, Sophy. I shall have to talk to Hart about the impropriety of filling his wife's head with such vulgar gossip."

"You'll do no such thing, Phineas," Sophy exclaimed crossly. "It is no concern of yours what Ned chooses to tell me."

"It damned well is when you contaminate my wife with your lurid stories," the earl fairly shouted, his face dark with fury.

Cassandra let out a gurgle of laughter. "You are being ridiculous again, my lord," she complained when the earl transferred his black gaze to her, eyebrows lowered ominously. "There is nothing lurid about Miss Rossani's amorous exploits—at least not the parts we are privy to. Wouldn't you agree, Sophy? And you may rest assured that your sister has not contaminated me, as you put it." She felt the laughter bubble up inside her again at the very idea. "I had not realized you were quite so stuffy in your notions, my lord," she added. "What is so dreadful about taking an interest in the latest *on-dits*? Or do you suppose that ladies spend all their time discussing new bonnets and the latest fashion plates?"

"This whole conversation is extremely improper," Lord Mansfield snapped. "You will oblige me, Cassandra, by not giving the subject another thought."

"Oh, I can't do that," she replied without thinking. "For one thing, it is highly diverting to speculate on Miss Rossani's next victim. Sophy believes it to be—"

"Cassie!" Lady Hart interjected hastily, rising from the settee and crossing the carpet in a rustle of silk. "I hate to admit it, but Phineas is right, you know. It was indiscreet of me to repeat Ned's confidences. Pray forget everything I said. And now I really must go," she added self-consciously, her lovely face pink with embarrassment. "Do you still plan to attend Lady Bradford's musicale tonight? We shall call for you at nine, my dear," she added, without waiting for a reply. "No, don't trouble yourself," she said as Cassandra rose to her feet. "I shall ask Dorset to have my carriage brought round. Until tonight, Cassie," She bestowed a hasty kiss on her sister-in-law's cheek and fled, leaving an uncomfortable silence in her wake.

"You will stay for tea, my lord?" Cassandra ventured to ask, after the silence had stretched to unbearable lengths.

Lord Mansfield lifted his gaze from the hearth and eyed her coldly. "Yes, " he said shortly. "And you will oblige me by explaining just who my sister believes to be—"

A discreet tap sounded at the door, and Cassandra let out her breath in relief as Dorset entered with the tea tray, which he proceeded to arrange on a low table beside her chair. The respite was short-lived, however, for no sooner, had the door closed behind the butler, than the earl repeated his question.

Cassandra took her time pouring her husband's tea and kept her eyes lowered as she handed him the delicate Wedgwood cup. Her wretched tongue had betrayed her again, she thought wryly. The momentary satisfaction she had derived from baiting his lordship must be paid for in blood. She might have guessed how it would be. Should she lie? she wondered. Or pretend ignorance? Or should she face up to a reality which, in spite of her protests to Lady Hart, she fully believed to be true?

"Well?"

Perhaps it was the sardonic tone of his voice that prompted her. Or was it the urgent need to show this autocratic man she had married that he meant nothing to her? she wondered. Or perhaps she needed, deep down in her heart, to prove to herself that his actions could not hurt her, that what she felt was disgust, not distress. Whatever the reason, she knew before she spoke what her answer would be.

He had not moved back to the hearth, but stood before her, the fragile teacup in his lean fingers. He stared down at her with ironic amusement flickering in the depths of his dark eyes. There was a challenge there, too, she decided, holding his gaze defiantly and allowing a little mocking smile to relax her lips. Did he think to intimidate her with that predatory stance? she mused. Well, it was time he learned that Miss Drayton was made of sterner stuff.

Her smile deepened imperceptibly. "Sophy tells me the diva's latest dupe is you, my lord."

In the silence that followed this calm pronouncement, Cassandra gently raised her cup and took a sip of tea.

"And do you believe her?" came the harsh response.

She shrugged. The earl's gaze was no longer ironic or amused. Cassandra glimpsed speculation there and perhaps a glimmer of surprise.

"Why should I not?" she countered, then added daringly, "unless you can disabuse me, my lord?"

When he made no attempt to do so, Cassandra calmly took another sip of tea, strangely pleased at her own fortitude in the face of this irrefutable evidence that her husband kept a mistress.

"You seem unconcerned," he drawled, moving back to stand before the hearth.

"Should I not be?" she asked coolly.

"You can hardly expect me to live like a monk," he remarked, ignoring her question.

"I cannot recall that our agreement called for any such sacrifice, my lord," she replied and could not resist adding, "I am well aware that you are not Stephen."

The reminder of his brother seemed to anger the earl, for he stiffened perceptibly. "Stephen was perfect, I gather?" he sneered.

"Of course," Cassandra replied with quiet conviction.

"He would never have set up a mistress?"

"No." Cassandra smiled wistfully. "Nor would he have embarrassed me in front of my friends.

"Will you have another cup of tea?" she inquired, quite as if they had been discussing the weather, when the earl did not immediately respond to her veiled reproach. After a moment he placed his empty cup on the mantel and came over to her. Before Cassandra could divine his intent, she found her chin firmly grasped in an iron grip and her face turned up to meet his cynical gaze. He gave a crack of humorless laughter as he raked her face insolently, and his lips curled up at one corner.

"If my brother was as perfect as you make him out to be, Cassandra," he growled from deep in his throat, "why did he succumb to the lures of your delectable person?" He grinned wolfishly at her gasp of dismay. "That sounds more like the kind of thing you might lay at my door, my dear. After all, I make no pretense at being your 'parfit, gentil knyght.'"

Cassandra tried to jerk her head out of his grasp, but he only tightened his hold on her, and a devilish gleam appeared in his eyes. "Do not expect me to dance to your tune, Cassandra. I am not perfect and have no intention of curbing my appetites. Do I make myself clear?"

"I had no such illusions, my lord," she replied frostily. "I realize that such a feat would be quite beyond you." She felt his fingers tighten spasmodically on her chin, and then he laughed.

"You amuse me, my dear." His gaze softened as it dropped to her lips. "But I would advise you not to provoke me, Cassandra. I will not answer for my actions if you do." His gaze met hers briefly before returning to her mouth, and suddenly Cassandra knew he was going to kiss her. Her body steeled itself for this invasion, but her heart fluttered wildly in anticipation, and she made no move to repulse him, as the earl dipped his head slowly and captured her lips.

Cassandra was unprepared for the softness and warmth of her husband's lips. They mesmerized her as they moved slowly, sensuously over her mouth, and she felt herself shudder quite uncontrollably. He increased the pressure, and his other hand came up to cradle her head. Cassandra was torn between a desire to break the spell of the earl's overpowering masculinity and the quite immodest urge to touch his face, his hair, his eyes with her fingertips, which tingled at the very thought. He made no demands on her, and it was all she could do to refrain from opening her mouth to him and inviting further intimacies. She was thankful she had not committed this impropriety, when he suddenly released her and laughed his old sardonic laugh.

"Well, well," he drawled lazily, gazing down at her averted face. "There is more to the vicar's daughter than meets the eye. We will explore that later, my dear. Meanwhile, it is time to dress for dinner. Yes," he added, in answer to her unspoken question. "I will dine at home tonight. You see, I intend to escort you to Lady Bradford's musicale. She is my aunt, you know."

"Yes. Sophy took me to call on her two weeks ago," Cassandra retorted stiffly. "But there is no need to put yourself out on my account, my lord. I am quite content to go with Ned and Sophy."

"I daresay you are, my dear. But it so happens that Lady Bradford is quite my favorite aunt. I would not disappoint her for the world." He laughed softly, as if at a private joke, and before she could think up a rejoinder, he was gone, the door of the Green Saloon closing gently behind him.

CHAPTER NINE

The Retreat

As far as Lord Mansfield was concerned, the musical evening at Lady Bradford's was a disaster. He had expected no less than the chilly reserve his wife maintained throughout dinner, but the frosty reception he received from Lady Hart when she discovered that he proposed to attach himself to her party seemed to him excessive. Even Lord Hart appeared ill at ease with his old friend as the two couples drove in relative silence to the Bradfords' town house on Clarges Street. When Cassandra pointedly ignored his assistance in descending from the carriage, Phineas began to lose his temper.

"What the deuce is the matter with everyone?" he muttered testily to his friend and erstwhile fellow rake as the gentlemen followed the ladies up the shallow steps and into Lady Bradford's spacious hall.

Lord Hart glanced at him apologetically as he allowed a footman to remove his topcoat. "The general opinion seems to be that you are a bit of a cad, old man," he remarked with less than his natural lightheartedness. "Sophy has taken it into her head that you are not the best of husbands to poor little Cassandra. Rather taken with your wife, is Sophy. Won't stand for your mistreating her."

"Poor little Cassandra, indeed!" Lord Mansfield growled. "What fustian nonsense will that sister of mine think up next? You don't actually believe such a Banbury tale, do you, Ned?" He glanced over at his wife—quietly elegant in plum-colored satin—who had removed her velvet cloak and was now ascending the stairs with Sophy toward the large saloon on the first floor where Lady Bradford held her frequent musical gatherings.

"Do you?" he repeated, suddenly conscious that Lord Hart had offered no response to his query and seemed to be studiously avoiding his friend's eyes as they followed the ladies up the staircase.

"Dash it all, Raven," Lord Hart muttered, fiddling nervously with his impeccable cravat. "Can't blame us for wondering what kind of rig you're running, old man, now can you? One minute you're in high gig over stepping into Weatherby's shoes with the diva when he gets himself shackled to his duchess. The next thing we know, you're rushing off to Kent on heaven knows what wild-goose chase, and then you appear in London with a wife. Good Lord, man! Even Sophy had no notion of what was in the wind. No wonder your friends don't know what to make of it."

"My marriage is none of their concern," Lord Mansfield said shortly.

Hart gave him a pitying look. "You're daft if you believe that, my lad," he remarked. "These are your friends you're talking about, Raven. The Seven Corinthians, remember? Of course, our numbers are dwindling under the encroachment of respectability. Chris Morville is rusticating in Dorset ever since he married that chit from Paris, and Simon Weatherby seems to be firmly fixed in Kent with his new duchess. And I no longer count myself one of the rakes since I married Sophy. Stands to reason that we would wonder about you, don't you see."

"No, I don't see," Lord Mansfield replied coolly. "What is there to wonder about?"

Lord Hart gave him another puzzled glance. "You ain't trying to bamboozle us into thinking yours is a love-match, are you, Raven? That won't fadge, believe me. For one thing, she ain't your style at all. Too good for you by half, if you want to know the truth, m'lad."

"I appreciate your overwhelming candor, Ned," Phineas said dryly. "But I fail to see what business it is of yours—or anyone else's for that matter—whom I marry and for what reasons."

"Wrong again, Raven," Lord Hart shot back. "We'd like to know why you broke the pact?"

"What pact?" Phineas replied automatically. But he realized exactly what his friend meant. Faced with the unexpected duty of providing a father for his brother's unborn child, he just hadn't considered it at all. It had simply not occurred to him to see a connection between that romantic pact made by a group of hotheaded young rakes fresh on the Town and the marriage of convenience he had entered into with Miss Drayton over a month ago.

"Don't play the innocent with me, Raven. After all, it was *your* father who gave us the idea. Wildest rake in all England saved by love. Or have you forgotten?"

"Leave my father out of this," Lord Mansfield said tersely.

"But we swore to live up to his Ideal Rake, remember? If you ask my father, of course he'll say we didn't come close to the notorious Earl of Mansfield. They were at Oxford together, you know. Only my father chose to retire to his estates rather than follow the example of your wild parent."

"I said, leave my father out of it." Phineas's voice had carried to the ladies, for Sophy turned and glared at him.

"What are you saying about Papa, Ned?"

Lord Hart winked at her. "I was merely reminding your brother that the late earl gave up his rakish ways when he fell in love with your mother, dearest. Just like us. Here, pet," he continued, offering his arm. "Allow me." He tucked Sophy's hand under his arm and patted it affectionately as the couple made their way to the top of the stair where Lady Bradford was waiting to greet them.

This desertion left Phineas little choice but to offer his arm to his wife, who placed her fingertips on his sleeve with such obvious reluctance that he grinned wryly. The sight of his little sister clinging so affectionately—some would call it snuggling, he mused—to her doting husband's arm gave Phineas pause. In the shock of Stephen's sudden death, he had forgotten all else except his dying brother's last plea to protect his beloved Miss Drayton's reputation. He saw once again Stephen's eyes, filled with pain and love and the growing awareness of death. Was it any wonder that Phineas had forgotten that youthful pact, made so many years ago by a group of young rabble rousers whose main ambition in life was to emulate the exploits of the most notorious rake of them all, his own father? He had been the most dedicated of all the Corinthians, their leader in fact, honor-bound by some code he had only half-consciously formulated to outdo his sire's reputation. His had been the most reckless, scandalous wagers, and any who so much as flinched at undertaking them was instantly cast out of their company until only the hardiest, most devil-may-care had remained. Seven of them. And Phineas grimaced at the memory of the more reprehensible of the acts they had committed in the name of sport and brotherhood.

He glanced down at the woman beside him, her profile calm and strangely remote. His wife, he thought, and felt a grimace twist his lips. Yes, he had broken the pact, all right. He had not married for love and reformed his ways as had Morville and Weatherby and Ned Greenley. He had not followed in his father's footsteps and taken a wife to his heart and pronounced the world well lost for love. No, indeed, he thought, suddenly uncomfortable with the feather-light weight of Cassandra's fingers on his arm. Ned had every right to throw his behavior in his face. And Phineas was wrong. Ned and the other Corinthians were his closest friends; more than that, they were his brothers, bound to him by the pact they had sworn to and tested in the fires of true friendship.

Impulsively, Lord Mansfield took his wife's gloved hand and slipped it into the crook of his arm, holding her hand firmly pressed against his side. She looked at him in surprise, her hazel eyes wide and questioning. But she made no move to pull away, for which Phineas was thankful. The Harts had moved forward into the Music Saloon, and the earl found himself being regarded none too cordially by his favorite aunt.

"My dear Cassandra," Lady Bradford said, enfolding Lady Mansfield in an affectionate embrace. "I am so happy to see you again, my dear. This ramshackle husband of yours has finally done his duty, I see. And you may well frown, Phineas," she continued, piercing her recalcitrant nephew with an accusing blue stare. "I never thought to see such scrambling manners in a Ravenville. Your father must be turning in his grave at the very notion of his son and heir behaving so shabbily. How long is it now since you arrived in Town, boy? Over a month, if I'm not mistaken. And only now do you deign to pay your old aunt a visit."

"Not quite a month, Aunt Agatha, but—" Phineas started to say.

"Not quite a month, he says. Can you believe it, my dear? What is the world coming to, I wonder, if a nephew cannot find a moment between his visits to Jackson's Saloon and White's to pay his respects to his mother's sister? Now if it had been Stephen, God rest his soul, the poor lamb," Lady Bradford continued, serenely oblivious of the effect of her words on the earl and his lady, "he would have been knocking on my door—" She stopped abruptly, her face showing alarming signs of crumpling into grief. "Oh, forgive me, Phineas. I had promised myself not to mention Stephen tonight, but I cannot bring myself to accept that he is gone from us . . . "

Lord Mansfield instinctively grasped his aunt's plump hand in his. "I know," he said gruffly. "Neither can I. But this is not the place, and besides, my brother would not want you to distress yourself, Aunt. He wouldn't wish to see his favorite aunt making a spectacle of herself in public." This last was said in a bracing tone touched with a trace of amusement, which seemed to restore Lady Bradford's equanimity.

"Go on with you," she responded sharply. "I am in danger of no such thing, Phineas." She waved them on and turned to welcome another group of guests.

Lord Mansfield glanced at his wife's pale face as he escorted her into the saloon. What could he say, he asked himself grimly, to alleviate some of the desolation she must be feeling at his aunt's unexpected mention of Stephen? He had felt her flinch and grasp his arm at Lady Bradford's words, but she had given no other indication of distress, other than the sudden paling of her cheeks. But Phineas knew that her heart must be aching. Although he had to admit that—thank goodness—he knew nothing of the pains of love himself, his heart ached, too, for his lost brother. So he could understand some of Cassandra's misery and was unexpectedly struck with a desire to alleviate it.

He covered her hand with his and gently loosened the rigid fingers from their grip on his arm. "You will ruin my coat, love," he said gently and was startled at the contempt in the gaze she turned upon him.

"That is all you care about, isn't it?" she hissed under her breath. "Fine clothes, fast horses, good wine." They had come to a halt just inside the door, and Phineas was all too conscious of the curious glances of his aunt's guests.

"Let us not brangle now, my dear," he said quietly. "I was merely teasing, anyway."

"And beautiful women, of course," his wife continued as though he had not spoken. "Let's not forget the beautiful women." Lady Mansfield smiled, but he could detect no warmth in her eyes, which glittered dangerously close to tears. "You care naught for anybody but yourself, do you, my lord?" she inquired almost dispassionately. "I regret the day I ever set eyes on you."

Phineas went cold at the suppressed fury and helplessness in her words.

Lady Hart beckoned to them, breaking up their private tableau of grief and anger. His wife pulled away from him, and he let her o, following her straight back with his eyes as the countess joined Lady Hart. It was only when Phineas noticed that his sister's group included the Marquess of Gresham and Mr. Hampton, both of whom greeted his wife with noticeable warmth, that Lord Mansfield made his way across the room to join them.

He would take her to Mansfield Grange he decided quite suddenly, as the musicians started to tune their instruments. And leave her there while he pursued his pleasure in London. The idea appealed to him. In one fell swoop he could put his wife out of the range of his ubiquitous cousin and free himself of the unreasonable feelings of guilt that had beset him lately.

Pleased with a decision that promised to dispose of an unwanted wife in an unexceptional fashion, Lord Mansfield settled himself to enjoy the concert.

Two days later, the Earl of Mansfield had put his plan into action much to the surprise of his wife and friends. Nothing that Sophy or her husband could say, however, made the least dent in Lord Mansfield's decision to depart London immediately for Nottingham. Cassandra refused to join her voice to her sister-in-law's loud protests against the earl's high-handed and—as Lady Hart perceived it—insensitive decision to separate his wife from her London friends and deprive her of the pleasures of the Little Season. She found herself almost glad to be quitting her husband's grand town house, where she had lived, for all intents and purposes, alone for over a month since her hasty marriage to the earl. Had it not been for her regret at leaving Sophy, Cassandra would have welcomed her return to the country, although she was under no illusion that Mansfield Grange would be anything like her father's small vicarage in Kent.

Since the Grange was situated over one hundred miles from London, Cassandra had expected to spend three nights on the road before they could reasonably expect to reach the village of Denton, the seat of the earls of Mansfield, four miles south of the more populous town of Grantham. But she had not counted on the luxury of having one's own horses stabled along the route north, and it was therefore late on the second day that the Mansfield traveling chaise swept through the ancient stone gates of the estate and came to a steaming halt before the impressive front doors.

Cassandra had not seen her husband since they stopped briefly for refreshments at the Green Man Inn in Stamford. He had cho sen to ride rather than to travel with her and her abigail in the ca riage, a decision she attributed more to his desire to avoid he than to any thoughtfulness on his part. She was stiff and tire from sitting for so many hours in the swaying carriage, wel sprung and luxurious though it undoubtedly was. Her head ache too, and she was naturally nervous about her first encounter wi the Dowager Countess of Mansfield, whose place at the Gran she would be expected to take. The thought depressed her. Sh had no right to such a position, she told herself honestly. Tru she was married to the earl, but their marriage was a farcic arrangement to which she ought never to have agreed. Would th dowager countess guess how matters stood between her eldest so and his new wife? she wondered. And if she did . . . But Cassan dra refused to tease her tired brain with useless speculations. Sh would have to wait and see.

"You will like Mama excessively," Sophy had confided to he when the two friends had said their teary farewells in Londo "She is the best of mothers and never nags and finds fault wit one as some mothers do."

"You are her only daughter, Sophy," Cassandra had remarke "No wonder she can find no fault with you."

"She is also my friend and supported me in my marriage Ned, even though he had such a terrible reputation as a rake. A most as bad as Phineas's it was, to tell the truth. But Mam merely smiled and talked Phineas into giving his approval, too."

"Your brother opposed the match?" Cassandra was surprised hear that Lord Mansfield possessed this streak of prudishness his character.

"Oh, yes!" Sophy laughed. "He refused—most adamantly, might add—Ned's first offer for me. He knew too many disrep utable details about my poor darling's career as a member of th Seven Corinthians, I suppose."

"The Seven Corinthians?"

"Yes. Hasn't Phineas told you about them?" It was Sophy turn to be surprised. "How like him to keep bits of himself secre like that. He has always done so, you know. Most provoking him."

"Perhaps he doesn't want me to know about his private af fairs," Cassandra suggested cautiously.

"Don't be a goose, Cassie. You are his wife now. And beside

why wouldn't he want you to know about the Corinthians? It's not such a grand secret anyway, if you want my frank opinion. Just a private club or some such—seven daredevils who met at Oxford and swore to become the greatest rakes in England. Of course, they never did achieve this disreputable goal, but they are still trying, as far as I know. Although there are only three left actually. No," she corrected herself quickly. "Only two, now that Phineas is married. Mama is delighted that he has finally reformed, Cassie, and is bound to welcome you with open arms."

"So your brother is no longer a rake?" Cassandra had inquired, a skeptical glint in her hazel eyes. "That is hard for me to believe, Sophy."

Lady Hart had looked at her friend askance, but any comment she might have made was interrupted by her brother, who appeared in the doorway demanding to know if his wife was ready to leave.

Cassandra wished that she had the courage to ask Lord Mansfield about this select group of gentlemen to which he belonged, but was glad when the opportunity did not present itself. No doubt he would resent her interest in his affairs anyway, she thought. Sophy's suggestion that her brother had reformed in any way was clearly ridiculous. And if the earl's mother labored under the same delusion, she was in for a nasty surprise if she ever discovered the real circumstances of her son's marriage to Miss Cassandra Drayton.

So it was with mixed emotions that Cassandra stretched her stiff limbs and prepared to descend from the carriage with the help of the footman. When the door was flung open, however, it was her husband who stood there, one gloved hand outstretched and a frown of impatience on his taciturn countenance. His many-capped greatcoat was misted with rain, which had started falling as they drove through Denton. His tall beaver was still on his head, and its brim shaded his eyes so that she could not tell what he was thinking.

"Welcome to Mansfield Grange, my lady," he said rather formally as she descended amongst the bustle of footmen unloading the chaise. "This is Burton," he added, acknowledging a stately, gray-haired butler who bowed and repeated his master's welcome.

"Her ladyship is awaiting you in the drawing room, milady," the butler added.

This proved to be not exactly true, Cassandra found when she entered the great hall, where two fires burned on either side of a wide staircase of Carrara marble leading to the upper stories. The Dowager Countess of Mansfield was waiting for them in the front hall and wasted no time in rushing forward to embrace her new daughter warmly.

"My dear Cassandra," she exclaimed, her face lit with a truly beautiful smile. "I can't tell you how happy I am to see you. And if I know anything about the way my son travels, you must be bone weary and starving to death, my dear. And as for you, Phineas," she added, moving into the open arms the earl held out to her and submitting to a bear hug, "you and I must have a serious talk about the impropriety of excluding your mother from your wedding plans, you thoughtless boy. Didn't it occur to you that I might have wished to be consulted on the matter?"

"Nonsense, Mother," Lord Mansfield replied carelessly. "Cassandra did suggest something of that nature, but you would only have made a huge fuss over everything, and you know how I hate that kind of affair. Much better the way we did it. Cassandra's father did the honors without any fuss at all. Then we stopped for a few days in London to refurbish her wardrobe—"

"Are you saying that you allowed the poor girl no time to prepare her trousseau?"

"Well, actually, yes," the earl confessed, slanting a rather wicked glance at his wife.

"Yes, *indeed!*" exclaimed Cassandra. "The villain forced me to say my marriage vows in a rag of a dress that was over five years old. I daresay I shall never recover from the embarrassment of it."

"And don't forget that abomination of a hat you wore on our wedding trip, my love," the earl said in a caressing voice quite unlike his usual bluntness.

"The one you ordered consigned to the rag-bag, my lord?" she responded with an archness edged with sarcasm.

The dowager gazed from one of her visitors to the other during this strangely antagonistic exchange, her lovely face showing a mixture of emotions.

"Have we missed dinner?" the earl asked abruptly. "I'm positively famished. We decided not to stop to eat on the road."

Cassandra met the dowager's bemused gaze and smiled.

"I presume his lordship means that *he* decided not to stop for dinner on the road. Am I not correct, my dear?"

With a sigh of relief Cassandra relaxed. The dowager was much friendlier than the new countess had any right to expect, given the circumstances of her precipitous addition to the family. And luckily, Lady Sybilla Mansfield also had a sense of humor. "I see that you are accustomed to your son's autocratic ways, your ladyship," Cassandra replied with a laugh. "And you are quite correct, of course. After a brief stop at Stamford, we barely paused to change horses." She cast a quelling glance at her husband who had listened to this exchange with an enigmatic expression in his gray eyes.

"Then you must come upstairs at once and rest before dinner, my child," the dowager said briskly, and Cassandra found herself whisked up the marble stairs to a suite of rooms whose splendor left her momentarily bereft of speech.

"Oh!" she exclaimed at last. "What a beautiful room, my lady. It reminds me of my childhood fantasies of fairyland." And indeed it was, she thought, advancing across a deeply piled carpet of woodland green, bedecked with a seemingly random assortment of meadow flowers in muted yellows, blues, and rose. She had the sudden urge to tear off her boots and stockings and run across it barefoot, as she used to run over the meadows near the vicarage at Walmer. All that seemed so long ago, although it was barely a few weeks in her past. Cassandra felt a pang of nostalgia for the land of her childhood, for the happy days before she had come to her present pass, before she had been forced into a farcical marriage, before her dreams of love had been ruthlessly trampled by a man who considered her an obstacle to his pleasure.

Cassandra felt tears sting her eyes. Now she *was* being missish, she told herself crossly. This would never do. Resolutely, she examined the rest of the furnishings, the delicate satinwood sofa before the crackling fire, the inlaid tables with slender bowed legs, the elegant gatelegged escritoire and matching chair, the deep armchair beside the hearth, invitingly upholstered in pale green leather and full of gay yellow velvet cushions. And finally the bed. Cassandra shivered. This was the bed in which generations of countesses of Mansfield had awaited the visits of their lords with varying degrees of dread, resignation, or even happy impatience, she thought. The bed in which those same countesses had given birth to innumerable little Mansfields over the centuries. Where Phineas himself had undoubtedly been born thirty-odd years ago. Stephen too, of course.

And now it was her turn to sleep in the countess's bed. It seemed to Cassandra almost sacrilegious that—under the normal course of events—her husband would have come to her in his mother's bed, the same bed in which he had been conceived and born. But hers was in no way the normal course of events, she reminded herself sadly. The present earl would not come to her in this bed. He would, in truth, not come to her at all. She would sleep here alone for the rest of her days. She found the prospect unexpectedly daunting.

But in spite of her lord's absence, this bed would soon see the birth of another Mansfield, she thought. A glow of warmth flooded through her at the notion that Stephen's child would be born within the circle of his own family—in his proper place and surrounded with love and caring. This was the reason she had accepted the inevitable, allowed herself to be bullied into a marriage of convenience with the earl. She must keep this fact firmly in mind if she were to find any sort of contentment in her position here at Mansfield Grange. After all, what did she care if her husband kept a mistress in London? He might keep two or three for all it mattered to her. She would dedicate her life to Stephen's son and find happiness in being a mother, not a wife.

If indeed her child was a son, a perverse voice within her murmured. A frisson of apprehension passed through her. The alternative wouldn't bear thinking of. Or would it?

Cassandra's gaze was drawn irresistibly back to the bed. It was covered with a warm eiderdown in the same shade as the carpet, but the scattered "flowers" had been sewn on in multihued drifts, their satin petals creating the illusion of a brightly colored wave, soft to the touch. Rich green velvet curtains hung around it, suspended from the quilted canopy and tied to the bedposts with gilded cords. How cozy it must be on a winter's night, she thought, curled up in the center of such a bed, protected from chill drafts by the closed curtains, cuddled in the arms of a loving husband.

Except, of course, she didn't have a loving husband, Cassandra reminded herself ruefully. Even in the event—which heaven forbid—that she gave birth to a baby daughter, Lord Mansfield would not be magically transformed into a loving husband. He would come to her then, she thought, a flutter of fear making her heart jump. Hadn't she agreed to that condition? But she would still be the wife he hadn't wanted, the unprepossessing female he had been obliged to wed for his brother's sake.

But at least this bed would be put to its proper use, that little voice murmured again. And she would not be quite so alone. Or would she? Quite suddenly, Cassandra was not as convinced as she had been that she wanted Stephen's child to be a girl.

CHAPTER TEN

Greeks Bearing Gifts

That first week at Mansfield Grange was the happiest Cassandra had yet experienced since leaving her beloved family in Kent. Her husband's family residence was everything she had ever dreamed a home should be. Stately and elegantly furnished it undoubtedly was, yet the new countess quickly discovered the comfort and warmth behind the imposing façade. The sense of friendliness and well-being that pervaded the house emanated, Cassandra realized after her first day in residence, from the dowager countess. Far from the stiff-rumped matron Cassandra had visualized, jealous of her son and resentful of his abrupt marriage to a penniless female far beneath his station, Lady Sybilla Mansfield soon showed herself to be as close to a fairy godmother as any new bride could wish.

Cassandra could not believe her good luck. Before the week was out, her initial apprehension had given way to admiration, and she felt as though she had known her mother-in-law for years instead of days. Such was the charm and genuine graciousness of the Dowager Countess of Mansfield, that Cassandra found herself wishing that she could open her heart to this woman about her real relationship with the earl. But that could never be, she told herself reluctantly. The dowager fairly doted on her sons and was still in deep mourning for Stephen, whom she invariably referred to as her baby. How could Cassandra tell this grieving mother what had actually transpired between her younger son and Miss Drayton before she became the wife of his elder brother?

The notion was clearly impossible. Cassandra could only hope that the charade of married bliss Lord Mansfield insisted on putting on for her ladyship's benefit appeared natural enough to allay any suspicions the dowager might have. It cut up Cassandra's peace of mind, however, but when she approached the earl on the matter, he only laughed at her, his lip curled in cynical amusement.

"There is no reason for alarm, my dear," he pointed out when she broached the topic on the second afternoon after their arrival. "I shall play my part to perfection, I can assure you."

"I hate the pretense of it all," she had replied, her voice betraying her agitation. "Are we to spend our whole lives deceiving your mother into believing that this is a real marriage?"

"Legally, it *is* a real marriage," he answered shortly.

She had colored up at the implications of his words. "You know that is not what I meant, my lord," she said stiffly.

Lord Mansfield gazed at her thoughtfully for several moments. Then his cynical smile appeared once more. "Are you suggesting that we not continue this pretense anymore, Cassandra?" His eyes slid over her caressingly, as if stripping her down to her shift, she thought, feeling a wave of heat wash over her. "That would be easy enough to do, my dear," he drawled. "And intensely pleasurable, I might add."

He took a step toward her. Cassandra shrank back, fascinated in spite of herself by the unmistakable message in his eyes. Part of her clamored to lose herself in their sensuous gray-green depths and forget that she had been brought up a lady. Ladies certainly did not feel the erotic yearnings that threatened to overwhelm her as she stared helplessly into her husband's eyes.

He took another step, and Cassandra realized that if she did not do something quickly, the earl would assume she was inviting him to ravish her. She raised a hand in protest. "You are being absurd, my lord," she said breathlessly. He caught her hand and raised it to his lips, pressing a kiss on each finger in succession. The warmth of his lips made her tremble in delight until it occurred to her that in all likelihood the earl was playing off his rakish tricks on her again. Undoubtedly this was all a game to him, an amusing make-believe of love. She forced herself to dredge up the picture of the amorous smile she had seen him bestow upon the Marchioness of Huntington in Hyde Park not many days ago. The unpleasant vision cooled her blood like magic, so that when her husband raised his amused gaze to her face, Cassandra was able to respond with a nonchalance she was far from feeling.

"I fear I am not so easily taken in by these gallant airs and graces as your numerous flirts, my lord," she remarked, one eyebrow raised derisively. "Your forget that I know you are not the reformed rake your mother believes you to be. Let us not deceive ourselves, my lord. 'Twould be foolish indeed to imagine that things are as they ought to be between us, wouldn't you agree?"

He had released her hand during this speech, and his eyes had lost their amused glitter. "And just how ought things to be between us, my lady wife?" His voice was harsh and his eyes shuttered, lips curled into a grimace that Cassandra had come to know only too well. He was clearly angry. Fleetingly, Cassandra wished that she had not provoked him.

"We do not share the marriage bed, that's true enough," he continued with a hint of sarcasm. "My mother will never know that from my lips, I can assure you, Cassandra." He laughed without humor. "And what is wrong with a little make-believe if it will save my mother any unnecessary unhappiness? She had such high hopes for me. Misplaced, of course, but I cannot change that now." He paused, and Cassandra saw that his gaze, though fixed on her, seemed not to see her at all. "I don't pretend to be like my father, and I cannot be Stephen," he continued abruptly. "Either for her or for you, Cassandra. And the sooner you realize that fact, the better it will be for all of us."

There was an intensity, a repressed anguish, in his voice that Cassandra had never heard in it before. For the first time she realized that the awkward relationship they shared was as unwanted and unrewarding for the earl as it was for her. It was pure selfishness to imagine that she had been the only victim in the arrangement. The thought was sobering.

He turned and strode to the door. Then he paused, hand on the knob as he looked back at her. "Tomorrow I will be gone." He smiled grimly. "That should make you happy, Cassandra."

And with that she would have to be content, she thought, listening to his footsteps growing fainter in the hall.

As if to fill the void the earl had left behind him, the very next morning after her husband's departure, Cassandra awoke with a headache and a queasy stomach, which she attributed to nerves over her quarrel with Lord Mansfield. She was later disabused when she suddenly lost her breakfast, her body racked by shudders and her face clammy. Bridget, her abigail, who had been in the process of selecting a morning gown for her mistress, rushed to her aid and gently wiped her face with a cloth dampened with lavender water.

"I must have eaten something that disagreed with me," Cassandra muttered, refusing her maid's insistence that she return to bed. "Those pickled oysters perhaps. Or the curried haddock . . . "

"If you'll forgive me the impertinence, my lady, I reckon it be more than oysters that have brought on this upset."

Cassandra glanced at her in surprise, but when she caught the knowing expression the abigail was doing her best to suppress, she blushed and climbed back into bed without further protest. "Perhaps I do need a little more sleep," she murmured.

"Shall I tell her ladyship, my lady?" Bridget wanted to know, and Cassandra could think of no acceptable reason for keeping the evidence of her condition from the child's grandmother.

As a result, the dowager countess came bursting into Cassandra's bedchamber less than five minutes later, her beautiful face ablaze with delight and her gray eyes glowing.

"My dearest Cassandra!" she exclaimed, sitting impulsively on the bed and clasping her daughter-in-law's hand in hers. "What splendid news this is. You have no idea how happy you have made me, child. A grandmother at last!" She paused and regarded Cassandra with a tiny frown. "You are quite sure, then, are you not? You *are* increasing?"

"Yes, I truly believe so, my lady." Cassandra smiled softly at the dowager's enthusiasm. "I had fancied over a week ago that something of that nature was occurring, but now I am sure of it."

"We must have Dr. Crenshaw in to take a look at you, my dear. Bridget, tell Burton I wish to see him right away." She pressed Cassandra's hand tenderly. "And of course we must send word to Phineas. Unless you have told him already. Have you dear?"

Cassandra shook her head. "No, I wanted to be sure before saying anything," she replied, conscious of the rush of color that invaded her cheeks. "And there is no need to disturb him in London, ma'am. We can tell him later."

Lady Mansfield regarded her curiously. "Phineas is not in London, dear. He is in Melton Mowbray at Lord Gresham's hunting lodge, less than fifteen miles away. Phineas and his friends spend much of their time there during the season. Didn't he tell you? What a careless nodcock he is, to be sure. I shall send for him right away."

"I am sure there is not need for that—"

"Nonsense, child," the dowager interrupted. "If he is anything like his father, he will want to know right away that his heir is on the way."

Cassandra recalled uneasily Lord Mansfield's words of the day before. He was not like his father, he had said. Would his pretense of being a loving husband draw him away from his friends and his hunting pleasure? For the first time Cassandra wished that her husband might share her own joy at the prospect of having Stephen's child. But with sudden insight she understood that Lord Mansfield—for all his good intentions toward his dead brother—might well find it difficult, perhaps even painful to pretend to be a substitute father. At least she was the child's real mother, she thought. But might not the specter of Stephen prevent her husband from relishing his role as father? She had sudden misgivings about the whole charade they had embarked upon and resolved to do everything in her power—however odious the earl might be upon occasion—to play her part with grace and tolerance.

Without quite knowing why she did so, Cassandra willed her husband to come home. Every stir in the front hall caused her heart to leap, and she began to wonder at her own foolishness.

When the days went by and he did not appear, however, she ceased to repine over his absence and poured her energies into pacifying the dowager, who did not let a single day go by without chastising her eldest son for his negligence and insensitivity. Cassandra put her own disappointment—which was sharper than she would have imagined a month ago—aside and concentrated on learning the running of a household as large and complex as Mansfield Grange and in helping the dowager with her preparations for the approaching Christmas season.

A brief note from his lordship—addressed to his mother, not his wife—arrived a week later with the curt message that they should not expect him at the Grange before mid-December, when he would be arriving with a party of friends.

When December the fifteenth came and went without a sign of Lord Mansfield or his guests, Cassandra could only believe that he was putting off the evil hour of acknowledging a situation he must find unpalatable, to say the least. The arrival of Lord and Lady Hart a week before Christmas went a long way toward lifting her spirits. She was particularly glad to renew her friendship with Lady Hart, who, upon discovering Cassandra's interesting condition, joined her mother in condemning Lord Mansfield's absence from his wife's side on such a happy occasion.

"It was ever so with Raven," she confided to Cassandra as the two ladies ascended to Lady Hart's rooms to change her traveling dress. "He can be the sweetest and most generous of brothers, but if he is in one of his moods, he becomes a veritable ogre of selfishness. Ned says that poor Raven is still feeling Papa's death. It's as though he no longer has a standard against which to measure his outrageous behavior. I find it difficult to believe that anyone would actually take pride in giving rise to the most scandalous *on dits,* but Ned tells me that it is indeed so. Raven always did want to outdo Papa's reputation, you know."

"Your papa was a notorious rake, I take it? Although from what your mama has told me, he was a wonderful husband, too. She appears to be convinced that rakes make excellent husbands."

Lady Hart giggled, and Cassandra was glad to see that, for all her Town bronze and sophistication, Sophy could still behave like the nineteen-year-old she was. "And I can vouch for that, Cassie," she confided. "My darling Ned was one of them before he married me, you know. And you wouldn't believe the things he does when he gets amorous." She stopped abruptly and blushed as the indiscretion of this remark struck her. She glanced self-consciously at her friend. "But then, of course, you do, don't you? I expect you already know all about *that* from Raven," she added ingenuously. "I never imagined that marriage could be so much fun!" She giggled again.

Cassandra had to turn away to hide her embarrassment and consternation. How could she admit that she knew nothing of the joys of connubial bliss? Her brief experience with Stephen had happened so unexpectedly and was over so quickly that she retained only a blurred impression of what had actually transpired. Her principal memory was one of shocked disbelief that they had been guilty of such a monstrous indiscretion. And there had been that brief moment of pain amid the awkward fumblings of Stephen's eager hands, the unpleasant sensation of intrusion, and the aftermath of guilt and apologies. She realized with sudden shock that she had deliberately repressed the memory of Stephen's inexperienced lovemaking, preferring to remember only the sweet plethora of kisses and promises of a life spent together in unending happiness. How naive she had been, she thought. And how disloyal she felt now at the unexpected surge of longing that swept over her to experience the intimacies of marriage that Sophy obviously enjoyed with Lord Hart.

But to her horror, instead of the blond countenance of her beloved Stephen, a dark, saturnine face thrust itself into her consciousness. Cassandra shivered. The thought of having to endure marital intimacies with such a man as Raven had appalled her, but now, quite unexpectedly, she found herself remembering Lord Mansfield's softer moments, his caressing smile, the amusing glint in his eyes, the warmth of his hands on her waist. Try as she might, Cassandra could not conjure up his more sinister qualities, which seemed to have faded behind a mist of romantical fantasies. She shivered again at her own foolishness.

"Have I said something to offend you, Cassie?" Lady Hart inquired anxiously. "You look so pale. Are you all right?"

Cassandra pulled herself together with an effort, pushing these new and disturbing feelings about her husband firmly into a dark corner of her mind. "Of course I am, Sophy." She laughed. "I just hope you and Lady Mansfield are right about reforming rakes."

Lady Hart looked a little uncomfortable at this. "I don't doubt for a minute that Raven is truly reformed," she said defensively. "Why, only last week I ran into him coming out of Duval & Carrier's on Piccadilly. He would not admit it, but I can guess he was selecting your Christmas present, Cassie."

Cassandra failed to register the second part of this astonishing announcement. "Lord Mansfield is in London?" she asked sharply, as the ladies descended to the drawing room for tea.

"Why, yes, my dear. At least he was last week." Lady Hart seemed entirely unaware of the agitation her announcement had caused in her hostess. "I imagine he must be on his way up here by now. Gresham and Sweet Willy have promised to spend at least a month with us. They often do during the Christmas season, you know. Since neither gentleman is hanging out for a wife, they can come here to the Grange and be comfortable."

Cassandra hardly heard her. The news that her husband had left Melton Mowbray for London could only mean that he wished to visit his precious opera singer. She refused to believe that there was an innocent explanation to his removal to the Metropolis. How could there be? A present for her, indeed! More than likely the rogue was laying out his blunt on his latest bit of muslin. Though why such a conclusion should discompose her, she could not fathom. He was not worth it, she told herself resolutely, motioning to Burton to place the tea tray on the low inlaid table before her chair. Of that she was certain. All her recent tenderer feelings toward her roving husband had been grossly misplaced, she decided. She would have to avoid such foolish fantasies in the future.

As a result of these and other even less charitable resolutions concerning her wayward husband, Cassandra was able to display a cool demeanor toward the earl when he arrived the following afternoon, accompanied by Lord Gresham and Mr. Hampton. After greeting his mother warmly, Lord Mansfield approached his wife with a decided challenge in his eyes.

"I hear you are to be congratulated, my love," he remarked in an offhand manner, which immediately set Cassandra's back up. Under the watchful eye of the dowager, she could do no less than raise her face for his welcoming kiss, but while she fixed a fatuous smile on her lips, she refused to let him off scot-free.

"I knew you would be overjoyed at the news, my lord," she murmured archly while his broad shoulders hid her from the rest of the company. "I trust you enjoyed your stay in London."

As soon as this unwise remark had left her lips, she wished she could recall it, for the earl's rather grim expression relaxed into a smirk. She was saved from further exchange with him, however, when the dowager sent the gentlemen upstairs to get rid of their dirt before joining the ladies for tea in the drawing room.

The few remaining days before Christmas passed uneventfully for Lord Mansfield. He had felt both an unexpected sense of relief and a strange stab of resentment when his mother's urgent message concerning his wife's condition had reached him at the Marquess of Gresham's hunting lodge in Melton Mowbray. On the one hand, the news that Cassandra had not duped him into marriage on false pretenses set his mind at rest concerning her honesty. Not that he had actually suspected her of resorting to this feminine deception, he had told himself more than once. But the lingering possibility that he might have misread her character disturbed him. At least that doubt could be laid to rest. On the other hand, the certainty that his wife was indeed carrying his brother's child put him into such a black mood that his friends made no protest when he announced out of the blue one morning that he had urgent business in London.

This strange moodiness had persisted during the solitary ride down to the Metropolis, and for some reason thoughts of the visit he planned to pay to the delectable Giullietta failed to dispel the

blue-deviled cloud from his mind. Even when he deliberately
dwelt on the many erotic pleasures he expected to receive from
his latest ladybird, somehow the anticipation of these amorous ex-
ercises failed to arouse him as they normally would.

As a result of these uncharacteristic preoccupations, the
evening Raven spent at Curzon Street had not been an unqualified
success. To begin with, the diva had obviously not expected him,
and the uncharitable thought crossed the earl's mind that perhaps
his *amourette* had had other plans for the evening. Then Giullietta
had been less than overwhelmed by the Christmas gift he had
brought her. Rubies, she had pointed out rather petulantly, were
not her favorite stones, as he must have known.

And the wench had been right, he thought moodily as he accepted the delicate Wedgwood cup from his wife, who still refused to meet his eyes. He had certainly known of Giullietta's
predilection for diamonds. However, he had unaccountably become distracted upon entering Duval & Carrier's on Piccadilly to
purchase just such a diamond bauble by Monsieur Duval's assumption that the earl had come expressly to select a Christmas
gift for Lady Mansfield. With typical Gallic charm, the rotund
jeweler had reminded Lord Mansfield of his countess's fascination for pearls, and he had become absorbed for rather more than
half an hour making a careful selection of a pearl and diamond set
for Cassandra to add to the fur cloak he had already planned to
give her. He had also chosen an emerald brooch for his mother
and a similar one in sapphires for Sophy. It was only after Monsieur Duval, bowing politely, had handed him the neatly packaged
items that the earl had remembered Giullietta.

He glanced again at Cassandra, who was engaged in an animated argument with Willy Hampton about the advantages of
country living over the rigors of Town life, and wondered what
his wife would say if she knew that she had quite banished
thoughts of illicit dalliance from her lord's head. He smiled rather
grimly at the thought. No wonder he had randomly selected rubies
for Giullietta, adding the rather gaudy bracelet to his other purchases almost as an afterthought. An oversight for which he had
paid dearly later that evening, of course, he remembered wryly.
The sultry Giullietta had become almost comical in her childish
insistence that nothing but diamonds would do for the greatest of
all Italian divas.

Quite irrationally, Lord Mansfield wished he might share with his wife the humor of this encounter. He smiled at the absurdity of the notion.

Cassandra had resolutely put from her mind any thought of her husband's illicit activities in London during his recent absence. What concern was it of hers, after all? she thought. She had been unreasonable to expect him to be overjoyed at the prospect of acknowledging another man's child, even if that man was his own much loved brother. And yet she *had* expected something of the sort, hadn't she? How foolish of her! She should have realized that he could not and would not be another Stephen to her. He had told her so. And it was true that she had—more than once—compared Phineas unfavorably to his younger brother. More often than not she had done it in self-defense, using Stephen at first as a weapon against Lord Mansfield's autocratic and overbearing manner, and later as a shield against the insidious attraction he was beginning to exert on her confused emotions.

When he had finally arrived back at the Grange, he had been accompanied by the Marquess of Gresham and Mr. Hampton, for whose presence Cassandra was intensely grateful, for they diverted the earl's attention from her. Their presence had not prevented him from taking up once more the role of doting husband, however, although she did not think for a moment that either of these two seasoned gentlemen believed the charade for one minute. His manner had been nonchalant, but there had been a subtle challenge in the way he had slid an arm around her waist and kissed her on the lips in front of the roomful of people.

Cassandra had been rather pleased at her own calm response. She had received his kiss, warm and surprisingly tender, with the cool composure befitting a lady. In fact, she might have brushed through the encounter without a blush had not the errant thought flashed through her mind that it might be pleasant indeed to press herself against the lean length of him and surrender herself up to something more exciting than the chaste touching of lips witnessed by all those present, including the butler. But that was not meant to be, she had told herself sternly, moving deliberately away from him into the drawing room to order the tea.

In the days that followed, however, she had to repeat this reminder several times, particularly when his lordship drew her more blatantly into the charade they were playing for the benefit of the dowager. It seemed to amuse him to match some of Lord

Hart's besotted behavior with Sophy. He would encircle her waist with his arm, sit beside her and hold her hand, touch her hair in passing, and generally act the loving husband to her cool indifference. But his eyes never held that loving gleam that Lord Hart's always did when his gaze lingered on Sophy. The earl's were always full of cynical amusement, and Cassandra knew in her heart that he was baiting her, taunting her, tempting her to forget propriety and give herself up to the flirtation—and who knew what other delights—he was offering.

The more outrageous his assault, the firmer Cassandra became in her resolve to resist the lure of a meaningless flirtation. So when he came quite unexpectedly into her bedchamber on Christmas Eve, scratching at the connecting door while she was dressing for dinner, she steeled herself to be coolly unresponsive.

The earl was in an unusually mellow mood as he entered the room, followed by his valet carrying a large, obviously heavy white box.

"Put it down on the bed, Turner," he said, motioning toward the center of the room. "Thank you," he added, as the valet gently laid his burden on the green counterpane. "That will be all for now."

Cassandra dismissed her abigail with a nod and moved over to the bed, flustered in spite of herself at the unusual presence of her husband in her boudoir.

"What is this, my lord?" she asked apprehensively.

"Why don't you open it and see, my dear?" He leaned negligently against a bedpost and crossed his arms, a decidedly satanic grin on his face.

"Is it for m-me?" Cassandra murmured, suddenly shy at finding herself alone in this particular room with her husband. This was the first time he had set foot in her bedchamber since their arrival, and his presence aroused a confusing melange of emotions she had no time to disentangle.

"Of course it's for you, you silly widgeon. Who else would it be for? I don't see anyone else here, do you? It appears that we are quite alone for a change, my love." He laughed, and Cassandra noticed that his eyes had turned a dark gray flecked with green and were observing her as she imagined a fox might observe a plump pigeon.

She moved to untie the satin riband, but her fingers were inexplicably cold as they fumbled at the knot. Hoping he would not realize just how much his presence flustered her, she made a gargantuan effort to bring her riotous emotions back under control. Her excitement mounted as the riband fell away, and she swept the lid off, lifting several layers of tissue paper out of the box before its contents was revealed to her astonished gaze.

"O-oh!" she exclaimed, her breath escaping in a soft sigh of pure pleasure. "Oh, how utterly lovely, my lord. How did you know I have always wanted one of these?"

"I have some modest experience in these matters, my love," he replied with a salacious grin, which Cassandra chose to ignore.

Almost reverently, she reached out to run her fingers over the glossy sable. Emboldened, she picked up the outrageously beautiful cloak to find that it was lined with lush green velvet, evidently designed to be reversed at will. It was accompanied by a detachable hood and generous muff of the same fur. Cassandra shuddered at the thought of what it must have cost. Then she brushed the notion aside and gave herself up to the utter delight of possessing such an extravagantly gorgeous garment. Impulsively, she crushed it to her breast and buried her face in the warm fur before raising her eyes to the earl, knowing that the truth in her heart was revealed there.

He held her gaze steadily for several moments before his mouth curled lazily up at one corner and a gleam of amusement—quite unlike his usual cynical glitter—warmed the gray depths of his eyes with an emotion Cassandra had never seen in them before. She trembled to think what her own unguarded gaze might be revealing to this man who could shake her to the very depths of her soul with a mere flirtatious glance. For that's all it was, surely? He must be toying with her again, she thought, only much more dangerously this time, since she had, quite inexplicably, developed a vulnerability to his blandishments.

Suddenly self-conscious about this frightening admission, she dropped her eyes to the sensuous garment clutched to her breast. The fur was already taking on some of the heat from her body; she could feel the warmth of it radiating through her fingers and against her cheek. Without warning, she was overcome with the quite wanton desire to wrap herself in this glorious mantle of fur that so intimately connected her to her husband. Her body cried out for the warmth of its caress; she longed to feel it against her bare skin, against her breasts, her thighs . . .

Cassandra jerked her thoughts away from the dizzying sensuality that threatened to engulf her. What was she thinking of? she wondered, awed and frightened at the intensity of her own unbridled desires. Her life at the vicarage in Kent had ill prepared her to understand the avalanche of sensations, which suddenly threatened to sweep her into a spiral of sinful yearnings she knew not for what. She had never thought of herself as a passionate creature; indeed, she had never given the notion of passion much thought at all. Her experience with Stephen had been gentle and calm, filled with sweetness, not sensuality. And now . . .

Guiltily, she ventured another glance at the earl. He had not moved so much as a muscle. Only his eyes had changed. They had darkened perceptibly, taking on the color of wet slate on a stormy, moonless night. She was reminded forcibly of her first impression of him standing impatiently in the vicarage parlor that morning—was it only three months ago? She had seen him then—in all his insolence and devil-may-care arrogance—as the Fallen Angel himself come into her life to destroy her peace of mind, to bring about her downfall, the destruction of all she held dear. And he had done so, too, she realized with sudden insight, her gaze imprisoned against her will in the depths of his dark stare. With a sickening sense of impending doom, Cassandra saw a sudden glitter of triumph flash in the nebulous gray depths, like the flicker of lightning in a storm-laden night sky.

With every ounce of resolve she had left, Cassandra dragged her gaze away and nervously shook out the magnificent garment that had triggered the sensuous yearnings in her traitorous heart. Before she could throw it around her shoulders, she felt his warm fingers close over hers.

"Yes," he murmured softly, close to her ear. "Try it on, my love. Let me help you." He twitched the cloak from her nerveless fingers and wrapped it around her shoulders, turning her to face the cheval mirror as he did so. "There now, love. What do you think?"

What did she think, indeed? Cassandra hardly knew how she could think at all with her husband standing so close behind her, his hands still resting lightly on her shoulders. She gazed at their reflection in the mirror. Her head barely touched his chin, and she could distinctly see his breath moving tendrils of her hair. Determinedly she pulled her gaze back to her own fur-clad figure.

"It is truly magnificent, my lord," she whispered, overcome by much more than the beauty of his gift. "I don't know what to say, except thank you. Thank you very much, indeed."

He did not remove his hands, and Cassandra wondered how she could escape unobtrusively. She saw him smile crookedly.

"I see you are not entirely pleased, my dear. I am sorry."

Cassandra's reaction was impulsive and instantaneous. "Oh, but I am!" she exclaimed, turning to face him. "Truly I am," she repeated and then, distressed at the skepticism she saw in his eyes, she reached up and kissed him lightly on the cheek. "There!" She smiled coaxingly up at him. "Now you must believe me, sir. I am absolutely delighted with it. Nothing could have pleased me better."

She saw an arrested look flit across his face before he masked it with an amused laugh. "Then I must certainly believe you," he remarked easily. "But tell me, Cassandra. Is there something the matter with my lips?"

Again Cassandra reacted without thought. She focused her gaze on his mouth, and a frown creased her forehead. If she were honest, she thought, she would have to say that there was absolutely nothing the matter with her husband's lips. They were firm and slightly full, the bottom lip jutting aggressively and hinting at a restrained sensuality that provoked an unexpected sensation of heaviness in her stomach. Furthermore, they were blessed with a shape that a Greek sculptor might have found worthy of young Paris himself. Cassandra put her head to one side, trying to appear unaffected by her prolonged scrutiny of that most intriguing part of her husband's anatomy.

"N-no," she ventured at last, determined to respond intelligently to his odd question and pretend that it was an entirely normal occurrence to examine a gentleman's mouth so intently. "I don't see anything wrong with them, my lord. Why do you ask?"

She could have bitten her tongue as soon as the words were uttered, for Lord Mansfield's mouth widened into a diabolical grin. "I was merely wondering why you chose not to kiss them, my love," he said softly. "As a wife would if her husband's gift really pleased her."

The earl's words hung in the air between them like an accusation. Cassandra glanced nervously around for a way out of this unexpected dilemma. "You are roasting me, sir," she murmured, cursing herself for failing to recognize the trap he had set for her.

"Not at all." He shrugged his broad shoulders dismissively. "I suppose that is my answer, then? You are not quite as delighted as you would have me believe." His voice was full of cynical amusement again.

"That is simply not true, my lord," Cassandra protested, anger at this unexpected perversity overcoming her reticence.

"Prove it, then," he drawled, then added under his breath, "if you dare, my lady."

This was all it took to overrule any inhibition Cassandra might have felt had she stopped to consider the enormity of her actions. Quite simply, she lost her temper. Angrily, she took a step forward and pressed herself against him. She had to stand on tiptoe, for he made no move to touch her. Cassandra found she had to place one hand on his shoulder to steady herself, and stretch her neck to bring her face up to his level. Once there, she glared challengingly into his amused eyes as if daring her old nemesis, the Fallen Angel, to call Miss Drayton a coward.

The she placed her lips firmly, even defiantly, against his, as her dark lashes fluttered and closed under the strange intensity of his stare.

CHAPTER ELEVEN

The Sleigh Ride

"You see, Cassie, I *was* right after all."

Lady Hart cast her sister-in-law a roguish smile over her shoulder as she stood before the tall cheval mirror, the sable cloak draped over her slim figure. "I daresay this must have cost a king's ransom, my dear. Just the sort of Christmas gift a reformed rake would lavish on the female who has made him change his ways."

Cassandra looked skeptically at the fur-clad vision preening before her glass. "I am not at all convinced that your brother has changed his ways, Sophy," she replied repressively, the memory of Lord Mansfield's outrageous behavior during their recent encounter all too fresh in her mind. And what rankled most, of course, was her own foolish role in the highly improper incident. She really should not have lost her temper, she chided herself for perhaps the tenth time since her lord's unheralded invasion of her bedchamber before dinner that evening. If she had only behaved with ladylike decorum, there would have been no excuse for the earl to kiss her. Or at least not in that utterly shocking and licentious manner. A frisson of pure frustration shook her as she recalled the ungentlemanly way he had abused her moment of vulnerability. That diabolical glitter in his eyes as she had pressed her lips chastely to his unresisting mouth should have warned her, but she had been deceived by his immobility, his initial lack of response to her kiss.

Lady Hart laughed her tinkling laugh again, turning this way and that to inspect the elegant folds of the cloak as it fell almost to the floor. "You are funny, Cassie. But I will not be taken in by these missish airs, my dear. Raven must be totally besotted with you to have given you sable, of all things. And such a perfect color, too. These are only the very choicest pelts, you must know.

I declare, my old astrakhan seems a veritable rag in comparison."
She pouted prettily at her reflection in the glass.

It was Cassandra's turn to be amused. How little her friend
knew about his lordship's perversity, she thought wryly. If the
earl was besotted, it was definitely not with love for a plain
vicar's daughter from Kent. He was driven by an unruly desire to
possess her, body and soul, like the devil he was. What gentleman—a true gentleman that is—would kiss the woman he loved
with the savagery—there was no other word for it, she decided—
as Lord Mansfield had kissed her only hours ago? He had managed to turn her own kiss, one she had intended as a friendly
gesture of gratitude, into a quite shocking, erotic, and definitely
sinful experience for this plain vicar's daughter. Cassandra shuddered involuntarily at the memory of that shattering moment
when she had first glimpsed what it might mean to be the object
of her husband's animal passion. She drew a deep breath and
forced herself to listen to Lady Hart's chatter.

"It is too bad of Raven not to let me know he meant to be so
extravagant," Sophy complained petulantly. "I would have demanded that Ned do the same for me."

"But didn't you tell me that you have asked Lord Hart for a
ruby necklace, Sophy? Surely that is proof enough of his regard
for you?"

"Oh, yes, I know it is, Cassie. It's just that there are so many
beautiful things I would like to have. And of course, I know that
Ned would do anything for me. But it's just that I would be so
thrilled if he had given me something like this"—she caressed the
sable folds covetously with her fingertips—"as a total surprise,
the way Raven did for you. Weren't you devastated with the pleasure of it all? Confess that you were, Cassie."

"Why, yes," Cassandra replied hesitantly. "I would say that de-
scribes my feelings exactly." And just how true that was, dear
Sophy would never know, she thought. Devastation was mild
compared to what she had felt when that unprincipled beast had
slipped an arm round her waist under the cloak and drawn her
roughly against him. Tonight's embrace had been nothing like the
warm, tender kiss he had given her in London the evening of
Lady Bradford's musicale. Oh, good gracious no, she thought,
wondering if she would ever be free of the hot imprint of his
mouth on her face, her cheeks, her poor innocent lips. She had felt
positively devoured! If this was what physical passion between a

man and a woman was all about, she wanted none of it. She did not want her nerves to be set jangling and her peace of mind to shatter like glass. *Or did she?* a little voice whispered quite rebelliously from the depths of her consciousness. Cassandra thrust this preposterous notion aside and picked up her warm gloves from the dresser.

"Come on, Sophy. We must not keep your mother and the gentlemen waiting."

Reluctantly, Lady Hart relinquished the fur garment to Bridget, who wrapped it snugly around her mistress's shoulders. "You were so quiet at dinner, Cassie, I wondered if Raven had been badgering you again. But now I see that you were merely daydreaming about the dash you intend to cut at the Christmas service tonight. Shame on you for not letting me into your secret, my dear."

Cassandra regarded her friend silently as Lady Hart allowed Bridget to wrap her warmly into her curly black astrakhan mantle and fit the matching shako onto her blond head. "You are making a great to-do about nothing, Sophy, and that's a fact," she responded rather tartly. If truth be told, she had been petrified at the thought of having to face Lord Mansfield at the dinner table after the intimacies to which he had subjected her. She could hardly have felt more embarrassment and chagrin if he had laid her down on the imposing four-poster and ravished her, she thought. Indeed, she wondered if it had been the dinner gong alone that had saved her from that ignominious fate or whether his lordship had come to his senses in the nick of time to prevent that irrevocable breach of the promise he had made her back at the vicarage in Kent.

That day of her precipitous marriage to Lord Mansfield, a wedding fatally marred by the shock and pain of Stephen's death, seemed to belong to another lifetime, Cassandra mused as she accompanied Lady Hart downstairs where Burton was assisting the Marquess of Gresham into his greatcoat. The earl, already swathed in his outdoor clothes and with his curly brimmed beaver already perched on his dark head, stood facing the stairs. Cassandra resisted the temptation to cast him a withering glance. She had endured his amused gaze all through dinner and parried his after-dinner attempts to draw her into conversation with blunt, monosyllabic rejoinders. As soon as she could, she had escaped upstairs with Sophy to fetch their wraps for the projected sleigh ride into the village for the Christmas Eve service at the local church.

The cross-country sleigh ride had been a tradition in the Ravenville household for many generations, the dowager informed Cassandra over dinner that evening. "Except for that one year when the snow came too late to allow the sleighs to cross the fields safely," she added. "Phineas was ten at the time, I believe, and Sophy a mere toddler."

"Oh, I remember that clearly, Mama," Lady Hart remarked. "We had to take the carriages instead. I declare it was the greatest disappointment to me. But after yesterday's storm the snow is at its best for sleigh riding. You will enjoy it, Cassie. It is so romantic." She had exchanged a frankly amorous glance with Lord Hart at this point, and Cassandra experienced a sharp stab of envy, which she quickly suppressed. She deliberately avoided her husband's eyes, but could well imagine the cynical grin his young sister's remark had elicited.

Cassandra squared her shoulders as she descended the last few steps into the Hall. The fur mantle felt warm and heavy on her shoulders, but she had been apprehensive about wearing it. The mere feel of it against her skin brought other, more riotous memories flooding into her mind, which she knew would be hard if not impossible to forget. But she would have to forget them, wouldn't she? How else was she to continue this charade of being a happy new bride and expectant mother if she allowed her heart to become entangled with a rakehell who was only amusing himself at her expense?

Her resolution to remain aloof from Lord Mansfield was put to the test sooner than Cassandra anticipated. As the Grange party milled out of the warm Hall into the frosty evening, Cassandra kept up a vivacious conversation with the marquess, hoping that she would not have to ride with her husband. This strategy was doomed to failure as soon as the group clustered round the two brightly painted sleighs, each drawn by a four-horse team decked with ribands and bells.

"You'll drive one, won't you, Robert?" Lord Mansfield inquired, suddenly appearing at his wife's side and slipping a hand beneath her elbow. "I'll drive the other. You will come with me, Cassandra. And I will entrust my mother to you, Cousin, if you will be so kind." Before she could protest this high-handed disposition of her person, Cassandra found herself standing beside the first sleigh, her husband's arm firmly around her waist. To her dismay, she saw that Lord Hart was already occupying the back-seat, his irrepressible Sophy snuggled beside him. They appeared to have eyes for none but themselves.

"As Sophy said, my dear, there's something romantic about a sleigh ride," the earl murmured in her ear. "You look enchanting, Cassandra," he added laconically. "There is something about sable I find irresistible."

Thankful that the dim light hid her blushes at this unmistakable reference to her indiscretion, Cassandra struggled to free herself. "You are insupportable," she hissed between gritted teeth. His only response was a crack of laughter as he tossed her up onto the seat beside the driver.

Except for an occasional murmur from the couple in the back, the drive to the village was accomplished in silence. Cassandra pulled the hood of her cloak closely about her face against the chilly air and tried to focus on the beauty of the night around her. Instead of taking the driveway, the earl guided his team across the Park and through the Home Wood. Cassandra was surprised at the eerie mystery of the snow-laden boughs and the sparkle of the moonlight on the icicles, which resembled nothing so much as fairy-tale decorations of nature. By the time they reached the small sixteenth-century church in Denton, the fascination of the night had worked its magic on her spirit and she felt strangely comforted.

Inevitably, at the sight of the village church, Cassandra's thoughts flew to her family in Kent. Everything about the scene reminded her of her former home in Walmer. She knew that, even as her husband swung her down from the sleigh, her father would be donning his gown in the tiny vestry, preparatory to commencing the service he always delivered on Christmas Eve. Old Mr. Donovan, the sexton, would be in the middle of his customary diatribe about his errant sons, who rarely came home to spend the holidays with their parents. Mrs. Mason, if she was not laid up with her rheumatism, would be helping Drusilla light the candles on the altar. The seasonal smells of holly and spruce, with which the church had been decorated for as long as Cassandra could remember, enveloped her as though she were there instead of far away in Nottingham, on the arm of a man she hardly knew.

Nostalgia for the safety and warmth of that life she had left behind forever washed over her so strongly that she felt the tears start in her eyes. Withdrawing a hand from her muff, she brushed them away before her distress was noticed.

"Are you all right, Cassandra?" The earl's voice was unnaturally soft and low.

She nodded, unwilling to trust the steadiness of her voice.

"That's a whisker if ever I heard one," he shot back. "What are you thinking about, love? You are blue-deviled about something—besides me, of course, so don't pretend otherwise."

She wished he would not use that casual endearment, which he could not possibly mean. It only emphasized the falseness of their marriage. Resolutely, she pulled herself together. "I was thinking about Christmases at home in Kent," she murmured. "And I miss my family."

After a slight pause, he remarked, "I trust you will say no such thing to my mother, Cassandra. She would be most distressed to learn that you do not consider the Grange your home. *We* are your family now, you must know."

"Her ladyship has been most kind," Cassandra replied colorlessly.

He laughed. "And I have not? Is that what you are implying, you ungrateful wench?"

That was precisely what she had meant, but she did not dare say so. At that moment Lady Mansfield descended from the second sleigh and called to Cassandra. "Sit next to me, my dear. I want everyone to see the beautiful daughter-in-law my feckless son has finally brought home to me." She linked her arm companionably through Cassandra's and drew her into the church. This genuine kindness on the dowager's part caused a lump to form in Cassandra's throat. But it embarrassed her, too, and she was careful not to meet the earl's eyes.

Cassandra remembered little of that Christmas service, distraught as she was with memories of her dear papa and Drusilla, and plagued by the palpable presence of the Earl of Mansfield—her husband, she kept reminding herself—by her side in the Ravenville pew. Behind her she heard the Marquess of Gresham's strong baritone competing with Lord Mansfield's and Mr. Hampton's in the well-loved Christmas hymns. The dowager sang in a clear contralto, which contrasted pleasingly with Sophy's fresh soprano. Mrs. Henshaw—a distant cousin of the dowager's who had spent her holidays at the Grange since becoming a widow, and accompanied her hostess to the service—sang in a trembling, slightly off-key voice, which was—perhaps fortuitously, Cassandra thought, drowned out by the enthusiastic voices of the congregation.

Cassandra herself could not sing at all. Her pent-up emotions threatened to overcome her when the organist struck the opening chords of "Oh, Come, All Ye Faithful," her father's favorite hymn. By the time the last note echoed throughout the crowded church, tears were running unchecked down her cheeks. She could not be sure whether she cried for her lost love, Stephen, or for her absent family, or for herself. Her tears might equally well have been for the gentle dowager who had taken Cassandra so unreservedly to her bosom.

It was only later that Cassandra admitted to herself that she may have shed her tears for the Earl of Mansfield, that cynical autocratic, unattainable man to whom she was perilously close to losing her heart.

Phineas found the ride home infinitely more enjoyable than the drive to the village church. It was also infinitely more disturbing. As their party left the church, Ned had good-naturedly agreed to drive the sleigh home. Mansfield told himself that he merely wished to set his wife's back up by forcing her to endure his company in the cozy backseat of the sleigh. It was not until he had settled his reluctant wife into the sleigh and climbed in beside her that he admitted to himself that he found the close proximity of her fur-clad figure strangely enticing.

"Still angry with me, Cassandra?" he inquired playfully, as Ned tooled the restive team out of the churchyard.

When his countess pretended not to hear him, Raven grinned wolfishly into the starlit night. So the chit was still smarting from the thorough kissing she had received at his hands earlier that evening, was she? Well, he would never confess it to her, of course, but he had not been entirely unaffected himself. What had started out as a lighthearted game on his part—to steal a kiss she had obviously been unwilling to give—had suddenly turned into a dangerously arousing embrace. Raven grimaced to himself at the memory of his wife's startled expression when he had pulled her against him and taken possession of her mouth in ways she had obviously not expected. Nor even dreamed of, he suspected.

A rueful smile relaxed his lips. The wench had been a total innocent, after all, he remembered. She had not known how to react to his passionate assault, nor had she known how to reject him or signal her disapproval of his advances. His wife had not even seemed aware of the seductive way her body had melted against his. If he had not known otherwise, he might have taken her lack of resistance for compliance. As it was, her unexpected acquiescence had incensed him and driven him to explore her with his mouth and hands in ways he had never intended. One did not, after all, treat one's wife as if she were one's fancy piece, a voice of reason had murmured from somewhere in the recesses of his mind. But the lure of her soft curves and unexpected meekness had clouded his brain and had very nearly caused him to lose his head completely. Had it not been for the dinner bell, which finally penetrated his overwrought senses, he might have disgraced himself in her eyes forever.

He looked down at the object of his aborted desire and shuddered at the thought of what might have happened had he followed his inclinations and taken his wife to bed. Meekness? he thought wryly, conscious of the stubborn set of the countess's small chin. How could he have imagined for a moment that this little spitfire had been meek? It was not meekness that had robbed his wife of her resistance, but innocence and inexperience in the ways of men. And shock. He had seen that all too plainly in her eyes the instant he had released her. She was clearly unaccustomed to such intimacies, and he had frightened her thoroughly.

Not for the first time, Phineas wondered how the devil his brother had managed to get a child on this woman without waking her up to the realities of male desire. She must think him a veritable savage, he thought with sudden misgivings. Perhaps if he kissed her again in a more civilized manner, he might redeem himself. He glanced at her pale face in the light of the sleigh lanterns and wondered at his own lack of address. When was the last time the notorious Raven had been so insecure, so unsure of his ability to please a woman? The notion that an insignificant vicar's daughter, with little or no beauty to boast of and a terrible temper to boot, could cause the much sought after Earl of Mansfield a moment's uneasiness seemed too ridiculous to take seriously.

Yet it was true, Phineas thought wryly. Here he was alone with the lady in the coziest of circumstances, with the star-studded night sky and snow-decked trees as romantic backdrop, and he could not make up his mind whether to kiss her or not. Obviously drastic measures were called for.

The earl placed his arm over his countess's shoulders and drew her against him.

He had half hoped that Cassandra would snuggle up to him as Sophy was unabashedly doing with Lord Hart in the driver's seat of the sleigh, but he might have known that she was not to be so easily placated. The rigidity of her small figure aroused his cynical amusement.

"Ah!" he sighed into her ear. "I have offended the sensibilities of the vicar's daughter, have I, my love? Why don't you just ring a peal over my head and get it over with, Cassandra? It will seem deucedly odd if you ignore me when you see the surprise I have in store for you, my dear."

"I have had quite enough of your surprises for one evening, thank you very much, my lord," came the arctic reply.

Phineas laughed. "I daresay you will change your mind when you see it," he remarked, content that he had provoked a response, however astringent, from the prickly Miss Drayton. And if he knew anything about women, he thought, as the sleigh drew up before the brightly lit Grange, his countess would become considerably mellowed toward him before the evening was out.

A tempting late supper had been laid out in the Great Hall of the Grange, which seemed very warm and snug to Cassandra after the drive in the open sleigh. She had managed to avoid further contact with the earl by stepping down from the sleigh as soon as it came to a standstill and moving to join the dowager and Mrs. Henshaw as the party entered the front hall. Behind her she could hear the voices of the men raised in jovial exchange with Sophy, who was regaling Willy Hampton on the advantages of the married life.

"The leg-shackled state is all very well for some, my dear Sophy," Hampton remarked laughingly as the footmen bustled about removing greatcoats and cloaks and taking charge of hats and gloves. "And I don't deny for a moment that old Ned here has found himself a rare treasure. But Robert and I have yet to be tempted to take that momentous step. Wouldn't you say so, Robert?"

"We can't all be such lucky dogs as Ned and Raven," the marquess remarked with his rich laugh. "And who will uphold the glorious reputation of the Corinthians if we all succumb to the blandishments of the ladies? There's only you and I left, Willy, m'lad. Now that old Raven has thrown in the towel." He met Cassandra's sharp glance with a bland smile.

By this time the group had reached the Great Hall, which had been thrown open for the occasion, and the dowager and Mrs. Henshaw ensconced themselves before one of the blazing fires that burned at each end of the cavernous room. Anxious to change the subject, Cassandra turned to the dowager with a smile.

"I believe we can be very satisfied with our decorations, my lady," she remarked, glancing around at the branches of spruce, sprays of holly, and mistletoe the dowager had ordered brought in and the clusters of potted palms provided by the estate greenhouses.

"Ah! But there is not nearly enough mistletoe, Cassandra," remarked Mr. Hampton, his merry countenance wreathed in smiles.

"You make the selfsame observation every year, Willy," the dowager chided him. "And yet it seems to me that you always manage to catch more than your fair share of unwary ladies."

"It must be all those years of practice, Mama," Sophy volunteered. "I was one of those poor unwary ladies, you see." She turned to Cassandra with a teasing smile. "Sweet Willy gave me my first kiss when I was sixteen in this very room. It was delightful," she added, blushing prettily.

"Thank you, my dear. I shall endeavor to do so again as soon as the opportunity arises," Willy said gallantly, raising Sophy's small hand and saluting it reverently.

"You are a shameless hussy, Sophy," Lord Hart said with mock severity. "And Hampton, I'll thank you to unhand my wife. If I catch you kissing her, I'll draw your cork for you," he added belligerently.

Hampton laughed good-naturedly. "Then we must make sure you don't catch us, old man." He winked playfully at Sophy. "And what about Robert?" he demanded. "Are you planning to draw his cork too, Ned? Now, that I would like to see. After all, he has kissed Sophy under the mistletoe every year just as I have. And so did you, m'lad, if memory serves me."

"Sophy is married now," Lord Hart said rather defiantly.

"What a dog in the manger you've turned out to be, Ned," the marquess drawled. "Who'd have thought that Ned Greenley would cavil at a few chaste Christmas kisses? You disappoint me, old boy. Truly you do." He turned away to accept a glass of champagne from Burton's tray.

"Chaste, indeed!" Lord Hart snorted.

"I think it is too bad of you to condemn us married ladies to such unnecessary privation, Ned," the dowager put in gently. "I am sure Phineas would not do anything so absolutely Gothic, and he is even more recently wed than you and Sophy."

Sophy giggled delightedly at her mother's unexpected support, but Cassandra felt her cheeks grow warm. All this talk of kissing was making her nervous. She glanced at the earl and found him observing her with a curious smile.

"What makes you think I will be any the less possessive than Ned, Mama?" he inquired pleasantly.

"You are both being odiously antiquated," Sophy burst out impatiently. "Anyone would think that Cassie and I do not know how to behave with proper decorum. What do you take us for, Raven? A couple of—"

"Sophy!" the dowager interrupted mildly. "Watch what you say, dearest."

"Yes," Lord Mansfield drawled, motioning a footman to bring forward a large silver tray laden with gaily wrapped parcels. "Let's not forget that we have a vicar's daughter in our midst now. We must try to live up to her expectations, not sink ourselves beneath reproach." He selected a gift from the tray and carried it over to his mother. "Mama, it's time to open the gifts." He bent to kiss the dowager's upturned face and stood by her side as she untied the elegant ribands.

No sooner had the dowager expressed her pleasure over the delicate emerald brooch, than Lord Mansfield approached his wife with another parcel, which from its shape could only be a jeweler's box. Cassandra looked up at him in amazement.

"B-but you have already given me my gift, my lord," she stammered, meeting his eyes that were full of cynical amusement again.

"Yes, and very delighted I was with your reception of it, Cassandra," he murmured. "Dare I hope that this one will reap a similar reward, my love?"

Cassandra felt her face flame, and her fingers trembled as she took the neatly wrapped parcel. Dimly, she heard a happy shriek from Sophy as she opened her own gifts, and the murmuring of the dowager and Mrs. Henshaw as they compared their various treasures. Then she was gazing down in astonishment at the pair of exquisitely crafted pearl and diamond earbobs that lay nestled in the black velvet case. They were a perfect match for the pearl ring Lord Mansfield had given her on that sunny afternoon in London a month ago when she had imagined—for a short and heady hour or two—that she might find happiness in her marriage after all.

She raised her gaze and saw that the earl was regarding her quizzically, all trace of cynicism gone from eyes that were dark as pewter. Tentatively, she smiled. "Thank you, my lord," she said quietly.

"The name is Phineas, Cassandra."

"Thank you, Phineas," she repeated, savoring the sound of his name on her tongue. "They are truly beautiful. But there was no need—"

"Nonsense, my dear," interrupted the dowager. "Never let gentlemen know that we love them with or without expensive gifts, Cassandra. They might just believe us, and then where would we be?"

This sally was greeted with much amusement by the gentlemen in question, and both younger ladies were immediately called upon to confirm or deny the dowager's advice.

"I have to agree with you, Mama," Sophy said with an arch look at her husband. "Although I do love to receive gifts, as Ned well knows."

"I'll wager he does, my girl," her brother said dampeningly. "But what about you, Cassandra? Do you agree with my mother that a woman's love is not dependent on the quantity of baubles she receives?"

Cassandra felt all eyes upon her in the silence that followed the earl's question. She smiled slightly at the frivolity of the notion that love could be bought with trinkets, no matter how expensive. She had loved Stephen with all her heart, hadn't she? And he had never had the funds to afford the kind of gifts Lord Mansfield had given her. No, she mused, love did not look for anything in exchange. Except to be loved in return, of course.

"Yes, indeed I do," she said finally. "If we are speaking of true love, of course. A love that must be kept alive with baubles and trinkets is not worth having, I should say." Then, fearing she had sounded too much like the vicar's daughter her husband had accused her of being, she added with a touch of humor, "Of course, a gentleman who arrives bearing unexpected gifts must always be sure of a welcome."

"I second that," the marquess interjected, his deep baritone laced with amusement. "And just to make sure of my welcome, my lady, I beg you will accept this little token of my esteem." He placed another slim box in Cassandra's hands, which she opened with no little apprehension.

Cassandra stared at the delicate gold chain that lay coiled around a lustrous teardrop pearl pendant of quite indecent size and perfection. She could do nothing but gape for several seconds, her breath suspended with the rush of mixed emotions that assailed her. Before she could recover from her astonishment and pleasure, Mr. Hampton deposited another small box in her hands, which revealed an exquisite pearl and diamond bracelet.

"Another mere bagatelle, my dear lady," he said dismissively. "But one which conveys—as no doubt Gresham's also does—our heartfelt admiration for one who has achieved the near impossible." He twinkled down at her with such friendliness in his blue eyes that Cassandra felt her apprehension evaporate. It was replaced by a warm rush of pleasure at the kindness these strangers had showered upon her. Three months ago she had known only Sophy and then only as a childhood friend. These gentlemen, including her husband—for she could not count that first frightening encounter with the Fallen Angel—had been complete strangers to her. And now, for the first time since her hasty marriage, Cassandra suddenly felt that she had a place within this family circle. She felt the warmth of their regard envelop her; she felt herself a part of the holiday festivities, sharing the joy of giving and receiving gifts. They actually liked her, she realized, marveling at the revelation. Except for Lord Mansfield, of course.

Involuntarily her eyes flew to him, and her heart sank. There was nothing there but cool derision, she thought, and a glitter of something very like anger, which he repressed even as she stared at him.

"I am speechless with delight, as you see, gentlemen," she managed to say finally, her voice husky with emotion. "Thank you both very much. I am happy to know that I have such good friends."

"Aren't you going to tell us what the impossible is that Cassie has achieved, Willy?" Sophy interrupted suddenly, and Cassandra felt her fingers tremble as she fumbled with the catch on the pearl bracelet. She had a very good suspicion what impossible feat Hampton had had in mind, and she wished that, for once, Sophy had controlled her insatiable curiosity.

Hampton laughed good-naturedly. "You are a pea-goose, Sophy, and no mistake. Our Cassandra has managed to get the most notable of the Corinthians to come up to scratch, my dear. No small achievement when you consider the avalanche of eligible hopefuls who have been thrown at his head over the past ten years. Here, my dear," he added, as the bracelet threatened to slip from Cassandra's cold fingers. "Allow me to assist you."

Mutely, Cassandra held out her wrist as Willy adroitly fastened the clasp for her. "Thank you, Willy," she murmured, not daring to look at the earl, who had not uttered a word during this exchange.

"I take exception to your calling Raven the most notorious of the Corinthians, Willy," the marquess drawled in his bored voice. "I had always considered that dear old Beau Weatherby had better claim to that title until he up and married that chit of a duchess."

"Yes, Simon was a wild one, all right," Willy agreed. "But coming into his cousin's title sobered him more than I would have thought possible. Raven was a good choice to step into his shoes, I always thought."

The Earl of Mansfield let out a harsh crack of laughter, which seemed to disconcert the other three gentlemen. Cassandra noticed that Willy's face had gone a dull red.

"Sorry, old boy," he mumbled, casting an apologetic glance at the earl. "Didn't mean that at all, of course. Can't think what came over me." He tugged nervously at his cravat.

The marquess grinned at his friend's discomfort. "Perhaps that will teach you to watch your tongue around the ladies, Sweet Willy," he drawled, devilish amusement glinting in his intensely blue eyes. "And now," he added, turning to Cassandra, "I intend to claim the right to assist Lady Mansfield with the second clasp." He cast a defiant look at his host. "That is if Raven will promise not to call me out at the crack of dawn."

Before Cassandra could rouse herself, the marquess had picked up the pearl pendant in his long fingers and taken a stand behind her chair. She experienced a tremor of excitement as he placed the chain around her neck. The pearl fell into place between the swell of her exposed bosom, and the cool presence of the jewel in so intimate a place caused Cassandra a frisson of embarrassment.

The warmth of his fingertips on her neck as he fastened the clasp titillated her senses, and the thought flashed across her mind that the Marquess of Gresham was quite the most admirable and exciting man of her acquaintance. The thought was unworthy of a vicar's daughter, she told herself hastily, but she could not keep the flush of pleasure from her cheeks. She glanced guiltily at her husband to find him glaring at her with an arrested look in his gray eyes, which, even as she watched, changed to a thunderous scowl.

"If you have quite finished playing abigail to my wife, Cousin," he said in a voice that sounded perilously like a growl to Cassandra's heightened senses, "you might like to join us in our seasonal toasts." Cassandra distinctly heard the marquess's chuckle of amusement at his cousin's implied warning. None too pleased herself with her husband's churlish remark, she gave Gresham a deliberately glittering smile as he handed her a fresh glass of champagne and remained—in what she sensed was a perverse challenge to the irate earl—at her side for the rest of the evening.

CHAPTER TWELVE

The Quarrel

Although she was now almost four months advanced in her interesting condition, Cassandra suffered none of the lethargy and sickliness she had been led to expect. No longer bothered by nausea, she refused to lie abed until midmorning or submit to the affectionate coddling the dowager was eager to lavish upon her.

"It is not every day that a woman becomes a grandmother for the first time, my dear," the dowager countess declared as the two sat over the breakfast table together that Christmas morning. The four gentlemen had risen earlier and gone out riding. Mrs. Henshaw, who was a late riser, had as yet not left her room, so Cassandra and her mother-in-law had the cozy breakfast parlor to themselves.

"You cannot imagine how many years I have begged Phineas to bestir himself and take a wife, but he has always fobbed me off with the excuse that the succession was safe with Stephen." She paused, her countenance briefly clouded with somber thoughts. "But now that Stephen is gone, poor lamb, I imagine Phineas felt the need to set up his own nursery." She sighed audibly as she accepted Cassandra's offer of a second cup of tea. "I could have wished he had done so sooner and in a less precipitous fashion, naturally, but I have nothing but admiration for his choice, my dear," she added with a warm smile. "And now that you are to present him with an heir, my cup runs over."

Since the topic of her hasty marriage and imminent motherhood always made Cassandra uncomfortable, she invariably changed the subject.

"Burton tells me that the tenant baskets are ready, my lady," she said briskly. "Shall I ask him to have the tilbury loaded and brought round? You did say it will take us quite two hours to make the rounds, did you not?"

"That's right, dear," the dowager replied, pushing back her

chair and rising. "And let me warn you, Cassandra, it is never just a question of dropping off each basket. Many of the Mansfield tenants have been here longer than I have. There will be the usual offerings of currant and plum cakes and gooseberry tarts to sample, and gallons of elderberry and damson wine to taste, babies to cuddle, and expectant mothers to congratulate." She smiled at Cassandra, her lively eyes dancing in anticipation. "And I must confess, I enjoy every moment of it, my dear. Please see to the tilbury while I go upstairs to rouse that daughter of mine. I notice that the gentlemen have conveniently taken themselves off when they could be of some real use to us, so I suggest we take one of the grooms to carry the baskets."

Cassandra was secretly relieved that the gentlemen would not be accompanying them as they drove around the estate to distribute the traditional Christmas gifts to the Mansfield tenants. Although the earl had said nothing further to her last night, Cassandra had recognized his displeasure in the stern set of his lips and the devilish glitter in his dark eyes. She had not needed to be told that her husband was in one of his black moods, and although the dowager had serenely ignored the earl's unnatural silence, Cassandra had been acutely aware of his disapproving stare the entire evening.

It was almost noon before the ladies returned, tired but satisfied, with an empty tilbury, but only Lady Hart chose to join the gentlemen for the light nuncheon, which had been set out for them in the Great Hall. Cassandra was glad of the excuse to accompany the dowager down to the kitchens to supervise the holiday baking and roasting that had been going on steadily for the past few days in preparation for the traditional Christmas festivities at the Grange. The dowager countess had—unobtrusively and with innate generosity—gone to considerable pains to show the new lady of the manor the finer points of managing a large household like the Mansfield family seat, and Cassandra was growing accustomed to the domestics coming to her for their daily instructions. She was well aware that she had the dowager to thank for the smooth transition and for paving the way for her acceptance by the neighboring gentry.

The seasonal gathering that evening—including as it naturally would all the prominent local families—was to be her first official function as the new Countess of Mansfield, and Cassandra was determined to enjoy the festivities in spite of her lord's continued moodiness.

She had dressed carefully for this momentous occasion and, at the dowager's insistence that she leave off her mourning, had chosen a new satin gown of a deep, iridescent green that brought out the matching lights in her hazel eyes. It was plain almost to the point of severity, its sole ornament a sash of green velvet caught under her small bosom, a band of moonlight glittering with tiny seed pearls and falling almost to her green kid slippers in front. Rich folds rustling around her hips hinted at her slim figure, and the daringly low décolletage and tiny dropped sleeves revealed a delectable glow of ivory throat and breast that vied with the luminosity of the pearls for attention.

On her wrist she had clasped Willy's Christmas gift, and her husband's pearl earbobs gleamed in her ears. After some hesitation she had fastened Lord Gresham's flawless pearl pendant around her neck, sensing that the delicately wrought gold chain was more her style than the heavy strands of heirloom pearls Lord Mansfield had sent to her chamber as she was dressing, with the peremptory command that it was high time she assumed the trappings as well as the title of his countess.

Should she be the dutiful wife and wear the pearls? she wondered, gazing with awe at the massive strands of translucent gems. Had he not ordered her to do so, perhaps she would have suppressed her own preference for the marquess's exquisite pendant. And then again, perhaps not, she mused, torn between keeping the peace on that special evening and showing his lordship that Miss Drayton was not to be bullied so easily into doing his bidding. Finally, she closed the lid of the jeweler's box with a snap and put it into her dresser drawer. If his lordship found her actions objectionable, she reasoned, he could hardly become more objectionable himself than he already was. With that thought to console her, Cassandra went in search for the dowager.

"A wise choice, my dear," that lady remarked as Cassandra entered her sitting room.

"The pearls are lovely," Cassandra began, anxious not to offend by belittling the heirloom strands. "But—"

"Yes, I know," the dowager interrupted with a smile. "They are more fitting for a stout matron than a mere slip of a girl like you, dear. I remember saying something to that effect when Phineas's father insisted I wear them as a new bride thirty years ago."

"And did you, madam?"

The dowager laughed outright. "No, indeed, I did not. I told my dear Kendall he should get out of the habit of ordering my wardrobe if he aspired to having a well turned-out wife. He didn't like that one bit, let me tell you. But he did try to mend, I must say that for him." She paused to examine Cassandra's gown closely. "You are a credit to us, my love. Even without those pompous pearls."

Cassandra blushed at her ladyship's praise and fingered her pendant nervously. "I did feel that this chain is rather too long, madam. What do you think?"

The dowager regarded her searchingly for a moment and then smiled roguishly. "You truly are an innocent, Cassie dearest. When you know my nephew Robert as well as I do, you would not doubt that he ordered the chain deliberately long so that the pendant might lie exactly where it does." She gestured toward the offending bauble resting in the valley of Cassandra's exposed bosom.

Cassandra glanced down and blushed. The teardrop pearl lay snugly in the cleft between her breasts. Was this by accident or design? she wondered. And why hadn't she seen any significance to this fact before?

"I cannot believe the marquess would be so devious," she protested.

"Then you have a lot to learn about men, my dear. And my dear nephew Robert is as much a born flirt as his father, the Duke of Wexley, was at his age. Wexley is my brother, you know, so I know whereof I speak."

"I shall shorten it immediately," Cassandra declared, her cheeks glowing at the thought of this masculine depravity.

"I wouldn't be so foolish, if I were you," the dowager remarked, taking up her gloves and Norwich shawl. "That is if you don't wish the rogue to know you have seen through his nefarious intentions, which might prove rather embarrassing, child. Robert would doubtless derive considerable pleasure from the notion that you are aware of the intimacies he hints at."

"What am I to do then?"

"Nothing, of course," the dowager replied sensibly. "I have always thought you handle Robert rather well, my dear. He is so used to females toadying up to him or swooning over him, as is Phineas. You should merely feign Olympic innocence, Cassandra.

That will thwart him if anything can." The dowager shot a frankly amused glance at her and added, *sotto voce,* "I cannot wait to see dear Robert's frustration. It will be amusing to best the delightful rake at his own game."

Cassandra immediately recognized the wisdom of this advice. Hadn't she used much the same strategy to keep Lord Mansfield at bay? That and her shrewish tongue.

As she accompanied the dowager downstairs, Cassandra reminded herself that she intended to enjoy herself tonight. If this meant playing the innocent or the shrew, either with her own husband or any other predatory male, she would do so without a qualm.

The entrance of the two countesses into the Great Hall—arm in arm and smiling at their shared amusement—caused various reactions among those guests already gathered before the blazing fireplace. Lord Mansfield immediately came to meet them, followed closely by the marquess. Cassandra felt the dowager squeeze her arm and turned to find a mischievous gleam in her ladyship's gray eyes.

"Are you ready, dear?"

Cassandra didn't pretend to misunderstand the dowager's playful reference to their previous conversation and smiled her reply before turning to gaze limpidly at the two gentlemen who were bearing down on them. The devil take the pair of them, she thought crossly. Two more dangerously attractive and elegantly attired men would be difficult to imagine. The earl's darker coloring and crop of black curls gave him the more rakish, threatening air, while the marquess's dark blondness and easy address made him dazzlingly handsome. When his sapphire-blue eyes glittered with ill-concealed delight as they lighted on the pendant, Cassandra felt a shiver of apprehension traverse her spine.

Lord Mansfield greeted his mother with an affectionate salute, but wasted no time in turning to his wife, the hint of scowl on his chiseled countenance. He raised her unresisting fingers to his lips in a courtly gesture, but the viselike pressure of his grip belied the outward appearance of harmony between them. Cassandra's stomach tightened as she saw his eyes drop to the pendant displayed so brazenly between her breasts.

He raised his gaze to her face, which she strove to keep expressionless. "I distinctly remember sending you the Ravenville pearls o wear tonight, my dear wife," he growled in a low voice. "May I nquire why you have chosen to wear this trumpery gewgaw intead?" His words were deliberately contemptuous and intended, Cassandra had no doubt, to reach the ears of the marquess, engaged in pleasantries with the dowager.

Cassandra's temper flared, but she forced herself to smile up nto her husband's scowling face.

"You are teasing me, my lord," she simpered with feigned sweetness. "There is nothing trumpery about this wonderful pearl." She caught the pendant between her fingers and pretended to examine it. The ruse gave her a chance to avoid the blazing fury growing hotter by the moment in the earl's gray eyes.

"It cannot compare to the Ravenville pearls, you silly chit," he snapped.

"I doubt it was meant to, my lord," she replied blandly. "And besides, it suits my mood tonight much better than your stuffy old pearls," she added daringly, knowing full well that she was adding tinder to an already highly flammable situation.

The marquess, who was waiting to greet his hostess, let out a crack of laughter at Cassandra's deliberate rudeness. "I am enchanted to see that you have such good taste, my lady," he murmured, as he raised her fingers for a rather lingering salute.

"Good taste be damned," the earl snarled. "You will not encourage my wife in this foolishness, Gresham. I'm warning you. And you"—he turned his smoldering gaze back to Cassandra—"you will return that cheap bauble to his lordship immediately."

Cassandra stared at him, her eyes wide with feigned astonishment. "Do not tell me you are disguised so early in the evening, my lord," she remarked evenly. "Such overindulgence will be the ruin of you, sir, as I have told you before."

"I am not drunk, damn it!" Lord Mansfield exclaimed impatiently. "And you will do as I say, Cassandra. I will not have you accepting extravagant gifts from other gentlemen."

"But you have just remarked that Lord Gresham's gift is a mere gewgaw, my lord," Cassandra pointed out reasonably. She turned her limpid gaze on the grinning marquess. "And besides," she added with infinite sweetness, goaded by the gleam of triumph in his blue eyes, "I naturally do not think of his lordship as a gentleman but as a cousin and friend. He *is* a good friend to both of us, is he not?" She let the question hang in the air between them, deriving considerable satisfaction when the gloating expression in the marquess's eyes faded.

The earl snorted with amusement at his cousin's set-back. "Touché, old man." He turned back to Cassandra. "As a vicar's daughter, you should know it is unseemly to accept gifts from other men, gentlemen *or* friends."

"I do know it is unseemly to be rude to *anyone*," Cassandra snapped, her temper aroused again. "And I refuse to insult either his lordship or Mr. Hampton by doing anything so churlish as throwing their holiday gifts in their teeth. And I think it is too bad of you to suggest that I do so, my lord."

"Touché, old man," the marquess echoed, obviously enjoying the earl's discomfort.

Lord Mansfield glared menacingly at his friend, and Cassandra saw the familiar sneer replace the marquess's momentary good humor. They held this challenging stance for so long that Cassandra could bear the mounting tension no longer. Whatever did they think they were about? she wondered, quarrelling over her as though she were some ignorant light-skirt who might be impressed by this show of empty masculine bravado. She was suddenly tired of the whole ridiculous posturing and playacting.

"You are both being exceedingly silly," she remarked with acerbity. "Would it make you feel better if I promise to wear the pearls as soon as I feel equal to that honor, my lord?"

Her husband glared at her. "And when would that be, my lady?"

Cassandra gave in to temptation. "When I am old and stout and matronly, of course," she flashed back. "And in the meantime, I suggest we join the others before they finish all the punch."

She thrust one small hand around the earl's elbow and, imperiously signaling to the marquess to give her his arm, drew them toward the group by the fire, conscious of Sophy's curious stare and the dowager's enigmatic little smile.

Fortunately for the success of the holiday season at Mansfield Grange, no further mention was made of the Ravenville pearls, which Cassandra later returned to the steward, Mr. Jeremiah Matthews, for safekeeping in the estate safe. Cassandra put Lord Gresham's notorious pendant away in her jewel box determined not to wear it again until her husband showed signs of becoming less irascible on the subject.

The sudden tension that had erupted between the two cousins n the evening of Christmas Day disturbed her. During her duties s hostess that evening, Cassandra found herself wondering about e cause of this strange flare-up of animosity between gentlemen ho called each other friend and certainly acted as if they were ost of the time. At the dowager's instigation, they had ceased to owl at each other like two dogs spoiling for a fight, but the ten- on remained. Cassandra was conscious of their eyes upon her as e moved among the guests gathered in the Great Hall to share e traditional good cheer of the season.

"I wish you would tell me what maggot has got into those two innies," she complained to Willy Hampton, when that gentleman ined her in contemplating the ill-disguised efforts of a number f fresh-faced young boys to maneuver unwary young ladies nder the kissing boughs.

"There seem to be an inordinate number of ninnies here night," Willy replied with a wide smile. "Which ones do you ean, my dear?"

Cassandra threw him a calculating glance. "You know very ell which ninnies I am referring to, sir." She laughed ruefully. But I daresay you will deny that anything untoward happened etween them just before dinner." She looked at him quizzically, nd he returned a bland smile, but his eyes were twinkling mer- ly.

"The two gentlemen you refer to have always been most com- etitive, my dear Cassandra. Somewhat like those two cow- anded moonlings over there trying to inveigle that redheaded hit out of a kiss. As clever as she can hold together that pretty vidgeon is, unless I mistake the matter. No! No, lads," he mur- nured under his breath. "That will never do the trick. There! Vhat did I tell you. She's given them the slip, the naughty little uss." He grinned at her. "Those shuttleheads have much to learn n the art of stealing kisses, wouldn't you say, my lady?"

"You are the avowed expert in such matters, Willy," Cassandra eplied, comfortable with his lighthearted bantering.

"My prowess has been vastly overrated, I assure you, Cassan- ra. But let us leave the youngsters to their pranks and seek out a lass of that excellent Mansfield punch."

Cassandra allowed herself to be led toward the dining room, ut when her companion paused on the threshold, she looked at im inquiringly.

"This is how the experts do it, my lady," he said with a wide grin on his pleasant face. "Confess that you have been fairly caught and must forfeit a kiss."

Cassandra glanced quickly about her at several smiling faces and then looked up to see that Willy had indeed spoken the truth. She was standing squarely under an unobtrusive kissing bough.

"Now I know, to my sorrow, why you have such a fearsome reputation among the ladies, Willy." She was chagrined at the ease with which she had been caught, but willingly conceded the kiss, which Willy claimed with a lightness and charm that delighted the spectators.

"I see that dear Willy has added you to his long list of conquests," Lady Hart remarked a little later as the two ladies stood together in an alcove to take a moment's respite from the heat and boisterous revelry.

"He is a smooth-talking rogue," Cassandra replied with a rueful laugh. "I was quite taken in by his off-handed manner. I never suspected—"

"You have to watch these rogues every instant, Cassie," Sophy cut in. "There is no limit to their devious tricks. And what are *you* grinning at, Robert?" she demanded of the marquess, who had sauntered up unnoticed and now stood regarding the ladies with hooded eyes and a sardonic smile on his well-shaped lips.

"I am rather in a quandary," he replied. "I have caught two fair nymphs under the mistletoe, and slap me if I can choose which one of you to kiss first."

"Oh, go on with you," Sophy squeaked in mock horror. "You are a cheat, Cousin. There is no kissing bough here, so you can take yourself off, you wretch, or I shall tell Ned."

"And just what is it you will tell Ned?" Lord Hart demanded, appearing quite suddenly beside his flustered wife.

"Robert is trying to steal kisses from us without the benefit of mistletoe, my lord." Sophy pouted prettily up at her husband.

Lord Hart glanced up and then grinned mischievously at his wife. "I believe Robert has the right of it, and it is you ladies who are craven, my love," he remarked, slipping an arm round Sophy's slender waist. "If you look carefully, you will see a twig of mistletoe up there." He pointed to the arch high above their heads. "And I for one will insist on collecting the forfeit, sweetheart." He wasted no time in clasping Sophy in a bear hug that effectively silenced her protests.

Cassandra glanced up to find Lord Gresham staring at her intently with glittering eyes. Before he could step forward to claim his kiss, however, he was shouldered aside and Cassandra was pulled—none too gently—into her husband's arms.

"I believe I have precedence here, Cousin," the earl said shortly, tightening his hold on Cassandra's waist until she felt breathless.

The marquess's face went still and expressionless. He sketched Cassandra a brief bow. "Another time, my lady," he murmured politely and turned away in amusement.

Lord Mansfield did not seem to notice his cousin's departure. His eyes held no sign of tenderness that Cassandra could discern, only a fleeting gleam of triumph as he dipped his head to claim his kiss.

Two weeks into a damp and chilly January, Raven finally admitted that he was thoroughly disgusted with himself. Although he knew he should—and even wished to in his better moments—he was quite unable to apologize to Robert for his boorish behavior on Christmas Eve. The marquess had taken to observing him with sardonic amusement as if waiting for his next outburst. It made Raven feel like a recalcitrant child and did nothing to improve his temper, already stretched paper thin. He deeply regretted his angry moodiness, but could not seem to shake it.

Part of the problem, he knew, had to do with his ambiguous feelings toward his wife. *His wife,* he mused, still unaccustomed to the cold fact that he, the notorious Phineas Ravenville, was irrevocably leg-shackled to a countrified chit. His mother had accepted Cassandra with surprising affection, especially after she learned about the child, he thought, with a pang of guilt. And his featherheaded sister had been easily gulled into believing that her childhood friend was actually his own choice of a bride. But the Corinthians were not fooled for a moment. Apart from Ned's oblique reference at Lady Bradford's musicale to their disappointment in what they considered his betrayal, however, and the small ruckus over his trysts with Lady Huntington in the Park, nothing had been said.

No, nothing had been said, but the tension had grown almost unbearable since his impulsive confrontation with Gresham over the pearls. He stood at the tall French window in the library, gazing out at the leafless sycamores. There had been sycamores in the garden at the vicarage, he remembered—sycamores, and masses of lilacs, and a rose garden, depleted of its summer beauty. A sparrow, damp and puffed up with cold, huddled on a bare branch in silent misery. The plain, unobtrusive little bird reminded him suddenly of Cassandra, and he felt a tug of pity for the drab young woman he had coerced into this . . . what had she called it? Inconvenient. Yes, that was it, an inconvenient marriage.

The earl pulled himself together impatiently. It was pointless to waste his pity on the silly wench. Hadn't she known, when she lay down with his brother, what the outcome of their amorous rompings would be? He ran his fingers through his unruly hair impatiently. No, he corrected himself. What the innocent Cassandra had not known was that her lover would be violently taken from her and that she would be left to face the consequences of their indiscretion on her own.

Raven crossed to the sideboard and poured himself a large brandy. Even that simple action—one he was taking more frequently of late—reminded him of his wife. Hadn't she chided him—none too gently, he remembered with a grim smile, on his habit of reaching for the decanter to steady his nerves? The devil take the impertinent chit, he thought, taking a large swig of the fiery liquor and holding it in his mouth for a moment before letting it run smoothly down his throat. He had needed the false courage the drink had given him to get through that unpleasant interview at the vicarage, he remembered. And as if it were not enough that he had sacrificed his own freedom for her, she had the effrontery to lambaste him with her prudish notions.

He took another draft of the amber liquid, refilled his glass, and moved back to the window. The prospect was not encouraging. He had spent a rather amusing time this winter with his friends, he thought, between his cousin's hunting lodge in Melton Mowbray and shooting parties at the Grange. It had seemed almost like old times, before Morville and Weatherby and Ned Greenley had succumbed to parson's mousetrap. Before young Harry Davenport and Nick Bellington had gone off to join Wellington on the Peninsula.

No, he thought, taking another long pull at the brandy. It had not been like those carefree days of his youth at all. Too many of the Corinthians were missing; too many of his good friends had taken another turn at the crossroads and gone on to become, if not exactly respectable, at least reformed. And husbands. Raven grimaced. He had become one himself. And a soon-to-be father. He stared moodily down at the brandy. It wasn't working today, he thought. He had drunk heavily at luncheon and had intended to spend the winter afternoon in a painless haze before the library fire. There would be no getting out of the house today, he realized morosely. A blizzard had swept through the region during the night, leaving snowdrifts, broken trees, and icy roads in its wake. The sun had not shown its face at all and by midmorning the snow had resumed, soon turning to sleet and icy rain. Raven shivered as a gust of wind rattled the windows. The sparrow had disappeared, and he wondered idly if the silly bird had taken refuge in the stables, where it would be relatively warm.

The devil take it, he thought irritably. He was getting maudlin. Irrationally, he wondered if Cassandra were happy at the Grange, or whether his house and his name were merely a refuge for a drab little chit who had been caught in the storm of life.

Silently he cursed himself for a half-bosky, sentimental fool. The opening of the door was a welcome distraction, and he grinned as Willy stuck his head in.

"There you are, old man. Sulking again, are you? Drink ain't going to cure what ails you, Raven. You can take my word for it."

Raven felt his grin slip into a scowl. Sweet Willy was nothing if not direct and never minced his words. The suggestion that there was anything the matter with him was galling, however, and Raven's scowl deepened. "What do you want?" he growled.

Willy grinned at this rudeness. "Ned and Robert have suggested a game of deep basset to while away a nasty afternoon, Raven. Like to join us, lad?"

The notion of a game of chance appealed to Raven, and his face brightened. He felt restless and reckless and edgy as a coiled spring. Perhaps he could induce his cousin to wager that handsome bay mare he had ridden to hounds last month. The idea of besting the marquess dispelled the gloom like magic, and it was not long before he was deep in play with the other Corinthians in the game room, a decanter of brandy within easy reach.

Two hours later, the wagers had risen and the level of the decanters had diminished considerably. Raven had indeed won the coveted bay mare from Gresham, but lost it almost immediately to Lord Hart, who promptly wagered it against another of the marquess's horses and lost.

Lord Gresham smiled his mirthless, sardonic smile and regarded his cousin through half-closed lids. "Still interested in the mare, Raven?" he drawled, his tongue barely slurring the words. "Tell you what." He grinned with Machiavellian charm. "I'll put up the mare against the little lady-bird you keep on Curzon Street." He smiled satanically. "Interested?"

The room became suddenly very still as Raven stared across the card table at his rival for the diva's favors. His *former* rival, he corrected himself. The greedy little tart had accepted Mansfield's offer rather than Gresham's, to the latter's infinite chagrin.

Of course, under normal circumstances, he would have discontinued his liaison with Giullietta upon his marriage. Except that his was not a normal marriage at all, only a sham one. Raven wished he could unburden himself to these men seated round the table with him. They were his closest friends, and on more than one occasion their advice and support had saved his bacon. But it was not his secret alone. Cassandra—whatever her failing as a wife—was under his protection and had trusted him to keep her safe.

Raven grinned wolfishly at his opponent. "Not trying to tell me something, are you, Gresham?" he drawled. "I am not yet ready to give up that fancy piece. You can keep your blasted mare."

Gresham's eyes glittered dangerously, but whatever he might have responded was interrupted by Lady Hart, who burst unceremoniously into the card room, dragging Cassandra with her.

"Here they are, Cassie. I told you we would find them cooped up in this stuffy room."

"Drinking and gambling," Cassandra remarked, her nose wrinkling in disgust. Raven watched it with a flash of amusement. She had a particularly pert nose, he thought, lounging back in his chair and regarding his wife lazily. An enticing mouth, too, come to think of it. At the moment, it was pursed primly as her hazel eyes took in the scattered cards and markers and the empty decanters on the sideboard. Raven noticed that she avoided meeting his gaze and grinned in perverse amusement.

"My dear Cassie, you should know by now that men are apt to sink into quagmires of depravity unless we ladies engage them in seemlier pastimes," Sophy stated with an air of long suffering that elicited a guffaw of laughter from her husband and Willy Hampton.

"And what seemlier pastimes did you have in mind, sweetheart?" Lord Hart inquired with a suggestiveness that brought a fiery blush to Sophy's cheeks.

"We t-thought it might be amusing to d-dress up and play charades, Ned," Sophy replied, stumbling a little in her embarrassment. "But I see that you are all hopelessly castaway and no fit company for ladies." She would have turned away, but Lord Hart reached out and grasped her wrist, drawing her closer.

"Don't run away, my love," he drawled, his voice noticeably slurred. "You have not yet told us what other seemlier pastimes you have to offer, dearest."

"You *are* bosky," Sophy exclaimed, unable to resist a nervous giggle. "Let me go at once, Ned."

"Oh, come now, Sophy. You'll not refuse your husband a little buss now, will you?" And before his wife could protest, he had pulled her onto his lap and began nuzzling her cheek.

Raven grinned at his sister's discomposure. He wondered vaguely whether he should remonstrate with Ned about his highly irregular behavior, but Sophy did not seem to mind, so he transferred his gaze to his own wife instead. She was staring at the raffish scene with no small alarm, as well she might, Raven thought. He rather enjoyed seeing her cool poise shattered for once. And Ned was right. He, too, could think of far more entertaining pastimes for a rainy winter afternoon than playing cards and drinking oneself under the table. Quite unexpectedly, he felt a sudden tightening of arousal. He gazed at his wife speculatively.

"Cassandra." His voice was low and urgent, and he had not meant to speak aloud. It surprised them both, for she turned startled eyes to his face and stared at him. "Come here, lass," he commanded, holding out an imperious hand. "We cannot allow these lovebirds to have all the fun now, can we?" He enunciated each word with careful deliberation.

"Go to the devil," came the quelling response. "You have all taken leave of your senses."

Both Gresham and Hampton let out raucous snorts of laughter at this, and Raven instantly bristled. "I said come here, wife," he repeated with ominous calm.

"And I told you to go to the devil, sir," Cassandra snapped back, a faint echo of panic in her voice. She glanced over her shoulder at the door, and Raven used that momentary distraction to lean forward and grasp his wife's wrist, jerking her roughly onto his lap.

She squirmed briefly then sat, rigid and hostile, but the warmth of her derriere caused his arousal to grow more pronounced. The idea that he could display desire for his wife before a roomful of guests amused and excited him. He reached for her chin with his long fingers.

"Come, love," he murmured in her ear. "One kiss won't do either of us any harm. I'm your husband, after all."

"And I'm your *wife*, not your light-skirt," Cassandra hissed furiously, her hazel eyes flashing dangerously. "And you can release me immediately, or I shall box your ears."

Goaded by this obstinate resistance, which had caused Lord Gresham's eyebrows to rise quizzically, Raven gripped his wife's chin more firmly and forced her to look at him. "If you won't behave like a wife, you cannot expect to be treated like one," he growled, suddenly determined to teach this country shrew a lesson she would never forget. He slowly lowered his mouth to hers. Hell and damnation, he thought fuzzily, luxuriating in the cool softness of his wife's lips. If the wench escapes bedding tonight, it won't be for want of opportunity.

"I say, old man," Willy broke in plaintively. "This is not at all the thing, you know. The lady has a point, Raven. You are being deucedly offensive. Not right to force the lady to kiss you if she don't want to. Even if she is your wife—"

Raven never heard the end of Willy's lecture. Cassandra slapped his face so forcefully and unexpectedly that Raven felt his ears ring. In a flash she sprang loose and swept majestically out of the room, slamming the door viciously behind her.

"Oh!" Sophy cried out in dismay, jumping up from Lord Hart's lap and smoothing her skirts down nervously. "What an odious beast you are, Raven, to torment poor Cassie with your vulgar starts. You are always spoiling everything. I hate you." She glared around the room belligerently. "In fact, I hate the whole pack of you. And that includes you," she added, pointing a quivering finger at her astonished husband. "I wish you were all dead." On this cheerful note, Lady Hart whirled and stalked out of the room, leaving utter silence behind her.

"So much for married bliss," remarked the marquess gently. "I shall ask Burton for some more brandy. I think we all need it."

Raven stared at the closed door, an odd smile on his face.

CHAPTER THIRTEEN

Burning Bridges

So incensed was Cassandra at the earl's unmannerly behavior and insulting insinuations in the card room that afternoon, that she refused to come down to tea and sent word that she had been afflicted with a severe megrim when the time came to assemble for dinner.

"It's that son of mine again, is it not?" the dowager inquired, stopping in to check on her daughter-in-law before going down to dinner. "What has the fiend done now, dear?" she added solicitously. "Sophy has told me something of the unspeakably ill-bred scene that took place this afternoon. You have every reason to feel offended, Cassandra. After all, the role of a husband is to cherish and protect his wife, not maul her about in public. I am quite disgusted with Phineas myself, and so I told him. He owes you an abject apology, and you shall get it if it is the last thing I do."

Rarely had Cassandra seen the dowager so put out, and she saw that her own peevish behavior did nothing to help matters. "Please do not tease yourself on my account, ma'am," she pleaded. "His lordship was severely under the weather this afternoon, and doubtless that was the cause of his . . . of his . . . "

"Of his unpardonable conduct you mean, don't you, dear? And he was frankly foxed from what Sophy tells me. Foxed and lewd, those were her exact words. As was Lord Hart. My darling Sophy is quite as inconsolable by this disgusting incident as you are, Cassandra. The poor thing has gone to bed with a splitting headache. Even now her abigail is applying rose water to relieve the throbbing. You should have Bridget do the same for you, dear. It is most beneficial."

After the dowager had gone, Cassandra rang for her abigail. For the sake of appearance, it might be wise to follow Sophy's lead and order an application of rose water. She wondered if

Sophy had really come down with a megrim or whether she was merely trying to avoid—as she was herself—an encounter with the offending gentlemen. To tell the truth, she thought uncharitably, Sophy had not seemed too shocked at her husband's lascivious behavior. In fact, Cassandra would have said her friend had rather enjoyed the intimate horseplay. And well she might, Cassandra thought philosophically. Sophy's was a love match, after all, and her Ned fairly doted on her, foxed or sober. While her own—

Her morbid thoughts were interrupted by the arrival of Bridget with a blue porcelain bowl of cool rose water. Cassandra closed her eyes and submitted to the ministrations of the abigail, but her thoughts flew back to the dreadful scene in the card room. Lord Mansfield had been quite indisputably disguised, she remembered. There could be no other reasonable explanation for the hot, frankly sensual glaze in his eyes as he had stared at her. Suddenly, she recalled how the earl had admitted, bluntly and without any flicker of shame, on that first painful day at the vicarage, that gentlemen often turned to lewdness when in their cups. Presumably he had meant himself, and now she had been treated to a disgusting exhibition of that very lewdness directed—for reasons she hesitated to examine too closely—at her person.

Could that exhibition of conjugal privilege have been merely part of the inexplicable male game Lord Mansfield was playing with the marquess? she wondered. Probably so, which meant that it was also a mockery of their marriage, a mockery of her. If she could only discover what drove him to such perversity, she might know what he expected of her. As it was, she was at a loss to understand his sudden fits of passion, knowing as she did that in his soberer moments he considered her more of a nuisance than anything else. There could be no question of affection, much less anything stronger. She resolutely shied away from even thinking about love. No, there was no love in Lord Mansfield's heart for her, she told herself firmly. If it was love she had felt for Stephen—and what else could it have been?—then the turmoil of emotions that Lord Mansfield stirred up in her breast must be something else, something quite painful and uncomfortable. She wished it would go away.

A small, nagging thought teased at her mind. If Raven had been making some primitive show of force for his cousin's benefit, why had his hand slid so caressingly from her waist to her hip and lingered there so possessively, suggestively, against her thigh? Why had he pressed her closer to him? Closer to that hardness that had shocked her into rigidity when she had glimpsed its deforming shape against the clean, taut lines of his well-cut breeches, felt its unmistakable imprint against her thigh? Surely the marquess had seen nothing of that horrendous impropriety? Or had he? Was that why he had smiled that peculiar little smile when she had made the mistake of glancing his way? Her cheeks flamed at the notion that perhaps the libertine had known what Raven was doing to her beneath the level of the table.

"You are coming down with a fever, milady," Bridget announced sententiously, gently dabbing at her mistress's overheated cheeks with the cool cloth. "It don't look good to me. No, sir. I shall ask her ladyship to call in the sawbones. Don't you think so, milady?"

"No, I do not think so, Bridget," Cassandra replied. "And you may go down to see to my dinner tray now. I am feeling quite sharp set."

"Begging your pardon, milady. You should not eat too heartily if you have a fever. That's what my mum always used to say."

"I do *not* have a fever, Bridget," Cassandra repeated sharply. "Only a mild headache. Lady Hart has one, too. It must have been something we ate for luncheon."

If she were not careful, she thought gloomily after the abigail had left the room, she would bring on a real megrim with her fanciful notions. And she had not eaten enough of anything at the rather boisterous luncheon the Grange guests had enjoyed to make a sparrow sick. The gentlemen had already been mildly topheavy even then, she remembered. No wonder that by midafternoon they were three sheets to the wind.

She shook her head angrily. There was nothing to be gained by dwelling on that unpleasant scene yet again, she thought. She would change into her night things, enjoy a cozy dinner, and spend the rest of the evening before the blazing fire with one of Mrs. Radcliffe's latest romances, which had recently arrived from London. And the devil fly away with all rakes and libertines, she thought smugly. And husbands, too, for that matter.

She had achieved the first two of these goals and was comfortably ensconced on her boudoir settee with a rug tucked around her, deep in the adventures of a spirited heroine who seemed equal to all of life's vicissitudes, when the door adjoining the earl's chambers swung open with a crash.

The Earl of Mansfield stood glaring at his wife with undisguised belligerence. "I understood that you were indisposed, my lady," he said harshly. "And here I find you still up and about at this advanced hour."

Cassandra glanced nervously at the ormolu clock on the mantel and was surprised to see that it marked the hour of one o'clock. She studied her husband covertly. He had removed his coat and cravat, and his hair was disheveled, falling in Byronesque curls over his forehead. He was really rather romantically handsome, she reflected irrationally—almost the living image of the dashing, elusive gentleman the heroine of Mrs. Radcliffe's novel was pursuing so relentlessly. And here he was in her bedchamber, she mused. Her romantic heroine would undoubtedly have given much to entrap her hero in a like situation, as perchance she would as the story progressed. The thought almost made her want to smile. Then she noticed his eyes, and all thoughts of mirth fled. Was the earl still foxed? she wondered, a flicker of panic stirring in her stomach. If so, he might well have come to renew the scene she had interrupted with a slap in the card room.

Cassandra suddenly felt very vulnerable indeed. The rogue must be induced to leave immediately, she decided. She would be pleasantly firm and not lose her temper under any circumstances.

"If you knew I had the megrim and expected to find me asleep, my lord," she began in a reasonable tone, "then I fail to see the purpose of your presence here." She regarded him warily.

"I saw the light still on," he replied brusquely. "My mother informs me that I owe you an apology, but I can hardly comply if you insist on skulking in your room."

"I am not skulking, my lord." Cassandra made a valiant effort to sound calm. "But your apology is accepted, nevertheless."

He laughed. "I have not made one, you silly twit." He paused, and Cassandra felt his eyes, harsh and comfortless as the wave-lashed cliffs of her native Kent, rake her face and slide down her throat to the open neck of her dressing gown.

"And I have no intention of doing so." His lips—lips that had been so recently seductive against her own—twisted into a sardonic grimace. "I see no reason for an apology. Why should a man apologize for kissing his own wife? Can you tell me that, my lady?"

When Cassandra failed to answer, the earl continued with a sneer. "No, I thought as much. You would do well to learn from my sister that a dutiful wife does as she is told." He grinned humorlessly, and Cassandra felt her heart grow suddenly cold with fright. She must pull herself together, or she would soon be bullied into admitting that she had been in the wrong.

"If being a dutiful wife entails countenancing the repulsive liberties I witnessed this afternoon, then I have no wish to be one," she said disdainfully. "Lady Hart is welcome to allow herself to be mauled by as many bosky libertines as she wishes, but do not expect me to make such a disgusting spectacle of myself, my lord."

A considerable pause ensued before he asked in a taut voice: "Are you calling my sister's behavior disgusting?"

"Of course I am not," she cried, her temper slipping. "It was Lord Hart's that was disgusting. And yours," she added before she could stop her wretched tongue. Too late, she saw the flash of anger in his eyes and wished she had not been so impulsive.

The earl, who had been leaning negligently against the mantel, moved slowly toward her, a diabolical smile on his face. To her dismay, he sat down on the settee beside her, casually draping an arm over the back, barely inches from her hair.

"I see you are in dire need of a lesson in wifely obedience," he drawled, picking up a stray curl and twisting it idly in his long fingers.

When those fingers moved to caress her cheek and edge tantalizingly down her neck, Cassandra threw the rug to the floor and jumped to her feet. "It is time for you to leave, my lord," she said firmly, disregarding the odd trembling of her knees. "It is late, as you pointed out, and I wish to go to bed."

He smiled, and she did not like the look of it at all. "Oh, you do, do you? Well, don't let me stop you, sweetheart. In fact, I shall be more than happy to accompany you." His voice was strangely soft and his eyes no longer cold but warmly suggestive. Dangerously so, she thought, like a large, sleek cat about to pounce on a terrified, drab little field mouse.

Resolutely, she turned to face him as he rose lazily to his feet, reaching down inside herself for the courage to meet his eyes. "Thank you," she said primly. "But that won't be necessary." When he made no move to leave, she added with a mixture of defiance and desperation. "And I wouldn't want you to break the promise you made to me under my father's roof."

His reaction was immediate and explosive. In one swift motion he grasped both her wrists and pulled her roughly against him. Stubbornly, she refused to raise her eyes, concentrating on the open neckline of his fine cambric shirt. Only when she became aware of the pulse throbbing at the base of his throat and the black hairs curling out of the open shirt, did she close her eyes in despair. The assault of his touch, his smell, his masculine aura on her senses was too, too much. His breath moved her hair as he laughed, and she could well imagine his cynical mouth grinning down at her.

"The devil take that promise," he growled, slipping an arm round her waist and easing her into the curve of his body. "'Tis easily broken, as are all promises, my love. 'Twas an unreasonable one to ask of a man, anyway. Now, give me that kiss you denied me this afternoon, Cassie. 'Tis only fair, don't you agree? Then we will decide what else you have to give me." Still clasping one of her hands in his, he used his knuckle to raise her reluctant chin and took her mouth in his.

Cassandra was paralyzed with alarm. The warmth and gentleness of his mouth surprised her. She had expected violence from him, but the movement of his lips on hers, and the insistent probings of his tongue against her clenched teeth threatened to undo her resistance. This man was truly a devil, she thought in panic. Only a devil would know how to seduce a woman who had no desire to be seduced, wouldn't he? Only a devil would know how to create that warm melting sensation that seemed to be invading her limbs and obscuring her will to resist. Only a devil would know that sooner or later she would begin returning his kisses, his caresses, and responding to his passion, his desires, with the wave of yearnings she felt, even now, welling up inside her. With a supreme effort she wrenched her mouth free.

"Why are you doing this to me?" she demanded in a low, hoarse whisper.

"Doing what, sweetheart?" His mouth traced a path of pure delight down the exposed side of her neck.

"This," she heard herself whimper. The pathetic sound of her own voice startled Cassandra into action. This would never do, she thought. No man could be expected to believe that such a weak-spirited creature actually meant to resist him. Gathering her anger in a cloak around her, she struggled so violently that the earl was caught off guard.

Suddenly, she was free. "Why are you toying with me like this, you blackguard?" she lashed out in a blind fury. "Trying to seduce me merely because you are bored with yourself and your odious friends? You don't give a tinker's damn about me, do you? Not really. Not the way—" Had she really been about to bring up Stephen again? she wondered wildly. That gentle boy who had loved her had no place in this ugly quarrel. "Yet you choose to amuse yourself at my expense," she continued, stamping her foot angrily. "Yes, you only think to amuse yourself and those rakes you call friends by hurting defenseless women."

She was almost shouting now, her fury whipped into a frenzy. "You are a shameless libertine, concerned only for your own selfish pleasure. What gives you the right to humiliate me publicly, as you did this afternoon? Can you tell me? Do you think I have no feelings? Do you think I don't care what disgusting things you force me to do?"

"You are distraught, Cassandra. Let's discuss—" the earl made a threatening move toward her, but she whirled out of reach. "Of course, I'm distraught, you clodhead. What decent woman wouldn't be? I believed you when you promised . . . when you promised not to hurt me. And now I find that even I, your wife, am not safe from your drunken excesses."

She paused for breath and glared at him, wondering what evil thoughts flickered behind the opaque stare of those hard gray eyes.

"You are exaggerating, my dear," he said coldly. "And I must ask you not to shout at me in the middle of the night. You will raise the household."

"Ha!" she snorted angrily. "Let us by all means raise the household. I can't wait to tell everyone what a base, revolting, drunken lecher you really are."

He recoiled visibly at these words, uttered with unmistakable loathing. "No, you wouldn't, you silly wench," he snarled. "Only consider what my mother, my sister, what the whole household would think if they knew your sordid little secret." He paused, and Cassandra saw the anger die out of his eyes. He looked suddenly bored with the whole scene. "This hoydenish melodrama serves no useful purpose, my dear—"

"My love for Stephen was *never* sordid," she interrupted, her face pale with rage. "*You* are the only sordid thing in my life." Cassandra knew she had already said too much, too many ugly, violent things to this husband of hers. He would never forgive her. But she could not stop. "I wish you would just leave me alone," she muttered disjointedly "Go back to London. Go back to that unfortunate woman you *pay* to satisfy your depravity. I hear you have never lacked—"

She stopped in midsentence, suddenly cowed by the murderous look that had sprung into Lord Mansfield's eyes. He stood transfixed for several moments before he relaxed and smiled grimly.

"You are right, of course. The treats in London are vastly superior to anything I might find in my own home, with my own prudish, countrified, shrewish wife." Cassandra quailed beneath the look of utter bleakness on her lord's face and, for some inexplicable reason, she felt she had just lost something infinitely precious.

"I wish you good night, my lady," he said with cold finality "And pleasant dreams."

It was some time later, before she fell into an uneasy slumber, that Cassandra realized the enormity of what she had done. Like the innocent she was, she had thoroughly alienated the man who had—probably without even being aware of it—invaded her heart.

The weather had cleared during the night, and the weak winter sun shone bravely into the breakfast parlor when Raven came down that morning. He was already on his second cup of coffee when Lord Gresham sauntered in, immaculate as ever, in spite of having been ruthlessly rousted from his warm bed by his host not an hour since.

"I trust you have a satisfactory explanation for this rag-mannered start, Raven," he drawled, accepting a heaping plate of coddled eggs, several thick rashers of bacon, and a serving of kidneys from Burton. "I can't say I relish having my rest disturbed at the best of times, but this is the outside of enough, old chap. What can possibly be so urgent that it could not wait until a more respectable hour?"

"We are leaving within the hour," Raven said cryptically. He had not slept at all well, and when his heavy-lidded eyes had finally closed, his dreams had been haunted by a fleeing female figure dressed in a drab brown kerseymere gown of outmoded, unrecognizable style. Every time the figure glanced back at him, he was distraught at the terror he saw in the huge hazel eyes. She was terrified of him. He didn't know how he knew this, but it was definitely so. The knowledge that he was a terrifying threat to this woman, who was important to him for reasons shrouded in the mysteries of such dreams, distressed him enormously. He woke up unrested and strangely tense. It was then that his midnight altercation with Cassandra came back to him in all its ugly details. The decision to leave the Grange had seemed entirely rational at that predawn hour. Now it had become imperative.

Lord Gresham raised an elegant eyebrow, a forkful of eggs suspended midway to his mouth. "We are? And where, pray tell, are we going?"

"To Melton Mowbray, of course." Raven had not previously given his destination much thought. Go back to London, she had told him, hadn't she? He was strangely reluctant to put that much distance between them, however. A ridiculous notion, when he considered it rationally. There was already an infinite, unbridgeable distance between them, he thought wryly. What did a few extra miles matter?

"Oh, I see." Gresham resumed eating, his face inscrutable. "I am absolutely delighted that my humble lodgings meet with your approval, Raven. What is the occasion for this precipitous flight, or dare I ask?"

"Don't ask," Raven replied shortly.

There was a short pause during which the marquess regarded him searchingly, his startling blue eyes unusually serious. "I devoutly trust," he began carefully, "speaking as your cousin and fellow Corinthian, and as *nothing else,* you understand," he added meaningfully, "that you have done nothing irreconcilable, Raven."

So rarely did the imperturbable, notoriously cold-blooded Marquess of Gresham let down his emotional guard, that Raven was momentarily taken aback. He returned his cousin's inscrutable stare, with the sudden realization that Robert had also obliquely acknowledged their long-standing and often ruthless rivalry, another taboo topic between them. Ever since he could remember, Raven had pitted himself against the marquess's enviable prowess in every conceivable form of sports, carousing, and women. Especially women, he thought with a grim quirk of his mouth, remembering his cousin's barely concealed chagrin when the voluptuous

Giullietta had made her momentous decision in favor of Lord Mansfield.

Raven had difficulty believing he had heard aright. Knowing how his cousin's mind worked, however, it was clear as a pikestaff that the marquess had, in a subtle, carefully tactful and oblique fashion, just informed his host that he would be a bloody fool to burn his bridges with Cassandra. In light of Robert's thinly disguised attempts at flirtation with the countess, this announcement could only mean that the marquess was withdrawing from the lists. This in itself was also highly unusual. In the past their challenges, acknowledged or otherwise, had been pursued to the bitter, bloody end—until both contestants had exhausted every possible and impossible rouse, trick, sleight of hand, and bribe to win the wager or trophy. In just such a way had Raven bested Gresham with Giullietta, offering the greedy little baggage a diamond parure that would have not looked out of place on a duchess. Raven guessed—again from his previous experience with his rival—that this bitter defeat was at least partially responsible for the marquess's amorous assault on Lady Mansfield. Just to even the score somewhat, Raven thought, and to provoke an amusing confrontation between them. Cassandra was right, he thought with sudden remorse, he had used her—they both had used her—to prolong their personal vendetta.

But what was Robert up to now? he wondered. He continued to meet the cool blue stare, trying to understand the complicated machinations of his cousin's mind. He had never—since Cassandra's first memorable encounter with the marquess—imagined that his wife stood in any real danger of being seduced. She had seemed impervious to Gresham's famous charm, and it was unthinkable that the marquess might entertain any serious designs against the innocent, countrified countess. She was not his type at all. Just as she was not Raven's type. It was ludicrous to imagine that two such well turned-out Town Beaux, fastidious to a fault in matters of dress, should look twice at a female who could appear in public wearing that hideous gown and aberrant monstrosity of a hat she had worn the day of her marriage.

Gresham was obviously still waiting for an answer to his question. He raised one eyebrow quizzically, and it suddenly occurred to Raven to wonder if perhaps Robert had not begun to feel the conflicting emotions that Cassandra had aroused in his own breast. Could it be, miracle of miracles, that the man whose icy indifference to every reigning Beauty on the Marriage Mart had been the despair of so many hopeful mothers had been touched at last? If this were true, then it well might be that Gresham was making one of his rare gestures of disinterested generosity.

The irony of it all struck him, and he grinned wryly. "There's no secret about that, Robert," he drawled mockingly, making light of what had suddenly begun to seem like a tragedy of major proportions. "I've been given my marching papers, if you must know. Told to go back to London. Back to that ladybird whom I *pay*—her very words—to cater to my depravity. It's a lost cause, old man." He cast a bleak look out the window at the intensely blue and cloudless sky. "To borrow one of your more weighty pronouncements, Cousin, so much for married bliss."

"Perhaps things are not quite as bad as you think, Raven," the marquess ventured.

"My dear Robert," Raven answered somberly. "If Cassandra tells you to go to the devil, you go. No two ways about it." He was silent for a moment and then added impulsively. "Still interested in the diva, Robert? If so, she's yours. Cost you a pretty penny, no doubt, but I'm withdrawing from that particular love nest."

The marquess glanced at him in surprise. "Found something more worthwhile, I daresay?"

Again Raven could not misunderstand his friend's meaning. He shrugged. "Perhaps," he answered evasively. "I need some time to think, that's all. Where the devil is Willy?"

Before the words had left his mouth, that gentleman strode into the breakfast parlor, his face wreathed in smiles. "Here I am, old man. No sense flying up into the boughs, Raven. What's afoot anyway?"

"It seems we are on our way to Melton Mowbray, Willy," the marquess remarked, picking up the newspaper that his host had cast impatiently aside. "And if you don't look sharp, my lad, you won't get any breakfast. Raven here is all hot to go."

CHAPTER FOURTEEN

Return to Kent

By late morning the four gentlemen were comfortably installed in Lord Gresham's luxurious hunting lodge just outside the village of Melton Mowbray. They had ridden down the twelve odd miles from Denton at a leisurely pace, trailed by Raven's light traveling chaise transporting their valets and the absolute minimum baggage to ensure the comfort and presentability of four fashionable gentlemen relaxing for a few days in the country. After a hearty luncheon provided on the spur of the moment by the marquess's housekeeper, Lord Hart suggested getting up a hand of hazard. This was enthusiastically endorsed by Willy Hampton, whose luck with the dice was legendary. Although Raven was more concerned with the contents of the marquess's liquor cabinet than with games of chance, he soon joined his friends around the green baize table in the front parlor, a decanter of French brandy conveniently at hand.

By midafternoon Raven had lost a considerable sum of money, plus two of his best hunters. He had won little or nothing for the past hour—his heart not being in the game—but was feeling relatively at peace with the world when there was an unexpected interruption from the housekeeper, who announced the arrival of two ladies.

The marquess leaned back in his chair and stretched. "Show them into the drawing room, Mrs. Cooper, if you please. And perhaps we should offer them some refreshments or other. Tea, perhaps?" He glanced questioningly at his housekeeper's carefully impassive face.

"Certainly, my lord," Mrs. Cooper said and bustled out.

"*Ladies?*" Lord Hart inquired in mock horror. "What *ladies* would visit a single gentleman's hunting lodge, my dear Robert?"

"More than you would think possible, old man," the marquess drawled in some amusement. "But relax, Ned. Your virtue is safe.

I have a very good notion these barques of frailty are particularly interested in our Raven here," he added with a faint smile.

Raven met Lord Gresham's calculating gaze calmly. He had indulged himself—as what red-blooded gentleman had not?—in many of the past orgies the marquess had hosted at his lodge. Indeed, Robert seemed to know every light-skirt and demi-rep within fifty miles of Melton Mowbray, and most of them had, at one time or another, enlivened the lodge with their charming presence. But today Raven's thoughts lay in another direction, and he shook his head in answer to his friend's unspoken suggestion.

"Count me out, Robert," he said softly, pouring another measure of brandy into his empty glass. "I seem to have lost my taste for dalliance."

The marquess grinned sardonically as he rose to lead the way into the drawing room, where two fashionably dressed ladies sat at their ease on the bronze striped settee.

"My dear Lady Huntington," he murmured caressingly over the gloved hand of that fair-haired Beauty. "What a welcome breath of fresh air to our poor jaded senses. And Mrs. Handcock, how delightful to renew our acquaintance." He glanced at the other gentlemen, who stepped forward to make their bows to the lovely visitors. "I believe you two charming ladies already know these reprobates?" he drawled, one eyebrow cocked in cynical amusement.

"Indeed we do, Robert," Lady Huntington replied in her husky, seductive voice. "Raven, you naughty man. I am glad to see you are not still immured at The Grange. Geraldine was only remarking to me this morning how dreadfully you have neglected us. You are thoroughly in disgrace with her, you must know."

Raven smiled faintly at this attempted witticism and stepped forward to take Geraldine Handcock's plump fingers in his. "I trust I am not sunk beyond redemption, ma'am," he said smoothly, while his mind registered the overblown charms of one of London's most notorious widows. Two of a kind they were, he reflected, Mrs. Handcock and the dashing, exquisitely gowned, perpetually bored Lady Chloe Huntington. The faint aroma of scandal hung about both of them, although their wealth and family connections still guaranteed their acceptance by all but the most highly starched matrons.

"I had imagined you escaped from the rigors of the country long ago, Chloe," remarked Mr. Hampton genially. "Never thought to see you so far from London in weather like this, my dear."

Lady Huntington bestowed a practiced, glittering smile on Willy, but Raven felt her restless blue eyes on him as he listened politely to Mrs. Handcock's unfavorable comparisons between Handcock Hall—the country seat of her elderly brother-in-law, Sir Thomas Handcock—and the elegant luxury of Lady Huntington's London residence where she had been a guest for several weeks.

"So overrun with children," she complained in her simpering nasal voice, quite as though children were some kind of contagious disease, Raven thought in disgust. "My dear sister has no less than eight of the little terrors, and is even now in the process of delivering a ninth. I applaud her desire to do her duty by her lord, of course, but such ridiculous devotion is quite beyond the pale of what is agreeable. Don't you think so, my lord."

"I'm rather fond of children myself," Raven found himself saying a little defiantly, much to the startlement of his friends, who were more accustomed to hearing him bemoan the need to breed brats to secure the succession. "In fact, Lady Mansfield is herself in that happy condition." Had anyone told him he would actually think, much less say anything so smacking of the besotted husband, he would have laughed them to scorn. He wondered what Cassandra would have to say about this indiscretion when she heard. *If* she heard, he corrected himself quickly. As things now stood, it was highly unlikely that she would ever know that he had so openly acknowledged his approaching fatherhood.

He felt Lady Huntington's inviting glance suddenly sharpen. "You have not wasted any time, I see," she remarked, her voice a consummate balance between taunting sweetness and malice. He distinctly heard Mrs. Handcock's shocked intake of breath, which confirmed his suspicion that malice had been the primary motive behind the marchioness's comment.

In the silence that followed this indecorous and ill-advised remark, Raven gazed steadily at the fair Chloe and wondered idly what had ever attracted him to this shallow, self-centered, vicious creature. He smiled faintly and said nothing, his glance drawn instead to his cousin, who lounged against the mantelpiece, his handsome face reflecting Raven's own cynical smile. The lifting of one aristocratic eyebrow told Raven more plainly than any words that the marquess had read his mind like a book. It also de-

fused Lady Huntington's barb into a shared jest at the expense of
the obviously jealous lady.

With enviable skill Lord Gresham dispelled the awkward moment by engaging her ladyship in the flirtatious banter at which
both excelled until the tea tray appeared. By that time Lady Huntington had forgotten her momentary flare of mean-spiritedness,
and her tinkling laugh echoed delightedly in unison with Mrs.
Handcock's husky contralto. She was in her element, and Raven,
suddenly sick of the meaningless charade the lovely Chloe demanded of her admirers, took the opportunity to slip out of the
room and escape to the small yet well-equipped stables which
housed Lord Gresham's flawless cattle.

Once out of earshot of the glittering laughter and flirtatious
pleasantries that seemed such an essential part of the world inhab-
ited by women like Lady Huntington and Mrs. Handcock, Raven
reverted to morose speculations about his rift with Cassandra.
Perhaps he should have stayed and confronted her this morning,
he thought. If he could only bring himself to confess his regrets
over the harsh words spoken in anger, for his unnecessary rough-
ness, for the stolen kisses. But no, he corrected himself. He could
not regret the kisses; the sweet innocence of her had excited him
as no other woman, demi-rep or light-skirt, had ever done before.
Why hadn't he recognized that startling fact? he wondered, disgusted at his own obtuseness. His visit to her last night might
have ended very differently, indeed, had he left his anger behind
and approached her . . . How *should* he have approached his
wife? he wondered. An experienced seducer such as Phineas
Ravenville should have had no trouble in convincing the innocent
Cassandra to give up the treasures of her body to him. He should
have begged her to release him from that ill-conceived promise,
but what had he done instead? He recalled only too clearly his
very words. Promises are easy to break, he had boasted, and in
doing so, he had destroyed the very foundation of trust upon
which their tenuous relationship had been built. The thought was
painful to him.

He glanced around the stable, and his eye fell on his big roan
gelding, Hannibal, munching contentedly in his stall. It suddenly
occurred to him that if he saddled up and rode out now, he could
be back at the Grange in just under an hour. She would be in the
Blue Silk Drawing Room, taking tea with his mother and Mrs.
Henshaw. He could change out of his riding gear and join them.

He could make himself pleasant so that she would sense his repentance. And after Burton had removed the tea things, he might catch her alone, and then—

Raven was jolted out of this pleasant reverie by a brittle, teasing laugh. "My dear Raven," Lady Huntington trilled, advancing purposefully toward him across the stable yard. "I do believe you are jealous of our darling Robert and have fled the scene rather than witness his extravagant compliments." She come to a halt very close to him, her breasts, revealed almost in their lush entirety and pushed up in tantalizing peaks by her low, tight bodice, almost touching his brocade waistcoat.

She tilted her head coquettishly to one side and looked up at him through her thick dark lashes, her lips parted suggestively in a frankly sensuous smile. Raven remembered a time when he would have been aroused by this brazen Beauty; he would have taken what she offered without considering anything but his own immediate gratification. Now the lady's obvious display of her charms failed to quicken his blood, and he found himself noting—as he never had before—that the gorgeous Lady Huntington had applied a subtle blush of color to her perfect cheeks and that a delicate web of lines marred the smoothness around her magnificent eyes. The rest of her charms were real enough, Raven knew from having held the Beauty in his arms on several previous occasions. Her lips had been soft and pliable, too, he remembered, but hadn't her kisses been too calculated, her passion too controlled, her sighs a shade too rehearsed to be genuine?

He gazed down into her glittering green eyes and wondered how he could tell this supremely self-confident seductress that he had no desire to sample her wares. She must have glimpsed something of his reticence in his eyes, for her smile became a fraction more forced as she swayed against him until he felt the heaviness of her breasts through the material of his waistcoat. Without conscious thought, he stepped back, causing the Beauty to stagger slightly. She pulled herself upright immediately and glared at him defiantly.

"I see," she murmured harshly, bitter in the defeat she must have sensed. "The intrepid Raven has become the dutiful husband. How very tiresome of you!" She regarded him silently for a moment. Then a spark of malice flared in her eyes. "Fallen in love with the little chit, have you?" She laughed her brittle, scornful laugh. "How terribly bourgeois to be sure, my dear. Or had you forgot that only the lower classes indulge in such romantical nonsense as falling in love. Shame on you, Raven. What a delightful *on-dit* this will make when I return to Town," she crowed in a show of triumph, her beautiful face suddenly transformed into a tight mask of rage. "Don't come crying to me when your passion for that whey-faced vicar's daughter begins to wane, my lord," she concluded waspishly and stalked back to the lodge without another word.

Raven looked after her departing figure, a strange arrested look on his face. Love? he thought. How absurd! True, he cared for the silly widgeon more than he had thought possible, and Robert had been in the right of it—he had found something worthwhile in his wife. But that was only natural, wasn't it? He felt as though one suffocating weight had been lifted from his shoulders only to be replaced by another, more perplexing one in his heart. But at last he now knew what he had to do. All unwittingly Lady Huntington had cleared his brain of any doubts in that respect. He would go home to his wife.

He was reaching eagerly for his gear, when the sound of a new arrival made him pause. Shrugging his shoulders, he led Hannibal out into the yard and threw the saddle on his back. The sight of Robert's groom walking a glossy chestnut gelding made him pause again, and a frown appeared on his face as he examined the animal. It was one of his own, he noticed with a stab of anxiety. Had he been sent for? he wondered, his thoughts flying to his wife. Leaving a stable lad to finish saddling Hannibal, he strode purposefully toward the lodge.

Before he reached the door of the drawing room, he could hear the cloying sweetness of Lady Huntington's voice raised in a maliciously suggestive explanation. "I can assure you, my dear Lady Mansfield, that I left your husband even now out in the stables. He is such a charming conversationalist," she continued, and Raven clearly heard the smirk in her tone, "that he had me quite enthralled. It is *sooo* generous of you to share him with us poor lonely widows," she concluded mendaciously, with a delightful trill of laughter that put Raven's teeth on edge. "Oh, there you are, my dear Raven," she called out, quite undaunted by the silence of her stunned audience. "Lady Mansfield has just arrived to protect you from us, I daresay. And not a moment too soon, either. I declare, Raven, you should at least brush the straw out of your hair before appearing before your wife." She smiled cynically at this malicious innuendo.

Raven did not waste a glance on the marchioness. His gaze was riveted on Cassandra, pale and wide-eyed, standing next to Lord Gresham, who supported her with a hand under her elbow.

"Steady, lass," the marquess murmured, as Lady Mansfield seemed to sway on her feet. "And pay no heed to Chloe, my dear. She is being her usual catty self."

A gurgle of laughter escaped Mrs. Handcock, who threw up a hand to repress it. Lady Huntington cast her a chagrined glance and turned back to the marquess. "You are a good one to talk, Robert," she remarked archly. "What do you know of marriage, anyway. Husbands are such brutes, don't you agree, Lady Mansfield? One cannot trust them to behave with any degree of propriety. I never let my poor dear Huntington out of my sight for an instant."

"Oh, do shut up, Chloe," Willy said, so sharply that everyone stared at him. "And Raven, don't just stand there. Do something!"

Raven had been rooted to the floor with shock at Lady Huntington's hideous distortion of the truth, and at his wife's pale, frightened face that tore at his heart. He strode across the room toward her, only to see her flinch against Gresham's arm. "What the devil are you doing here, Cassandra?" he barked. No sooner had the words left his lips than he saw the flicker of warning in Gresham's eyes and cursed himself for a gauche, thoughtless clodpole.

"Is something amiss at the Grange?" he inquired, endeavoring to keep a rein on his impatience and anxiety. This new attempt only caused the marquess to roll his eyes toward the ceiling.

"Please get me out of here," he heard his wife whisper through lips that trembled visibly.

Raven glared threateningly at Lord Gresham, but the latter appeared not to notice. He brushed Lord Mansfield aside and whisked Cassandra out of the room before Raven realized what he was about.

"I would say you have a little competition there, my dear Raven," purred the marchioness, her little white teeth bared in a feline smile.

Raven bolted out of the room, but Lord Gresham had already thrown Cassandra up into her saddle before he reached them.

"Cassandra, listen to me," he cried, reaching for the reins, but she whirled her horse and flew off down the drive at breakneck speed.

Raven cursed loudly and fluently, staring after the fleeing figure with a scowl.

"Want me to escort her?" the marquess inquired quietly.

"No, I'll go," Raven threw over his shoulder as he raced to the stable yard and snatched Hannibal's reins from the openmouthed groom. In one swift motion he was in the saddle and heeling the gelding down the drive after the disappearing bay.

Cassandra became vaguely aware of a cool hand on her forehead. The hand was gentle and obviously belonged to someone who cared a great deal for her because the touch of the fingers was light and caressing. Drusilla, she thought dreamily. I must be home with Drusilla again. The feeling of being cared for was so comforting and restful that Cassandra made no attempt to stop herself from slipping back into sleep. When next she became aware of her surroundings, her first thought was that she had overslept. Strangely unwilling to open her eyes, Cassandra was nonetheless conscious of the sunny brightness of her room. Whatever was she doing still abed? she wondered. Was she really back at the vicarage or was that merely a fanciful dream? She could have sworn she had felt Drusilla's gentle fingers bathing her aching head with the lavender water their mother used to make. A surge of longing for her sweet sister, so intense that it made her want to sob, caught at her stomach.

"Drusilla," she muttered incoherently, moving her head restlessly, her throat suddenly parched. She felt the presence of a figure leaning over her.

"Cassandra, darling," a soft voice whispered. "Are you thirsty, dear? Here, drink this and you will feel better."

No, this isn't Drusilla, Cassandra thought rather forlornly, as someone raised her tenderly and held a glass to her lips. She drank avidly and then sighed as her head was laid back on the pillow. This was the dowager, she realized hazily. But why was the dowager countess tending Miss Drayton in such a fashion? She must still be in her room at the Grange, she thought, married to a man who . . . With an agonizing jolt, the memory of the recent painful events in her life started to come back to her. She had behaved like a complete wet goose, she knew. Proper countesses did not go madly chasing cross-country after their husbands to beg forgiveness for temper tantrums. Only the rag-mannered Miss Drayton of Walmer vicarage could have conceived such a hen-witted start, of course. And what had her good intentions brought her? She might have guessed that in the *beau monde* nobody cared a fig for good intentions. How they must all despise her for being so gauche as to show her feelings so frankly. No, she corrected herself, remembering the tender touch of the dowager's hands. Lady Sybilla Mansfield did not despise her, of that she was certain.

She moved restlessly again and to her dismay found her body sore and strangely listless. Had she contracted some terrible sickness? she wondered, forcing her eyes open. Then it all came back to her, and tears welled in her eyes. She saw again Lady Huntington's beautiful face laughing derisively at her and suggesting those terrible things about Raven. She remembered the marquess's firm hand on her elbow when her husband had burst into the room and she had swayed, wishing that she had never come on this fool's errand. She had only made herself look ridiculous and quite impossibly naive. Yes, she remembered, they had all been acutely embarrassed by her sudden appearance.

And Raven . . . but she didn't want to think about Raven. He had seemed angry with her again. Why was he always angry with her? she wondered, closing her eyes tightly to stop the tears that tickled the back of her throat. She had only wanted to repair some of the damage she had wrought with her own wretched temper. The marquess had realized that immediately, she remembered. She had seen the flash of sympathy in his marvelous blue eyes—eyes that missed nothing, she thought ruefully. Lord Gresham knew that she loved her husband. Why couldn't Raven see it, too? she wondered unhappily. She felt a warm tear slid down her cheek.

"Oh, the poor lamb is hurting, milady," Bridget's agitated voice cut through the haze of memory that had enveloped Cassandra. "Shall I run down to tell his lordship, milady? Ever so anxious he has been all day, he has, the poor gentleman."

Gentleman? What gentleman was the abigail talking about? Cassandra's head felt fuzzy again, as if it were wrapped in cotton wool. It was difficult to concentrate. Then suddenly she knew who the gentleman must be, and she opened her eyes, pushing herself up to look wildly about the room. "No!" she cried, her voice sounding like a croak.

"Hush, my dear." The dowager came quickly to her bedside, and Cassandra felt once more the coolness on her brow. "Do not distress yourself, Cassandra. And yes, Bridget, fetch his lordship at once."

"No!" Cassandra cried again weakly. "I will not see him. I cannot—"

"You are distraught, my dear," the dowager soothed her. "Of course, you must see Phineas, Cassandra. He has been like a caged animal all day, in and out of this room every ten minutes or so. We must put his mind at rest, dear. He is as devastated as you are over this tragic affair."

Tragic affair? What did the dowager mean? she wondered. Before she could demand an explanation, however, she heard a rush of steps in the hall, and suddenly the earl was standing at the foot of her bed, staring at her with strange intensity. Then he was beside her, her limp hand clasped in his strong fingers.

"Cassandra?" His voice was tentative, with a note of pleading in it that was very unlike his usual tone; but Cassandra was not about to be so taken in. She closed her eyes and turned her head away. In that quick glimpse Cassandra had seen a very different Lord Mansfield from the arrogant, overbearing man she was accustomed to. He had appeared haggard, and his gray eyes had flinched under her gaze. She felt the pressure of his fingers and the warmth of his lips, but she refused to respond. This was the man who had come to greet her with straw in his hair, fresh from a romp in the stables with that witch Huntington, she thought. The memory made her bitter, a new and painful experience for the practical Miss Drayton.

"Where is Dr. Crenshaw?" inquired the dowager in a low voice.

"He went down to the kitchen to have a look at Cook's burned hand," the earl replied. "He will be up presently."

There was a moment of silence. Cassandra kept her eyes firmly closed, even when she heard the door open to admit the local physician, Dr. Crenshaw, a tall, thin individual, she remembered, who had been called in only a week ago when the Mansfield cook had spilled hot grease all over her left hand.

"And how's our patient this afternoon?" he inquired briskly, and Cassandra sensed that the doctor had replaced Lord Mansfield at her bedside. "Has she mentioned anything about the accident yet?"

"She drank some water, but does not seem to remember anything," the dowager said, her voice full of anxiety. "Do you think it wise to tell her the truth, doctor?"

"There is no lasting physical damager, my lady, as I explained to you yesterday evening, but the countess must come to terms with the tragedy that has overtaken her if she is to become cured in her mind as well. I recommend that the sooner she knows the truth, the sooner she can begin to mend, my lady."

"Oh, Phineas, I simply cannot bear it," the dowager suddenly cried in a choked voice, and Cassandra distinctly heard the agitated rustle of her silks as she rushed from the room. What could have caused the dowager to react so strangely? Cassandra wondered. A cold nugget of fear began to mushroom inside her.

"If you will excuse me, my lord," she heard the doctor say, "I would like to examine my patient again, just to be on the safe side."

Cassandra heard the door open and close again. The room seemed oddly quiet and lonely without Raven, although it was illogical of her to be so missish.

She opened her eyes and encountered the doctor's calm gaze. She smiled feebly. "What is it that I am supposed to remember, Dr. Crenshaw?"

"You have been in a serious accident, Lady Mansfield," he replied without any of the roundaboutation she had anticipated. "Do you remember nothing at all?"

She frowned. There was so much about that dreadful encounter with Raven at Lord Gresham's lodge that she *did* remember and would give anything to forget. Why was it that she had no recollection of any accident. "I recall riding over to Melton Mowbray," she began tentatively. "I saw his lordship there. And several of his friends," she added lamely. "Then I must have ridden back, but I cannot seem to remember arriving at the Grange." She looked at the doctor expectantly.

"That is because you took a nasty tumble, my lady. You were unconscious when his lordship found you and brought you back home." He watched her attentively, and Cassandra wondered if there was anything he wasn't telling her.

"But I heard you say I suffered no physical damage, did I not, doctor?"

"Yes, my lady. You received several bumps and bruises, naturally, but in general terms, you are entirely healthy."

The nugget of fear suddenly ballooned alarmingly. She remembered it now, the mad gallop across the snow-covered field and the hedge looming up before her. The chestnut had stumbled, and he recalled the odd sensation of watching the accident happen to someone else.

"And in more particular terms, doctor?" she insisted. "What other damages are there?"

The doctor regarded her solemnly for several seconds. "You have sustained a tragic personal loss, my dear lady, which you must strive to put behind you. There will be other children, never fear."

Cassandra ceased to hear anything the doctor said. She could see his lips moving, but nothing reached her. She had lost Stephen's baby she thought, suddenly recalling the pain of the fall in all its intensity and the fear that had consumed her in that instant before everything went black. So she had known all along, she thought, amazed at the capacity of her own mind to hide the terrible truth behind the comforting haze of forgetfulness. She had not wanted to know; she had not wanted to face the truth.

She felt the tears trickling down her face and turned her head away, but there seemed to be no feeling left in her, only a great emptiness. Stephen was finally gone out of her life, she thought. I have failed him and lost him forever.

The doctor gave her hand a fatherly pat. "I shall send in his lordship to sit with you now, my lady. In a few days this will all seem like a bad dream."

No, she thought bitterly, listening to the doctor leave. It will always be a bad dream, one I shall never wake up from. She closed her eyes, ignoring her husband when he sat beside her and took her hand in his, ignoring the dowager's kindly attempts to interest her in a light dinner, specially prepared by Cook for her mistress, ignoring a frantic Sophy's tearful pleas to come back to them from whatever place it was her darling Cassie had withdrawn into.

Cassandra remained impervious to everything. Days after Dr. Crenshaw had told her she was quite strong enough to go down for a short while in the afternoons and should consider sitting for an hour or two in the sunny conservatory, she clung to her bed. At the dowager's suggestion that the earl carry her downstairs to take tea with the Marquess of Gresham and Mr. Hampton, who had ridden up to the Grange from Melton Mowbray for the third time since her accident to pay their respects, Cassandra only shook her head and closed her eyes with a sigh. They sent great bouquets of flowers; heaven alone knew where they obtained flowers in February, she thought, gazing listlessly at the monstrous yellow chrysanthemums and fragile tulips. From hothouses, no doubt, probably in London, at exorbitant prices. She wished she could find the energy to be grateful, but even that basic emotion seemed to require too much effort, at least more than she could bring herself to exert.

Dr. Crenshaw visited her regularly now, at the insistence of the dowager, who was becoming visibly distraught at Cassandra's lack of interest in anything except sitting by her boudoir window staring blindly in the direction of the small family cemetery two miles across the Park where Stephen lay buried.

Raven often came to sit with her, but he rarely asked her questions anymore, confining himself to recounting his plans for the estate during the coming year. At first he had tried to talk to her about Stephen, but Cassandra's silent tears would invariably indicate her distress at this choice of topic. This afternoon he had brought her some early peaches from the estate hothouses, sent he explained—by McGinniss, the head gardener, who hoped that her ladyship would consider a visit to the domain that had so intrigued her before the accident. He had also brought a letter from Drusilla, one of the many from her sister that had arrived at the Grange in the past month.

After he had gone, the dowager came to take tea with her and invite her to come down to dinner, as she did almost every afternoon.

"I think not, my lady," Cassandra murmured gently.

"Please do, Cassandra," the dowager pleaded. "I don't know my son anymore; he has become as silent and reserved as you are. Whatever wrong he has done you, and I know it must be grievous, I wish you would tell me, dearest—"

"Believe me, ma'am, you wouldn't want to know," Cassandra interrupted with a gentle smile.

"Then do it for yourself, dearest Cassie. I cannot bear to see you pining away like this, my love. You heard what Dr. Crenshaw said. There can be other babies if you will only give poor Phineas a chance." The dowager suddenly seemed to realize what she had just said and blushed. "What I mean is that it takes two to overcome the kind of misunderstandings that arise between hus-

and and wife, my dear. One to forgive and one to reform. I found in living with my dear Kendall that forgiving is often the sweetest part of loving. Won't you *try* to forgive him, dear?"

Cassandra saw the pain in the dowager's handsome gray eyes, so like her son's that Cassandra felt a twist of anguish herself. The dear lady was genuinely unhappy at the open rift Cassandra stubbornly maintained with the earl. For the first time since the accident, she asked herself if perhaps she was being selfish in effectively punishing everyone in the household for her husband's perfidy. *Yes,* a little voice spoke up unexpectedly from inside her heart. But did she want her relationship with the earl to return to what it was before the accident? *No, of course not,"* the voice responded without hesitation.

She looked down at the letter from Drusilla in her lap. The milder climate of Kent would already be showing signs of the approaching spring, she thought. Drusilla had asked about their mother's roses. Should they be fertilized now or when they started to form buds? she wanted to know.

Cassandra gave a start. Unexpectedly, she had found the answer to her dilemma. She would go home to the vicarage for a month to sort things out. A month with Drusilla would do wonders for what she was beginning to see as her excessive self-pity. It would also give the Mansfields a respite from her moodiness. Yes, of course, she thought. Why hadn't she thought of this before? All she needed was the earl's consent.

She turned to the dowager with more animation than she had felt in over a month. "Yes, my dear lady, I shall certainly try. For your sake, and for Phineas, and for my own, too. But I will need a favor from him, which you may be able to help me achieve."

"Anything that is in my power," the dowager responded gladly.

"I need your son's permission to spend a month in Kent with my family. My sister has invited me, and I would dearly like to accept, but I fear that Lord Mansfield might not approve."

The dowager was jubilant. "You leave Phineas to me, my dear," she exclaimed happily. "I know he will approve of anything that will bring you back to health, Cassandra. He cares deeply for you, my dear, as no doubt you know."

Cassandra knew no such thing, of course, but she caught herself wishing devoutly that the dowager was right.

CHAPTER FIFTEEN

Raven's Return

A week later, the thing was done.

The cavalcade arriving late that blustery February afternoon at Mansfield Court on St. James's Square would have startled the aristocratic neighbors of that select address, Cassandra reflected, had any been on hand to witness it. As it was, few of these families had yet returned to Town for the coming Season, she assumed, since so many of the knockers on the Square had not been replaced.

The Dowager Countess of Mansfield had decided, on the spur of the moment, that she would accompany her dearest Cassandra to London to get a good start on her preparations for the Season. Or at least this was what she had told Cassandra, who suspected, however, that the dowager had not relished the loneliness of the Grange after her guests departed. The dowager had extracted a promise from Cassandra that she would bring Drusilla to London in April so that her ladyship would have the pleasure of sponsoring her come-out. Although Cassandra had reluctantly agreed to this kind suggestion, privately she considered that her beautiful sister would be far better off in Kent than rubbing elbows with the kind of rakes and libertines she was bound to meet at Mansfield Court.

The sight of Mansfield Court reminded her of the weeks she had spent there immediately following her own marriage to a rake and libertine. What might that marriage have been, she wondered, had her husband been a different kind of man? Impatiently, she shrugged off this idle speculation. She was on her way back home to Kent, she reminded herself, and while it pained her to say good-bye to the countess, there was no doubt in her mind that the earl would be glad to see her go.

But in escaping from the earl, she thought, watching him dismount from his big roan gelding and throw the reins to one of the grooms who had accompanied them, she was giving up the company of a number of people who had been unexpectedly kind to her. Well, she would not think of that, she decided, gathering her sable cloak about her and preparing to descend. After all, she had been happy enough in Kent before meeting any of them, hadn't she?

While this was undoubtedly true, her leave-taking from these very same friends the following morning was more wrenching than Cassandra had anticipated. Willy Hampton, who had ridden over with the marquess, with whom he was racking up for a few days, surprised her with an effusive buss on the cheek, while Lord Gresham disconcerted her by raising both her hands to his lips and looking at her searchingly with those inscrutable sapphire eyes of his.

"You *are* coming back, are you not, Cassandra?" he asked softly.

She was startled once again by his perceptiveness. How could he know that a part of her mind had toyed with the idea of cutting all ties with the *beau monde* and picking up the pieces of her old life at the vicarage? She smiled and shook her head. "Do I look as though I would do anything so bacon-brained, my lord?"

"Yes, indeed you do, my sweet innocent." He frowned. "Isn't it bad enough that Raven is behaving like a deuced Jackstraw, without you contemplating anything equally bird-witted?" he demanded.

"Are you insulting my wife, Robert?" Lord Mansfield appeared suddenly at her side and glared pointedly at their joined hands.

"Don't be daft, Raven." The marquess grinned and took his own sweet time in releasing her. Cassandra was conscious once again of the odd tension that ebbed and flowed between these two men.

"I wish you would change your mind and let me accompany you, Cassandra," the earl said, ignoring the marquess's presence.

They had already had several arguments on the subject, at least Raven had argued, and Cassandra had listened patiently and then shaken her head. She had absolutely no desire to arrive in Walmer in the company—and the custody, she thought privately—of a husband who would insist on her taking up residence with him at Seven Oaks. He had insisted on her staying there anyway, of course, but Cassandra had merely allowed him to assume that he had won that battle. Actually, she had no intention of going anywhere near the Kentish estate of the Mansfields where Stephen had spent so many happy months last summer.

The earl had also insisted that she take Bridget and a formidable array of gowns, bonnets, pelisses, and other accessories, which Cassandra had no intention of wearing. The dowager and Lady Hart had added some lavish gifts for Drusilla and the vicar, and entreated her to write often and get plenty of rest in preparation for the rigors of the coming Season. She was glad enough of Bridget's company, however, and once the well-sprung Mansfield traveling chaise had left the Metropolis behind, she began to share some of her abigail's enthusiasm for the countryside through which they drove.

Dusk was settling over the Kentish hills as the chaise turned off the Deal-to-Dover Road and drove into the village of Walmer. Cassandra felt not a little conspicuous as her fashionable carriage, escorted as it was by four outriders and two grooms besides old John Morton, the coachman, drew up in front of the vicarage. But all her misgivings disappeared when Drusilla, radiant as always in a blue muslin gown and her fair tresses tossing in riotous curls around her lovely face, raced out of the house and enveloped her sister in a warm hug.

After instructing the carriage to drive on to Seven Oaks with Bridget and the luggage, Cassandra gave herself up to the joy of homecoming. That first evening, spent by the cozy fireside of the vicarage with her father and Drusilla, was the happiest she had experienced in a long time. London and Mansfield Grange, and the months she had passed there, seemed to recede into the fog of memory until she could almost believe that she had never left to become a countess at all. Finally, she thought to herself as she gave Drusilla a good-night hug and climbed into her old bed, she had found peace.

Cassandra was to discover in the days that followed each other in lazy succession that she had misread her own heart. After two weeks of pastoral bliss, during which she tramped every inch of the countryside, rediscovering the secret hideaway places where she and Drusilla had played as children, and which she had later shared with Stephen in the full flush of their newly discovered love, she admitted to herself that she had not found the peace of mind she sought. It simply was not here to be found.

A far more crushing blow to her self-esteem, however, was the discovery that Drusilla had efficiently stepped into her shoes as chatelaine in the Drayton household. Cassandra was particularly hurt to be treated like a guest in her own house. Mrs. Hill, although overjoyed to see her old mistress again, no longer consulted Cassandra in the running of the vicarage. It also pained her that the villagers, like old Mrs. Mason and her daughter Molly Potter, with whom she had always been on such excellent terms, now seemed so inhibited in her presence and made so many curtsies to her that she felt like a stiff-necked stranger.

"You miss Lord Mansfield, don't you, Cassie?" her perceptive sister quietly asked one sunny afternoon as they sat on their favorite hill, looking east toward the sea. When Cassandra did not answer, she continued. "It's no use denying it, you know. I noticed it that first evening when you spoke of him, dearest. There is something in your voice when you say his name, and your face betrays you, Cassie." She grinned impishly. "I never thought to see you actually in love with that odious tyrant."

"He is *not* an odious tyrant," Cassandra retorted instinctively and not quite accurately. "And I am *not* in love with him. I miss Lady Mansfield, if you must know. She treated me just like her own daughter."

"Oh, yes. So you have told me before, dear. But what about your husband? How does *he* treat you, Cassie? Do you enjoy being married to him, after all?"

"It is highly improper of you to ask such questions, Drusilla," she said sternly, but could not prevent her cheeks from turning a delicate rose. "We get along tolerably well together, if you must know."

"Tolerably well!" Drusilla scoffed. "Whatever happened to all your dreams of romance and a doting husband, Cassie? And why is Lord Mansfield not staying at Seven Oaks with you? That is your new home now, you know."

"Are you trying to tell me I am not welcome here?" Cassandra's heart felt suddenly cold. "Oh, Dru," she burst out involuntarily, her voice quavering. "You make me feel like a stranger. It's horrible."

"What a peagoose you are, dearest!" Drusilla exclaimed bracingly, flinging her arms about her sister.

Drusilla's effusive embrace comforted her briefly, but after they had both dried their tears, Cassandra was once again abandoned to her own devices while her sister went off to the village on an errand for the vicar.

Cassandra took refuge in her room. She had taken to writing lengthy letters to the dowager, whose replies were so peppered with references to her amusing activities in London, where the Season was beginning to get under way, that Cassandra found herself nostalgic for the lively company of the Mansfield ladies. This made her feel disloyal to her father and Drusilla, who were both genuinely delighted to see her. But more and more frequently, Cassandra was made aware of the temporary nature of her presence in the Drayton household.

After a month had passed, Cassandra found that she depended on the dowager's lighthearted and affectionate chatter to keep from falling into the doldrums. The frequent mention of Lord Mansfield in her ladyship's correspondence did little to cheer Cassandra, although she read them avidly. She received—secondhand through the dowager—many assurances that her husband eagerly looked for her return to London in April, but Cassandra seriously doubted that Raven had anything to do with these kind messages. The fact was, he had not written her a single line since her departure, and she had no difficulty at all in imagining him disporting himself with his buxom opera singer.

It occurred to her one afternoon as she sat writing in her room—as she seemed to do more and more often lately—that unless the earl gave some definite sign of desiring her presence in London as his wife, her pride would never allow her to return. In spite of the dowager's repeated protestations to the contrary, Cassandra feared that he had not written because he did not care what happened to her. She reviewed, in excruciating detail, every ugly, offensive word he had ever spoken to her. Wasn't it madness to imagine that a gentleman would say such things to a lady he had any true regard for?

On the other hand, a little voice from her heart reminded her, he had not always been unkind or indifferent, had he? Cassandra glanced at the glowing pearl ring on her finger, and a flood of longing swept over her. He had been like a real husband that afternoon in London, she remembered—attentive, and kind, and generous to a fault. He would have been even more like a real husband on Christmas Eve, she thought, recalling the intoxicating pressure of his lips on her mouth, her neck, her . . . A frisson of desire stronger than any she had ever known shook her. Good God, she thought, the mere memory of his passionate embrace had the power to make her hot and breathless.

Cassandra stood up abruptly and went to stare blindly out of the window. No matter where she looked, however, her mind's eyes saw only the earl's intense gray eyes, dark with incipient passion, glaring at her fixedly as though he wanted nothing so much as to devour her. What sweet intimacies might not have been hers that night had the dinner bell not rung? But it did ring, you ninny, a practical voice of reason interrupted these maudlin reminiscences. And he came to his senses, didn't he? He saw that you were not the lithe and lovely Lady Huntington, or that luscious Italian diva he keeps closeted in London for his erotic pleasures. No, he must have suddenly realized he was making a Jack-pudding of himself over a plain vicar's daughter, and had hedged off as soon as he decently could. That was it, wasn't it?

Cassandra sighed gustily. There was no sense in wrapping up the truth in clean linen now, was there? Miss Cassandra Drayton of Walmer vicarage was no beauty and never would be. And the sad fact that she had—inadvertently, irrationally, and quite unwillingly—lost her heart to a rake of the first stare was a truth she had better start learning to live with. Plain females probably fall in love with handsome rakes all the time, she told herself sternly. But few if any of them go into a serious decline or die of a broken heart as a result. She would endure, but the thought gave her little comfort.

She returned to her spindle-legged escritoire and sat down. Should she write to him? she wondered. It might be better to know for certain that he intended to disown her than to prolong this agony of indecision. She took up a pen and had already addressed it in her neat hand before it dawned on her that it would only provoke his lordship's cynical amusement to be addressed as *My Dear Husband*. Cassandra crumpled the hot-pressed sheet and threw it vigorously from her. She had decided on the more impersonal *Dear Sir*, when Mrs. Hill tapped at her door to inform her that a gentleman was downstairs asking for her.

"A gentleman?" she repeated stupidly, quite unable to grasp the import of the housekeeper's words. "Are you sure he didn't ask for Drusilla?"

"No, milady," Mrs. Hill insisted. "The Countess of Mansfield is what 'e said, milady, and I reckon that must be you, milady. I put 'im in the front parlor."

"Did he give his name?" she inquired, her heart suddenly up in her throat with nervous anticipation.

"No, miss. That is, milady. Leastwise I didn't catch it. Lord something or other, I believe."

After the housekeeper left, Cassandra sat for several minutes, unable to control her shaking. Her legs felt quite incapable of supporting her, and when she finally rose, she leaned heavily on the escritoire to steady herself. This is ridiculous, she thought. Here you are, a grown woman of twenty-three behaving like the veriest schoolroom chit in the throes of puppy love. This stern admonition did nothing to calm the riotous thoughts that jostled her mind, however. The scene reminded her too vividly of a similar afternoon six months ago when she had received another visit from a gentleman caller, a visit that had changed her life forever.

Was history repeating itself? she wondered. Had he come back for her? Was it possible that he *did* care after all? Prudence warned her not to place any credence in such an about-face on the part of that particular gentleman, but her heart did not want to listen. The notion that the Earl of Mansfield, *her husband,* was waiting for her downstairs—no doubt with a thunderous scowl on his handsome face at being kept kicking his heels—impelled her into sudden action.

A quick glance in the mirror told her that she looked very much as she had six months ago when she had rushed pell-mell into the front parlor, expecting to encounter Stephen but finding her nemesis there instead. Her gown was just as dowdy and unfashionably modest, and several auburn curls had escaped the severe chignon she had confined them in this morning. Nothing much had changed, she thought fleetingly, at least on the outside. On the inside, her heart was singing.

A dazzling smile lit up her face as she tucked a curl or two back into place and raced—as no real countess ever would, she thought without remorse—down the stairs and flung open the door to the front parlor, her heart in her eyes.

"Oh!" She stood there for the merest second, feeling as though she had been turned to stone, before she recalled her manners and stepped forward to greet her caller. "What a lovely surprise, my lord!"

"You are a sweet liar, Cassandra. It's as plain as a pikestaff that you wish me in Jericho. You have no idea what a lovely smile you have, my dear," the Marquess of Gresham drawled, a glint of amusement in his perceptive blue eyes as he caught both her hands and raised them to his lips. "But it wasn't for me, was it, Cassandra?"

Cassandra had the grace to blush. "What ever do you mean, my lord?"

"You know very well what I mean, my dear. That dazzling smile was for Raven, unless I mistake the matter." He gazed at her intently for a moment, and Cassandra felt, not for the first time, that there was more to the marquess's words than mere teasing.

"Won't you please sit down, my lord?" she murmured to hide her embarrassment at this plain speaking, indicating a place beside her on the chintz-covered sofa.

"I am sorry to disappoint you, but I thought it was time I took things into my own hands." The marquess took up a stand in front of the hearth and continued to observe her keenly. "Raven is acting like a besotted fool; I can get no sense out of him at all. It is time for you to return to Town, Cassandra."

"Is he ill?" Cassandra could not keep the apprehension out of her voice, and the marquess grimaced.

"That depends entirely on how you define ill, my dear. All I can tell you is that he seems to have maggots in his head lately. He had a rare dust-up with poor old Willy just the other day and landed him a facer without any provocation. Now if he had drawn *my* cork, it would have made more sense." He regarded her enigmatically, a wry smile on his lips. "Indeed, it may well come to that. Raven is bound to fly into the devil of a pelter when he discovers I am down here."

"I doubt it will signify a jot to him, my lord," Cassandra remarked calmly. "He is doubtless too engrossed in the treats London has to offer him," she added, forcing herself to smile as if she didn't care how his lordship entertained himself. "I imagine Lady Huntington is back in Town?" she added and could have bitten her tongue for betraying her interest in Raven's *amourettes*.

"Of course our dear Chloe is back in London," the marquess retorted bluntly. "Where else would that rapacious Beauty be at this time of year? London is an ideal hunting ground for the type of prey she is after."

"You mean Raven, I presume?" Cassandra inquired with false nonchalance.

"That's one of the things I came to talk to you about, my dear," the marquess began, "since Raven refuses to tell you himself."

Cassandra felt her heart contract uncomfortably. "I really don't want to know," she interrupted, angrily aware that her voice was shaking.

"Oh, but you do, Cassandra," he said gently. "You see, Raven does not care a fig for our incomparable Chloe. Not now, anyway. And I can give you my word that he has never . . . never . . . that is to say . . . " He paused, so obviously at a loss to phrase what Cassandra imagined he had been about to say, that she took pity on him.

"If you mean to imply that Lady Huntington has never been Raven's mistress," she said quietly, feeling the rush of heat to her cheeks, "then how do you explain that disgusting little scene at your hunting lodge?"

"That was pure malicious fabrication on Chloe's part. No truth to it at all, believe me."

"He had straw in his hair," Cassandra muttered through clenched lips.

"He had no such thing," shot back the marquess. "If you had not rushed off in such a pelter, like the silly widgeon you are, you would have seen that for yourself." He glared at her, reminding her so much of Raven that she wanted to cry.

"That was another of Chloe's Banbury tricks, my dear," he continued in a gentler voice. "Raven had no straw in his hair or anywhere else, as you would have seen had you looked at him."

Cassandra went very still, and after a moment's painful consideration had to admit that she had not, in fact, seen any straw in her husband's hair. She had been so certain of his guilt she had believed what that dreadful woman had said without a second thought.

"You are right," she said slowly. "I behaved very badly, didn't I?" Another unpleasant truth struck her. "And because I didn't trust him enough and rushed off so recklessly . . . " She paused to consider the enormity of her guilt. "I never would have taken that hedge if I had not been such an addlepated gudgeon." Suddenly she felt like crying again and looked up at the marquess helplessly. "It's all my stupid fault, isn't it? This whole ghastly imbroglio could have been avoided if only I had . . . " Her voice tapered off into silence. There was no use repining over what could not be mended, she thought miserably.

"You're beginning to sound like Raven," Lord Gresham remarked dryly. "The devil take it, Cassandra! The man does nothing but mope about as though he were a damned moonling, my dear. A sore trial to his friends, let me tell you. And to top it off, he gave Chloe the cut direct at the theater last week, which had her bristling mad and not speaking to any of us."

"But surely he has other . . . other amusements?" she murmured, knowing she should not be mentioning these things, particularly to a gentleman, but unable to control her wretched tongue.

"Ah!" Lord Gresham exclaimed disgustedly. "There you have it, Cassandra. You will not credit it, but Raven has given his precious diva her congé. I believe that little ladybird is now safely under the protection of a fledgling duke, a veritable Bartholomew baby, with more hair than wit, but with pockets deep enough to keep the diva happy for some time, I imagine." He regarded her quizzically. "Of course, you are not supposed to know any of this, my dear. Most improper of me to bring it up, but it seems to be expedient that you know how the land lies with Raven."

Cassandra stared at him in astonishment and blurted out without thinking. "I thought that you . . . that is to say, Sophy told me that you were interested in . . . " She stumbled but tried again. "I thought you wanted—"

"If you mean did I not harbor indecent designs on the diva," he drawled, amusement in his eyes. "Then the answer is yes. Until recently, I would definitely have been interested in taking up with that lady. In fact, I think you should know that Raven suggested as much to me that morning we left the Grange together. He confessed that he had found something much more worthwhile." His sapphire eyes had deepened with some unspoken emotion, which Cassandra did not dare put a name to.

"Then why . . . ?" she began unsteadily, dropping her eye from his piercing gaze.

"Because I, too, have recently undergone a drastic change in taste, my dear. I now favor less flamboyant females with the bloom of the country still on their cheeks rather than paint. I am getting besotted in my dotage."

The notion that this gorgeous specimen of manhood before her could so describe himself seemed so ridiculous that Cassandra giggled nervously. His description also made her uneasy; it was too close to what she saw every morning in her mirror. "Now who is being absurd, my lord?" she chided gently. For a split second, she had been terrified that he was going to say something that might destroy their friendship. But she had misjudged him, of course. Lord Gresham was not the kind of cad who would make an improper declaration to the wife of his own cousin. This was as close as he would ever come to revealing his feelings, she realized, feeling a sudden pang of sympathy for him.

"Now, tell me again why I should go back to London," she demanded, firmly changing the subject. "I have heard nothing from Raven, you know."

"Raven's a bloody fool," the marquess declared scathingly. "But unless I have mistaken my man, which is not likely after all these years, he is even now springing his horses on his way down here to put a bullet through my hide."

Cassandra stared at him in astonishment. "Why ever would he want to do anything so barbaric?"

"I left a note with his mother, letting Raven know that I was coming to see you."

This still made no sense to her, so she tried again. "And for that he would want to shoot you? I confess I cannot see the logic in that, my lord."

Lord Gresham let out a loud crack of laughter. "Oh, you will, my dear. You see, I told your sapskull of a husband that I intended to persuade you to abscond with me to Paris." He looked at her quizzically, his blue eyes brimming with amusement. "Don't you think that was monstrously ingenious of me, my dear?"

Cassandra could only stare at him in utter consternation. Had the man taken leave of his senses? "You are insane, my lord," she whispered in horrified tones. "This is madness of the worst kind. That is to say"—she softened her rejection somewhat—"this is indeed a flattering offer, my lord, but it cannot be." Her voice trailed off disconsolately.

"Cheer up, Cassandra," he said with surprising good humor. "More than likely it won't come to that. By my calculations Raven must have arrived at Seven Oaks several minutes ago. He will be upon us before you know it, to rescue you from my lascivious grasp." This picture seemed to amuse him, for he smiled broadly.

Cassandra got shakily to her feet. Everybody seemed to have run mad. "But he will shoot you, Robert," she cried impatiently. "That is if he comes at all," she added, the euphoria of the moment subsiding as quickly as it had ballooned inside her.

"Oh, he will, my dear. Lady Mansfield assured me he would."

"The dowager *knows* about this . . . this Cheltenham farce?" Cassandra was struck with an overwhelming desire to burst into hysterical laughter.

"Of course." Lord Gresham grinned devilishly, evidently in high gig.

"And what if he does not come?" Cassandra inquired, sinking from the heights of delirium to the abyss of pessimism.

Lord Gresham observed her, his grin fading. "In that case, my dear, you are welcome to embark with me for Calais." He took her limp hands and held them against his chest, smiling down at her tenderly. "In fact, my love, I shall insist upon it. If that blackguard is so lacking in all sense of decency and good manners as to abandon you to the likes of me, he deserves to lose you, Cassandra." His voice took on a husky quality she had never heard in it before. "You deserve the best of everything, Cassandra. You deserve to be loved and cherished and protected by a man who can appreciate your charms, my dear. And, by God, you will be if it's the last thing I do," he added fiercely.

"Like hell you will," snarled a voice from the doorway. Both occupants of the room swung round to confront the new arrival, whose entrance had gone unnoticed in the emotion generated by the marquess's moving speech.

"Raven, my dear fellow," Lord Gresham remarked coolly, without releasing Cassandra's fingers, which had suddenly turned to ice. "What took you so long?"

CHAPTER SIXTEEN

Miss Drayton Prevails

The Earl of Mansfield stepped into the room and slammed the door behind him. He was anything but amused at the scene he had interrupted, and regarded his cousin's witticism as the vilest piece of impertinence.

"Trying to seduce my wife, Gresham?" He made no effort to keep the bitterness out of his voice and glared rigidly at the marquess, who had the bloody nerve, Raven realized, to stand there holding Cassandra's hands most tenderly.

Lord Gresham smiled serenely. "It's high time someone did, don't you agree, old man?" He regarded the earl pointedly.

The ambiguity of this answer made Raven pause, but he was too enraged to examine the myriad implications it contained. "No use trying to the dust in my eyes, Gresham," he snarled, taking a threatening step forward. "And you can take yourself off now. Your presence is definitely *de trop*. I will deal with you later."

The marquess raised one supercilious eyebrow. "Really, old man, you take too much upon yourself. I hadn't realized this house was yours. Surely it is for her ladyship to send me away if I have outstayed my welcome, not you, Raven." He bestowed one of his most dazzling smiles on the countess.

This further show of insolence was so typical of Lord Gresham's high-handedness in disposing of those who dared to cross him that, under normal circumstances, Raven would have been vastly amused at his cousin's panache. This was far from a normal circumstance, however. The damned smooth-talking rogue had had the effrontery, not only to dangle at his wife's shoestrings for months, but to leave him a note to the effect that he intended to take her to Paris, as if it were the most natural thing in the world to run off with another man's wife. Raven had been so incensed when he received the marquess's missive that he had ground his teeth for several seconds before trusting himself to speak. When he had regained his powers of speech, he had regaled his mother—since Gresham had exhibited his execrable bad taste in making the dowager his go-between—with a pithy and extremely unflattering description of his lordship's morals, behavior, and unsavory ancestors.

It was not until he was halfway down to Walmer that it had occurred to him that his mother had shown remarkable *sang-froid* upon hearing that her only son and the head of the family was about to take off precipitously for Kent with the object of putting a bullet through the Marquess of Gresham's arrogant hide. All she had said, he remembered uneasily, was to be sure to bring Cassandra and Drusilla back to London *tout de suite* since Madame Suzette was anxious to fit them for a bevy of new gowns.

Raven shook his head impatiently and returned his attention to the couple before him. "Take your hands off my wife, you bastard, or I'll draw your cork for you right here," he growled menacingly. "And you." He looked directly at Cassandra for the first time since his arrival and cursed himself for kicking his heels in London—where nothing seemed to amuse him anymore—when he could have been down here with this female he had heartily disliked on sight and who had been nothing but trouble since the unlucky day he had put a ring on her finger. He glared at her, standing so confidently and so close to Gresham it made him want to beat the marquess's brains out and take her pretty neck in his hands and shake some sense into her. No, he corrected himself quickly. If he were honest about it, he would have to admit that he wanted to put his arms about her and kiss her until she couldn't stand up, until she went all soft and pliant against him, until she begged him—with her eyes, her lips, her body—to take more than kisses from her and give her more of himself. And then he would lay her down and give himself to her as he had never done to any other woman. The desire for such a consummation was so intense that he felt himself harden as he held his wife's gaze.

If only he could overcome this barrier that stood between them, he thought distractedly, watching with fascination as the hazel of her pupils turned almost green with emotion. In all his dealings with women, Phineas Ravenville had never found himself at a loss for words. He had always had the glib compliment, the pretty turn of phrase, the suggestive flattery at the tip of his tongue. Why then, he asked himself morosely, could he not charm his wife with the same ease? He had given it much thought in the month he had been alone in London. Alone only in a manner of speaking, of course, but he had never felt such loneliness of spirit as he had during the past month. He had finally had to admit that the obstinate, shrewish chit had become necessary to his happiness. The implications of this admission scared him so much that he had refused to consider the obvious remedy. If he arrived in Kent and allowed his wife to see how essential she was to him, he would condemn himself to live under the cat's paw for the rest of his life. The notion that a mere vicar's daughter—one with scrambling manners and a sharp tongue into the bargain—could bring the notorious rake Phineas Ravenville to such straits appalled him.

And yet here he was, he thought grimly, still appalled yet inexorably drawn into a romantic entanglement he would have laughed to scorn six months ago. What had wrought such a change? he wondered, raking his wife with a critical gaze. It could not be her beauty, because she possessed none, as he had known from the beginning. Fine eyes she undoubtedly had, but then so had a hundred other young ladies of his acquaintance. And as for her taste in gowns . . . He noticed with sudden shock that the gown his wife was wearing was either the same abomination or a twin to the one she had worn the day of their marriage. The sight of it filled him with an unexpected rush of emotions, which threatened to unman him in front of the ubiquitous marquess.

To forestall any such embarrassment, Raven scowled at the object of his discomfort. "And you," he repeated savagely. "Must you go about rigged out like a damned governess? I thought I told you to throw that abomination into the rag-bag. It amuses you to thwart me at every turn, no doubt. Well, let me tell you, madam—"

He broke off in consternation as Cassandra's eyes filled with tears. She cast an imploring glance at the marquess before rushing past him, wrenching the door open, and disappearing into the hall beyond.

Both men stood transfixed, staring at the open door and listening to the countess's soft footsteps growing fainter in the distance.

The marquess sighed audibly. "If that don't beat the Dutch," he said disgustedly. "Rarely has it been my privilege to witness a more cow-handed handling of a delicate situation, Raven. You have outdone yourself, my lad. I wash my hands of you." His glance was frankly pitying. "What in Hades inspired you to rail at the chit over a deuced gown? What the devil does it matter what she wears, you nincompoop? You ain't married to the damned dress, are you?" He waved an elegant hand in the direction Cassandra had taken. "I shall leave you to pick up the pieces, Raven. And try not to be such a damned fool in future."

Before he could make good his words, however, a small, golden-haired fury in a pale blue muslin gown appeared in the doorway. "I might have known it would be you," this vision spat with suppressed venom, glaring at the earl. "You are an odious, tyrannical, heartless, absolutely intolerable beast!" she enunciated clearly and with evident relish. "My sister is upstairs, crying her eyes out, and what are you doing? Arguing over some stupid gown if I understood her correctly. You are an abomination, sir—"

"I couldn't agree more," put in the marquess admiringly.

"And who are you to agree with anything?" the tiny lady in blue interrupted him scathingly. "Another despicable, disgusting libertine, no doubt. Well, I'll have you know that creatures of your ilk are not welcome in this house." She turned back to the earl. "And that goes for you, too, you poor excuse for a husband. Where have you been for the past month, if I might ask? Disporting yourself in London, no doubt. You would be well served if my sister refused to see you ever again." She glared viciously at Lord Mansfield, her pansy-blue eyes flashing dangerously. "I shall certainly discourage her from subjecting herself to any more of your tyranny."

The earl gathered his wits about him enough to protest this piece of interference. "I wouldn't do that if I were you," he said. "She is my wife, and I have come to take her back to Seven Oaks where she belongs."

"Pshaw!" the diminutive virago snorted. "You don't deserve her."

"You are undoubtedly correct," the earl admitted ruefully. "But you will oblige me by telling Cassandra that I am waiting to drive her home, Drusilla."

"It's Miss Drayton to you," she snapped angrily. "And I hope my sister has enough sense to send you to the rightabout. I certainly would if I were in her shoes."

With this parting shot and a haughty toss of her silvery gold curls, Miss Drayton turned on her heel without another word and left them.

*   *   *

When Cassandra came downstairs twenty minutes later, dry-eyed and subdued, she had changed into her fashionable London gown, put on an appropriate hat, and thrown her fur cloak over her shoulders.

She found her husband alone in the front parlor. Lord Gresham, he informed her rather stiffly, conveyed his regrets for his hasty departure. "He remembered a rather pressing engagement in London," Lord Mansfield added noncommittally.

Cassandra felt as though her last moral support had crumbled. She had been counting on the marquess to help her through the uncomfortable evening ahead at Seven Oaks, and through the coming days and weeks and perhaps years she must endure in the company of a man who cared more for the gowns and bonnets she wore than for what was in her heart. He had made that only too plain in the ugly little scene in her father's front parlor. How many more such scenes would she have to endure throughout the years ahead? she wondered. She straightened her sagging shoulders defiantly. It was not like Miss Cassandra Drayton to give in to adversity like some spineless ninny, she told herself sternly. She would prevail, in spite of the odds against her.

For a brief, desperate moment she considered begging Drusilla to accompany her to Seven Oaks. But her outspoken sister was definitely in the earl's black books, having had the temerity to take up cudgels in her defense. They were barely on speaking terms. So she limited herself to giving Drusilla one last, desperate hug before allowing her husband to lift her into his curricle.

The drive to Seven Oaks was accomplished much too quickly for Cassandra's peace of mind, and before she was even halfway resigned to spending her first evening alone with her husband in months, Lord Mansfield was reaching up to lift her down again. She wished now that she had taken Drusilla's advice and sent the earl packing. She even considered briefly if perhaps she had missed a golden opportunity in rejecting Lord Gresham's invitation to accompany him to Paris. At least that would have put her out of reach of her husband's disdainful silence, which was harder to bear than his anger. Paris would be deliriously gay at this time of year, if what she had heard was true. And she would be escorted by one of the most dashingly handsome men of her acquaintance. She would be the envy of all the Parisian belles, she mused. Robert would be a most flattering and attentive companion, she had little doubt of that—so unlike the stern man who

stood regarding her speculatively in the tiled hall of his Kentish
estate. Then why did the thought of kissing the marquess leave
her absolutely unmoved? she wondered. She must be the worst
kind of lackwit if she could fail to be enchanted at the attentions
of London's most accomplished flirt. And by some odd quirk of
fate, this was so.

Her fantasies of Paris and Lord Gresham dissipated the instant
she set foot in the chamber the earl had assigned her. If he had deliberately set out to remind her that she was his private property,
he could not have chosen a more effective method. He had himself accompanied her upstairs and flung open the door, revealing
the comforting presence of Bridget, laying out one of her newest
evening gowns on a bed that seemed to her overheated senses to
dominate the center of the room. She glanced nervously at her
husband as the abigail came forward to take her cloak and noticed
that he was watching her with a strange little smile on his lips.
Was he remembering Christmas Eve at the Grange, when he had
come into her room to give her the cloak? she wondered. Did he
realize that he had stolen much more than a kiss from her that
night? She suddenly wished quite achingly that he had lost as
much as he had taken from her; but that, of course, was wishful
thinking, she knew. It would be easier for the proverbial leopard
to change his spots than for a rake as notorious as Phineas
Ravenville to lose his heart to a plain and simple country girl with
no taste for high fashion.

She would not be missish about it, she decided, after he had
gone off to dress for dinner and Bridget was brushing her auburn
hair into a riot of curls on top of her head. She would have preferred a more demure chignon to match her mood of quiet resignation, but Bridget was adamant.

"It ain't right to wear this beautiful hair all rolled into a bun
like some spinster at her last prayers, milady," she scolded. "His
lordship will want to see his wife looking beautiful tonight, unless
I mistake the matter."

Cassandra had opened her mouth to demand what was so special about tonight, when it came to her rather forcibly what the
abigail's words implied. She shut her mouth quickly and opened
her jewel case to take her mind off the ridiculous hope that had
flared briefly in her heart that Lord Mansfield might actually be
entertaining the notion of seducing her.

Now she was being nonsensical, she thought, rifling through

her jewels and coming up with Lord Gresham's pearl pendant. And why not? she asked herself defiantly, handing the heavy jewel to Bridget to clasp around her neck. The weight of the pearl between her breasts was somehow comforting, and if it served to remind his lordship that one of the most dazzling and sought-after men in London had found this vicar's daughter worthy of attention, so much the better, she thought rebelliously.

With this heartening thought to sustain her, Cassandra picked up a light shawl and went down to the drawing room.

Lord Mansfield had been standing before the fire, but he turned at her entrance and came across to take her hands and raise them to his lips. Cassandra could not tell if the glitter in his gray eyes when they lit on the pearl pendant signaled the beginning of another brangle between them, but she refused to be intimidated. When the earl reached out and casually picked up the pendant, resting his fingers briefly on her breast, she held her breath.

"I see Gresham is still with us," he said softly, raising his penetrating gaze to her face. He fingered the jewel pensively and then returned it to the cleft between her breasts, the warmth of his touch sending tremors of delight across her skin.

"Tell me, Cassandra," he inquired gently. "Would you have gone with Gresham to Paris?—or anywhere else, for that matter?—if I had not arrived in time to spike his guns."

He still held both her hands, and Cassandra felt the tension humming in him. So it was important for him to know if she had a *tendre* for the marquess, was it? She smiled to herself at the knowledge that he cared at least that much. Now would have been the time to tease him, she thought, to make him suffer a little for all the grief he had caused her with his own flirts. Coyness was foreign to her nature, however, so she told him the truth.

"No."

His mouth twisted into a smile, and Cassandra wondered if it was triumph or relief the earl felt. "Why not?" he insisted.

When confronted by this question, which she had not considered before, she found the answer absurdly simple. "Because Lord Gresham never had any intention of taking me to Paris," she replied, relinquishing this fantasy without the least twinge of regret.

"I think you underestimate yourself, my dear."

She shook her head. "That has nothing to do with anything,"

she said. "I think Robert was playing a deeper game than we imagined."

"Are you saying he was amusing himself at your expense?" The familiar frown brought his dark brows together threateningly.

"Oh, no!" she exclaimed quickly. "The marquess is the kindest and most perceptive man I know."

"Unlike me, I suppose?"

A less honest, more worldly-wise woman would have prettily denied such an aspersion. But once again, Cassandra did not flinch from the truth.

"Yes," she said softly, hoping he would not fly into one of his black rages. "Unlike you, my lord." She smiled hesitantly and added, as if to forestall his anger. "But I am sure you did not mean to be unkind—"

"Oh, but there you are wrong, my sweet," he exclaimed harshly. "I did mean it. I didn't care whom I hurt, if you must know." He dropped her hands and flung away to pace the room restlessly. "I behaved in the most reckless and unfeeling manner with someone entrusted to my care. Robert warned me that it would all come home to roost one day, and he has an annoying habit of always being right."

Dismayed at the unexpected anguish she heard in the earl's voice, Cassandra forgot her own anxieties. "It couldn't have been very pleasant to be saddled with a wife you hadn't planned on and never wanted, my lord. Believe me, the prospect might easily have irritated a saint."

Lord Mansfield let out a crack of harsh laughter. "Did it irritate you to be leg-shackled to a husband you didn't want, Cassandra? Because if anyone is a saint here, it's you, my sweet."

"Well, yes," she replied slowly. "I was annoyed at first, of course. But I tried to remember that it must be so much worse for you."

The earl looked at her strangely for a moment and then took her face gently between his hands. "I owe Drusilla an apology, my love. She is right about me. I *am* a heartless, selfish beast, and you *are* much too good for me. God's truth, Cassandra, you are quite extraordinary. No other woman I know would have said that." He seemed to be struggling with some inner emotion, for his eyes had gone dark, and Cassandra wondered what secret demons were harrowing him. She wanted to put her arms around him to comfort him, to hold his head on her breast and caress his hair with tender fingers, to smooth away the frown that marred his handsome face. A wave of longing shook her, so intense it made her light-headed, and she closed her eyes to hide the truth of her feelings from the man she most wished to know them.

A moment later she opened them and smiled up at him, catching an expression in his eyes that made her heart skip a beat. "You are exaggerating, my lord. You are not *quite* as irredeemable as you seem to believe."

His mouth quirked into a wry smile that tore at her heart. "Name one single redeeming thing about me, my lady," he challenged.

Heaven help her! She could name a dozen without even trying, a hundred if she gave the matter any thought at all. His eyes, to begin with. Eyes that had repelled her, frightened her, scorned her, but also attracted her like hard brilliant gray magnets, dark liquid pools of desire that hinted at unspeakable delights a vicar's daughter scarcely dared dream of. Eyes that were even now melting her resolve to be cool and complaisant with a man who—if Bridget were to be believed—might well have her seduction on his mind.

"You see," he teased, obviously mistaking her silence for defeat. "You cannot dredge up a single virtue in me. Confess it, Cassandra."

"Oh, but I can." She smiled, secretly delighted at his playfulness. "How many gentlemen would have agreed to wed a country nobody to save her from disgrace? Can you tell me? You have my eternal gratitude for that unselfish act, my lord. I realize I may not always have shown it, of course—"

His hands dropped to her shoulders, and he held her at arm's length. "Aha! Now I understand why you are always pulling caps with me, my dear. And all this time I thought you were a tiresome shrew." He sobered, and his eyes became shuttered. "Besides," he added lightly. "Even a rake has some sense of honor, Cassandra. I could do no less. For you. For Stephen. And for myself."

"Not everyone would have thought so." She watched the veil of cynicism he had used to mask his real thoughts and wondered how she was ever to earn his friendship, much less his affection. "I am glad you did," she added impulsively.

Something came alive in the depths of his eyes, and he smiled at her. "So am I, Cassandra. You have no idea just how glad I am, my dear."

Nervous at the unexpected glimpse she had caught of the earl's emotions, Cassandra rushed on recklessly. "Which only goes to prove what Robert told me."

"Robert?" He retreated again behind the safety of cynicism.

"Lord Gresham, that is."

"My cousin seems to have been unduly busy, " he said shortly, and Cassandra recognized yet again the bond—antagonistic though it often was, between the two men. Yes, she thought, Lord Gresham was still with them. This was another facet of her husband's life she would have to learn to live with.

"Lord Gresham tells me that you have reformed your ways, my lord. Is he right in that, too?"

She was surprised and hurt at his sudden withdrawal. He left her abruptly and strode over to the French windows to gaze out at the thickening twilight. Had she inadvertently trespassed on an area of his life that he had not wished revealed to her? she wondered. She knew from her own father that gentlemen had many odd little rules of behavior that must not be broken; so many little fantasies—she had no other word for them—about what they could or could not share with the women in their lives. Perhaps this was one such rule she had broken now, she thought with sudden insight. Perhaps this man, to whom she felt inextricably committed, found it intolerable to have his actions questioned by a mere female. It was also possible, she realized, that he was not yet ready to admit to being a reformed rake like so many of his fellow Corinthians and like his own father.

But because she was who she was, Cassandra could not be content with half measures. She must know if her husband's heart was free, or if it was still attached by insidious bonds to any of the scintillating, seductive women who shared his world—women with whom she could never hope to compete, she admitted without rancor.

"He told me that you cut poor Lady Huntington in public, and that you have given up your . . . " She paused, searching for the polite word. "Your other connection, my lord." She had been addressing his rigid back, but at these words he turned, and she found herself wondering if that glitter in his piercing gaze was anger or amusement. Then he smiled, and Cassandra relaxed.

"Our precious Robert has outdone himself," the earl drawled, strolling back toward her.

"He also pointed out to me that you had no straw in your hair," she rushed on before her courage failed her.

"No straw in my hair?" He looked puzzled for a moment, then his face relaxed into a grin. "No, as a matter of fact, I didn't." He placed his hands back on her shoulders and squeezed them gently, brushing her collarbone lightly with his thumbs.

"I should have seen it for myself," she whispered. "Why didn't you tell me?" She was feeling strangely breathless, and her heart was pounding in a highly irregular manner.

It took him several moments to reply. When he did, he sounded unexpectedly apologetic, as if he were admitting to some aberrant behavior unbefitting a gentleman. "I must confess to an odd desire to have my wife think a little more highly of me," he said slowly, and Cassandra's heart, which had been beating so wildly, suddenly seemed to stop in midbeat.

This was what she wanted, wasn't it? Her husband was admitting that he valued her regard for him. He wished her to be his friend. Then why didn't she feel elated? Was it because she wanted them to be so much more than friends? She knew it was, of course, and she also knew that she would be willing to settle for friends since he obviously could not love her. If he did, he would have said so, wouldn't he? Friends and lovers. Oh, yes, she thought resolutely. They would be lovers before the night was much older. How odd, she thought, that being lovers implied so much more than a joining of their bodies. They would make love, but they would not be in love, at least Raven would not. But she could always make believe, couldn't she? And she was determined not to allow another night to go by without becoming a real wife to her lord.

"Then Robert was right. You have changed, if not exactly reformed." She smiled up at him, her new decision giving her a feeling of wantonness that was oddly exhilarating.

His fingers dug into her shoulders. "Would it please you if I became another reformed rake, my dear?"

"Only if it pleases you, my lord," she answered primly, slanting her eyes at him provocatively.

His eyes crinkled with amusement, and he drew his knuckles slowly up her neck to cup her chin. "And what about you, Cassandra?"

She dropped her lashes as she had seen Sophy do a hundred times to poor besotted Lord Hart. "It might be pleasant not to have to wonder where you are and what you are doing, my lord," she answered demurely, but truthfully.

He brushed her lower lip with the soft pad of his thumb. "Do you mean to tell me that you have been wondering about me all this time?" His smile was infectious now, and she felt her heart flutter at the teasing tone of his voice.

"Well, not all the time, my lord. Only occasionally."

The pressure of his thumb or her lips increased slightly. "Only occasionally? What a monstrous, unkind thing to say, my pet. Did it never occur to you that I have been wondering about you, too?"

Not in a million years had such a thing occurred to her, of course. She raised her brows in disbelief. "Heavens, no! Why ever would you do such a thing, my lord?" He must be teasing her again, she thought, but at least this was better than being ignored or berated.

He slid one hand down her arm and encircled her waist, holding her loosely against him as his thumb still worked its magic on her lips. "Well, it's true," he said, gazing at her mouth as if the sight of his own thumb touching her entranced him. "Didn't our dear marquess tell you about that, too? Didn't he tell you what he called me?"

Cassandra had suddenly become aware that what she had prayed would happen was indeed happening. She was being seduced by her husband. In a momentary flash of panic she contemplated escape, but instantly discarded the notion as too missish by far. Miss Drayton—she must really stop thinking of herself as Miss Drayton, she decided—was surely made of sterner stuff than that. Hadn't she planned to seduce the earl into her bed tonight, anyway? With very little encouragement, he would save her the trouble. All she need do, she told herself, was let herself respond to him as she had always dreamed of doing. It shouldn't be difficult at all.

"And what was that, my lord?" she murmured, leaning ever so slightly against him so that his hand tightened on her waist.

He looked deeply into her eyes, and Cassandra realized that this was going to be much easier than she had imagined. His gaze was already hazy with incipient desire. "It is rather inelegant, I'm afraid, my dear. He called me a fish that has been hooked and landed, but still refuses to admit defeat. Rather accurate description, wouldn't you say?"

Cassandra placed one palm on the earl's lapel and looked at

him carefully. "I don't think you look anything like a fish, my
lord." She had spoken calmly, but her heart had jumped into her
throat again. Had the marquess—a man whose sharp eyes missed
none of his friends' foibles—meant what she thought he meant?
If so, she dared not consider who the happy angler might be.

"My sweet innocent." Lord Mansfield laughed, and Cassandra
heard a trace of self-mockery in it. "You are far too kind, sweetheart. But Gresham was right again, I fear. I am well and truly
caught this time." He pulled her closer against him. "There are
certain compensations for the loss of my freedom, however, as
Robert kindly pointed out to me."

Cassandra was not sure she followed this line of thought, but
the feel of his hardness against her thigh reassured her that things
were progressing as planned. "And what are those, my lord?" she
asked, relaxing a trifle so that her body could mold itself against
his with greater ease.

For answer, he dipped his head abruptly and took her lips in a
soft kiss. "You are one of the compensations, my sweet Cassie,"
he murmured against her mouth before invading it with the tip of
his tongue. She reached up to pull him down harder against her,
and the crispness of his hair made her fingers tingle deliciously.
He responded fully to her encouragement, and Cassandra felt herself growing warm and pliable under his hands and lips as they
seemed intent on capturing every inch of her with a sensuous
abandon that made her blood sing.

When he finally paused for breath, Cassandra returned to a subject that had been nagging at her. "What exactly did you mean
when you said I was a compensation, my lord?" she murmured
against his waistcoat. "I don't know that I like the idea."

The earl laughed, and Cassandra could hear the gentle rumble
in his chest, quite distinct from the thudding of his heart. "An unhappy choice of words on Robert's part, my sweet. Would you
prefer to be the love of my life?"

Cassandra held her breath. The seduction was going far better
than she had dared to hope, but what Raven was now suggesting
was not something she could joke about. She looked up at him
anxiously. "That sounds rather serious, my lord," she murmured,
unwilling to believe he meant what she hoped he did.

"I can't think of anything more serious than being in love,
Cassie. Can you?"

This admission was so unlike anything she had expected from

her rakish husband, and Cassandra was stunned. "I had no idea you were susceptible to such romantic notions, my lord," she responded warily. "I thought rakes prided themselves on the quantity of their conquests, not the quality."

"Ah!" He grinned and pulled her against him again. "But I am no longer a rake, my sweet. Remember?"

She gazed up into his beloved gray eyes and trembled at the glitter of desire now clearly apparent in them. Did he mean what he said about love? she wondered. Or was she merely imagining that the earl felt anything but the most basic attraction for her?

"So you say, my lord," she said dryly, making no move to return his embrace.

His hand came up to cradle her head, and Cassandra felt the pins fall from her carefully contrived coiffure. "You don't believe me, my love?" He ran his fingers through her hair, and she felt Bridget's creation disintegrate entirely. When his mouth came down to possess her, however, all thoughts of propriety fled in the rush of warmth that made her cling to him and snuggle into his tall frame with a tiny moan of unabashed and sensuous delight.

The result of this rash surrender was immediate and entirely beyond anything Cassandra had, even in her most erotic fantasies, imagined. She had thought that the earl's previous embrace had been everything that even the most romantic female could wish for, but what he was doing to her now, with his mouth, his hands, his now fully aroused body, made her understand with blinding clarity why some otherwise perfectly sober young females could commit the grossest improprieties for the love of a man. Raven was making her feel undressed and, to her horror, she reveled in it. Her clothes suddenly felt unbearably oppressive, and she found herself wishing to be rid of them. She ran her hand beneath his coat and felt the heat of his chest through the thin cambric of his shirt. The touch of him sent fire leaping through her blood, and heaven knows what might have happened, she thought, if she had not suddenly become conscious of a coolness on her shoulders.

She opened her eyes to discover that her husband had drawn her gown down to expose her breast, which lay nestled in his warm fingers. "My lord," she protested weakly, feeling for all the world like a heroine in the latest melodrama, "what are you doing?" The scandalous scene and her stupid question were so typical of the misadventures of vapid fictional females that Cassandra could not resist the urge to giggle.

Lord Mansfield raised his head and glared at her, black unruly curls falling over his forehead. "What is so funny, ma'am?" he growled.

Unself-consciously, Cassandra reached up to brush his curls back. She smiled tenderly into his passion-filled eyes. "You are, of course." Calmly she detached his fingers from her breast and pulled up her gown. "You are still behaving like a rake, my lord," she said primly. "I am most disappointed in you."

He stared at her for several moments, a baffled expression in his eyes. Then a glimmer of amusement began to crinkle his mouth. "You are, are you, my tiresome, adorable shrew?" he murmured, reaching for her again. "I thought I was showing quite admirable restraint, my love."

Throwing him a reproving glance, Cassandra slipped out of reach. She put her hands to her hair, now cascading indecorously down her back. "I shall have to go up and tidy myself, my lord. I can scarcely sit down to dinner, looking like this."

"You look adorable, Cassandra." The earl laughed, a deep-throated, sensuous sound that made her blood tingle. "I shall go up with you, my love. I intend to show you how a real rake behaves."

"What about dinner?" Cassandra asked. Now that the moment she had longed for had arrived, she was inexplicably beset by nervousness.

"I think we will send a message down to the kitchens to postpone dinner," he said smoothly, his eyes daring her to defy him.

She glanced at him from under her lashes and smiled enigmatically. She felt impelled to employ one last delaying tactic. "For half an hour?" she inquired, unable to disguise the tremor of anticipation in her voice. "That should be sufficient, I believe, my lord."

"Indefinitely."

"Indefinitely?"

"Yes, my sweet love, indefinitely. It will take me that long, perhaps longer, to show you what it means to be married to a reformed rake."

Cassandra smiled and lowered her lashes provocatively, a frankly flirtatious gesture that seemed to delight her husband, for he put an arm suggestively about her waist and smiled possessively down at her as he guided her up the wide staircase.

"Do you agree, my pet?"

"Oh, certainly," she replied promptly. "Lord Gresham said it was high time *somebody* seduced me."

"The devil take Lord Gresham," the earl said between his teeth. "But the rogue was right again." He opened the door to his lady's chamber.

"But I warn you, Cassandra," he said, and the loving light in his eyes gladdened her heart. "I don't want to hear that man's name mentioned again tonight. Is that clear?"

And for once, Cassandra felt not the slightest desire to gainsay her lord.